What the Shadow Knew

A Deacon Bishop Mystery

Michael Paulson

Chapter 1

It was a bright morning, in Austin. I went outside, lit a cigarette, and smiled at the shining sun. A day full of promise as my mother used to say when trying to motivate my childhood pursuits. Then I noticed the old lady, in the window of the flat next to mine, flashing me. Certain promises, clearly, were never intended for fulfillment. I waved her goodbye and climbed into the Buick. Then, I headed for Eggie's Diner.

Tuesday's breakfast special was steak and eggs. My favorite way to overload my arteries with cholesterol. I parked in the back, went inside and settled onto a stool in front of the service counter. Surprisingly, the waitress gave me more coffee than her usual outpouring of smart remarks. Some people have no understanding, when it comes to tipping frugality.

After finishing my meal, I drove to the Portland Building, and found a spot in the visitor's lot. In spite of the old lady's terrifying dance routine, my optimism was at an all-time high. Nothing could go wrong, today. Absolutely nothing.

Little did I know how quickly my prospects could change.

Dr. Paisley Firth was an optometrist with an office on the third floor. Two weeks before, give or take, Firth had hired me to spend an evening documenting his wife's extracurricular sexual activities. That was not my typical professional pursuit. But, at the time, my bank balance had been sucking air. So it was put telephoto lens to use, or go out of business. Unfortunately, my photographic safari had stretched from dusk until dawn. At which time, Mrs. Firth finally came up for air.

My delivery of the snapshots, to Dr. Firth, had closed the case. Or so I thought until his cell-phone call, on my drive to work this morning.

I caught the elevator up to Firth's offices, practicing my public relations smile. Follow-up calls, in my business, usually meant drawn-out haggles over my invoice. In Firth's case, I had been liberal with my expenses and somewhat excessive in the charges for equipment. But, after a night of filming Mrs. Firth's debaucheries, my strained eyes deserved extra compensation.

Firth's office was flashy. The amenities included the receptive smile from a marvelously proportioned redhead wearing the nametag 'Roxy'. There was also what could only be described as luxurious seating, by way of armchairs upholstered in suede leather. Moosic droned in the background, reminiscent of leisurely elevator rides, to provide a calming influence. Framed comic book covers decorated the walls, showing super heroes saving damsels in distress. These, I assumed, were for the benefit of the optometrist's younger patients rather than motivational materials for the easily influenced.

When I identified myself, Roxy said there was no need to fill out patient forms. The doctor had seen to that. I asked if he had seen to anything else. She ignored my sexual dig and said I'd be in Paisley's chair within a few.

I was not sure how to take that.

"Business good?" I asked, making conversation.

"Depends on what you mean by business?" she returned.

Roxy was lean and tanned. Her painted hair flowed away from a lovely face like dogwood bending in a summer breeze. She looked to be about thirty years of age. There were no rings on her fingers, so I assumed she was single.

"There's business and then there's business?" I asked.

"You might say Paisley's in the business of putting his hands in a lot of pies," she said, with a wink.

"Sounds like something in which I should invest."

I settled into one of the chairs not mentioning her boss' recent use of my investigative expertise. For some reason, Firth had insisted I not divulge our professional relationship during this visit. It was no skin off me. Firth had paid his bill.

"If I was a betting man, Roxy," I said. "I'd wager your boss relies upon your special talents."

The tip of her pink tongue traced the outline of her upper lip in a stirring manner.

"Cutie can't get enough," she cooed.

I crossed my legs, fighting earthy desires.

"Cutie?" I echoed.

"Dr. Firth. Cutie's his nickname."

I was about to press for the source of the moniker when the telephone rang. Roxy answered. From the instant flush to her cheeks, Roxy had focused her entire being upon the other end of the connection, and my presence was now part of her colorful history.

Twenty minutes later, I was in nicotine withdrawal and she was on her fifth telephone interaction. This time, Roxy was expounding the virtues of a vibrator with a g-spot attachment to someone named Rembrandt. I could not imagine anyone naming their daughter Rembrandt. But stranger things had happened. Apparently Rembrandt, based upon Roxy's side of their conversation, was keenly interested in pulsing oscillations. Something, according to Roxy, impossible to achieve without excessive battery wear.

A door labelled 'Examinations' opened.

From behind it, a squat, florid-faced man appeared. He was about forty-five years of age, with a light brown toupee balanced atop an egg-shaped head. Although he might be Cutie to those in his intimate circle, I knew the fellow as Dr. Paisley Firth.

He waved me over.

I got to my feet. After tossing the receptionist a wink, I did a quick-stride to the wig-adorned chubby. My nicotine cravings had put me past the point of mellow negotiations. In fact, armed retaliation to his as yet unstated demands fit my mood.

"Let's get down to brass tacks," I told him. "No refunds."

Dr. Firth leaned forward, his voice barely audible.

"Have you ever had a day when everything went wrong?" he asked.

"I was in Chicago last week, doing an in-depth investigative exploration concerning a multifaceted mystery, which became a non-discussable nightmare. So, stop whining about having a bad morning."

"How can you compare my writhing despair and suffocating anguish to you conning some broad into taking a trip to the Windy City?"

He was beginning to irritate me.

"As much as I would like to sympathize, Dr. Firth," I said, "my bleeding heart does not extend to discounts."

"It's not that, Mr. Bishop. Your check is in the mail." He took a ragged breath. "It's my wife: Connie."

As much as I appreciated his prompt handling of my bill, I gave Firth a determined head-shake.

"No way am I going down that bushy road again," I told him. "I've seen more of your wife exploring her own sexuality than any man should have to."

"Mr. Bishop, I'm scared."

"Trust me. It's normal to feel fear when viewing telephoto shots of your wife's mouth gobbling male genitalia."

"Connie's disappeared!"

That came as an unpleasant surprise. Mrs. Firth on the loose put every red-blooded American penis at risk. Perhaps, even the center for disease control.

"I think my wife's been murdered," he added.

Mrs. Firth dead could mean I had photographed her killer. Something I would not enjoy explaining in open court, what with the implications cast by her activities. But, what bothered me even more than professional humiliation, if such a thing was possible, was her husband's assumption his wife was dead. Most men with missing wives live in hope their loved one is still alive.

"Let's not jump to conclusions," I told him.

"Connie hasn't called," he whispered. "She always calls."

"I know. I heard. At the top of her lungs, I heard her."

"To give me details on her latest — engorgement." He tilted closer. "Connie likes something she can really grip."

"I can appreciate your concerns." I glanced at the ceiling. "But, your wife being gone can't be unusual — considering her hobby."

"Gone is normal." He sniffed audibly. "Not telephoning, isn't."

That gave me pause.

"She telephones you after each — outing?" I asked.

"There's nothing so fulfilling as open communication."

Most marital advisors would concur.

"Dr. Firth, your wife probably lost track of time," I suggested.

"That night I followed her, she went for hours… a full twelve hours working up a sweat. If the guy she was with hadn't begged off, I think she'd have gone another twelve."

"Connie's been gone for nine days?"

That put an exhaustive spin on things.

"You've tried her cell-phone?" I said.

"Of course. Hundreds of times." His lower lip trembled. "It always goes to voice mail." He paused, amidst a forlorn whimper. "Between Connie and me, voice mail is a big no-no."

"I'm glad something is." I looked at my watch. Ten minutes to nine. "Let's go someplace private. Then, we'll discuss your options." I didn't speak for a moment, and when I did my voice was a little desperate. "I assume you have ashtrays?"

"It's a nonsmoking building."

"Peachy."

Dr. Firth turned and waddled off down a short hallway. I shut the door and with my tongue slathering for the taste of burning tobacco, I followed.

A few strides later, we stopped in a room the size of a walk-in closet. It had been furnished with a tiny desk, a stool on wheels, an examination chair, a phoroptor mounted to a wheeled support, and a mirror on the wall opposite. He pointed to the chair. I went over and sat down.

"Let's start with who was she with," I said, taking out notebook and pen.

"Cutie," Firth whimpered.

"I get, from Roxy, that's your nickname. But, I prefer to keep our relationship on a business basis."

"No. His name's Cutie."

That was an unexpected. Two guys named Cutie in Texas? What happened to the machismo rednecks named Bill-Bob?

"What were Cutie's given and surname?" I asked.

"I knew him only as Cutie."

"I guy goes out with your wife and you don't ask for more than his moniker?"

"It's more exciting that way." He scratched his groin. "If it helps, Cutie's the man in your photographs."

At least I had a visual start. But, Texas was a big place.

"How many times did your wife date Cutie?" I asked.

"Four." Dr. Paisley Firth let go a whimpering sigh. "Sometimes, when she hooks a good one, she doesn't like to let go."

"So, I noticed." I silently mouthed a four-letter word. "Why do you think she's dead?"

"If your wife was gone nine days, what would you think?"

"Isn't it far more likely she's shopping for lubricants?"

A sob burst from his throat.

"How can you make jokes when I'm dying inside?" he moaned.

Everyone needed to love and be loved. Even the Firth's. So, I put on my sympathy face.

"Get hold of yourself," I said. "Had Cutie given you reason for concern, before your wife's disappearance?"

"No. Never."

"It's just that I photographed your wife cracking braided leather across his ass while he was screamed bloody murder about being a bad boy."

Firth offered a weak smile.

"Connie loves her whips," he sniveled.

"When was the last time your wife took money from an ATM?" I asked.

He weighed my question for a long moment.

"Not since the night you followed her." He sniffed wetly. "Not at all like Connie. ATM's, to her, are second only to sex."

"How long have you been married?"

"Twenty-seven blissful years."

"No serious disagreements?"

"None."

"Did your wife sign a prenuptial agreement?"

"Yes. Why?"

"Just considering possibilities."

"You think she'd dead, too?"

"Calm down," I told him. "No need to panic. Cutie's probably at home, right now, thanking God he's still alive and applying salve." I inhaled deeply, trying to grab a little Austin smog to tide me over, but my lungs came up empty. "You're wife's probably sitting on an icepack, shoving blue pills down his throat and praying for a rise in fortunes."

"I really want to believe that."

"Did Connie take any clothes on this last outing?"

"Just the usual lingerie in her overnight bag." Firth gave me a flash of teeth. "Sometimes a little mystery helps start the engine."

I raised a finger to focus his attention.

"Does she take along credit cards?" I asked

His head nodded beneath a stationary toupee.

"That's how Connie pays for the motel," Firth explained. Then, he croaked out a sob. "I'm worried I'll never again see another room charge."

"Have you notified the police?" I asked.

"Not yet."

That warning bell in my head started clanging suspicions like there was no tomorrow. When a man truly thinks his wife is dead, he notifies the police. Unless, of course, he was her killer.

"Why not?" I asked.

"That would mean explaining where Connie'd gone, with who and why." He wetted his lips. "She'd be totally embarrassed."

"If you don't notify the authorities, I will."

His eyes bugged, as he chewed the air for many seconds.

"Your investigations are supposed to be private," Firth eventually blurted.

"My investigations are. But, if your wife's absence is the result of foul play, the authorities will wonder why you didn't report it."

He dragged his hands across his face.

"All right," Firth said. "I'll do as you say. But, before we go any further, we should keep this visit official."

I frowned.

"How does one have an *unofficial* visit?" I asked.

"I didn't tell Roxy why you were coming."

"Neither did I."

"I told her you were a patient."

"The significance being?"

"I didn't want to shock her with Connie's disappearance."

"I've chatted with your receptionist," I said. "I've heard her on

the phone. Nothing would shock Roxy, except a battery shortage."
I raised my eyebrows. "Now, let's get back to your wife before my
nicotine addiction sends me up a wall."

"Those cigarettes'll kill you one day."

Firth had death on the brain.

"So, people keep telling me," I said. "How'd your wife first
hook up with Cutie?"

Firth plopped his ample backside onto the stool and skidded
over.

"Roxy introduced us." He smiled. "I chalk that up to my
personal hands-on employee training program."

It was easy to picture Paisley Firth instructing Roxy — hands-
on. Her sprawled across the reception desk. He frantically pressing
his point. But, as pleasant as that fantasy was, I had difficulty
explaining Roxy's interest in furthering Connie Firth's sexual
pursuits. Most women jealously guard their lovers; at least the
good ones.

"Will Roxy have Cutie's particulars?" I asked.

"I'm afraid not." He let out a disappointed sigh. "These days,
relationships are so casual."

"What else can you tell me about him?"

"That's it." Firth abruptly positioned the phoroptor in front of
my peepers. "Now, try to relax."

"What in hell are you doing?"

"We have to keep your cover."

"There's no cover."

The exam-room door abruptly opened and the receptionist
stuck her head in.

"Paisley?" Roxy cooed. "Charlene Holland's here."

"Now...let's try these, Mr. Bishop," Firth said, abruptly
spinning the dials on the phoroptor. "Thank you, Roxy."

The door closed on her exit.

Why had Roxy announced the arrival of that particular
patient? She had not done so when I made my entrance.

"What's so special about Charlene Holland?" I asked.

"Certain people require special handling."

"Meaning, females?"

"They're such delicate creatures, aren't they?"

"I know this Sicilian number, by the name of Rita Portello, who'll kick that idea out of your head."

Dr. Paisley Firth reached up and switched on the chart projector. Rows of letters appeared as reflections in the mirror, drawing my attention. Each was clearly legible. As far as I could tell, my eyes were functioning perfectly.

"When I find your wife," I said, "assuming Connie's no worse for wear, she may be reluctant to return."

"In view of what I saw in the pictures, understandably so."

"My point is, I can't force her to come back."

"She's dead, Mr. Bishop. Which means your concerns are moot."

Once more, he was directing me in a particularly unpleasant direction. Had he killed her? Was this all window dressing to underscore his innocence?

"Out loud, Mr. Bishop," he cut into my thoughts. "The lowest line you can read clearly."

"I don't need an eye exam."

"The letters, please?"

Rather than persist in arguing, I submitted to his request.

"A, R, N, D, O, H, T," I said.

"Perfect," he said. Firth screwed up his round face. "Was Connie screaming?"

"Screaming?"

"You know when Cutie was ringing her bells six ways from Sunday."

"Either that or she was coughing up a lung." I pushed the phoroptor off to one side and stood up. "Look, Dr. Firth, the sooner I get going the sooner I find Connie."

"What about orgasms?" Firth said, scrambling to his feet.

"Never before lunch." I held out one hand, palm open and up. "I'll need a grand up front."

He pulled out an overstuffed money-clip and peeled off ten hundred dollar bills.

"When you need more, let me know," he asked. "I'd spend my last dime searching for Connie."

A guy wanting to know if his wife was chipping around, I could understand. But, to mourn her assumed demise in one breath and revel in her indiscretions in the next? Either Firth was insane, or he was playing me.

On my way across the reception area I caught sight of a nicely built blonde, of the female variety. She was coiled up on one of the chairs. Her pink sweater covered the largest pair of mammaries I had ever seen. A gray skirt barely came down to her thighs. She smiled at me. I smiled back. Since the only other woman in the room was Roxy, it was safe to assume the current object of my lust was Charlene Holland.

"Paisley mentioned a guy named Cutie," I said to Roxy, when I reached her desk. "What can you tell me about him?"

"He's enormous," Roxy said.

"It's important I get in touch with him."

Roxy's shoulder's bobbed.

"I don't know how," she replied.

"Then, how do you and Cutie keep in contact?" I asked.

"Cutie gives me a ring when he's in the mood."

And people wonder why I love my job.

"When you and he do meet, where do you go?" I asked.

"No place special." Roxy gave off a natural scent that, if bottled, could garner a fortune. "But, if it helps, we always end up at my place."

"Where did you first meet Cutie?" I asked.

"Comic Con," Roxy said.

Comic Con was an annual event, in Austin. It was a venue to unite fans who love comics with comic artists. Part of this gathering featured masquerade contests. This allowed participants to become their favorite comic book hero, or heroine. It was usually attended by teens and preteens. But, comic book lovers of all ages would be present.

"Cutie dressed like the Phantom Vampire," she continued. "I wore my Vampirella costume." Her eyes widened and then Roxy laughed, as if tickled by memories. "It was mutual lust at first bite."

"What prompted you to introduce him to Mrs. Firth?"

"Connie and I were at a comic book collector's archive, looking for her favorite comic character's magazine."

"And that would be?"

"The Wanton Woman."

"Silly me for not realizing."

"Connie spotted Cutie and commented on his looks." Roxy pulled at an earring, self-consciously. "I told her I'd dated him a few times, and could recommend every inch." She cocked a telling eyebrow. "Connie said she was interested. But, didn't want to cut in on my fun." She traced her tongue along her lips. "I told her there was enough to go around."

I handed her one of my business cards.

"Next time Cutie calls," I said, "give me a ring."

When I got out to the Buick my cellular phone rang. Immediately my imagination went into overdrive as I pondered where to take Roxy on our first date. But, instead of her, the caller was Walter Osgood Kemp.

"What's shaking, Ozzie?" I asked.

"I need a P. I.," he said.

Kemp was an ex-con from my days as a police officer. I had lost track of him after my forced retirement. Not that we had been friends. Our relationship was more along corrupt financial lines.

"What for?" I asked.

According to Kemp, he had a problem only I could resolve. That sounded surprisingly profitable. When he paused for breath, I suggested a prompt consultation at my office culminating in a large cash advance. Kemp countered with a meeting at his place of business, tomorrow morning. Sundays, I reminded him, were meant for sleeping late, leisurely baths and uninhibited romps with wanton women. Kemp, however, said Sunday was the only day he could provide a witness to corroborate his situation. My schedule, for the next two weeks, was open. But, Walter Osgood Kemp was a notorious character lacking in every scruple. A lot like me, if the truth be told. So, I asked for details before making a commitment. He said it was too delicate to discuss, over the telephone.

Mentally, I formulated several excuses. But, in the end, greed prompted me to accept the appointment. Kemp provided an address, and then rang off.

Why would a loathsome scammer like Kemp insist upon meeting a Private Investigator, of questionable repute, on a Sunday morning? It was like Satan seeking salvation from a warlock.

Chapter 2

On the Sabbath, at the agreed upon time, I parked in front of the appointed place: 1417 Weston Avenue. The single-story limestone structure had served many masters over its multi-decade history: A bike store. A gas station. An automobile repair shop. And, for a very short time, a singles dating service. But, most recently, it had become a church. As a professional detective I had deduced the latter from two clews: First, bolted to the building's tile roof was a neon cross. This electrified Christian symbol blinked a blue promise of fellowship, and salvation. Second, above the front door was a plaque proclaiming the existence of *The Church of Hidden Salvation, Walter Osgood Kemp; Pastor*.

I climbed from the Buick, strolled beyond an elderly school bus, parked on an oil-stained drive, and went inside the unholy chapel.

Ahead of me, in the nave, were fifteen pews. Beyond, in the chancel, was an organ, a pulpit, an altar and a door. The latter, I suspected, offered access to the pastor's office. Walter Osgood Kemp stood behind the pulpit. From the look of his fancy garb, he was the latest malignancy to infest the mail-order-ministry. Perched upon the pews were seventeen people, men as well as women.

Kemp was droning a sermon to promote redemption, or something akin to it. I stood just inside the kirk — leaning my back against the front door — watching, listening and wondering. The parishioners looked to be street-people. Most of them appeared to be drifting in and out of what I suspected was a drug-induced slumber. All of them thickened the atmosphere with exudations from unwashed flesh.

"God's blessing is priceless," Kemp exalted, "and as pure as the air we breathe. Although precious, it can be had without money. You need only worketh and believeth and promiseth to lead a virtuous life and attend Church every Sunday - unless your sorry asses are banged in the joint."

Forty-some years ago the less than eloquent Walter Osgood Kemp, son of Mira and Jubal Kemp; grocers, bookies and illicit drug purveyors, came into this world kicking and screaming. It was as though the act of birth had instilled, in him, an irrepressible desire to carry forward his parents' criminal pursuits. During Kemp's childhood he had rocketed from diapers to knee-pants with a few stops, along the way, at several detention centers. By the time he reached the luxury of long trousers and the need for a razor, Kemp had enjoyed more than one stay in Huntsville Prison.

"At this point, brothers and sisters," continued the less than ecclesiastical cleric, "I paraphrase from First Corinthians: 'For no other foundation can a man lay than that which is Jesus Christ."

Osgood Kemp looked the part of a holy-man. He wore crimson and cream, in the form of brocaded Pallium, Chasuble and Fanon. Even his voice sounded close to the hallowed mark. However, there was something fishy in his shepherding demeanor. Something which would, should he draw near, make an honest man investigate the safety of his wallet.

"But anyone who buildeth upon that foundation," persisted Kemp, "without me gettin' my cut, will be in deep shit."

My first exposure to the ignominious Walter Osgood Kemp occurred during a stint in Vice, while I was a detective with Austin P-D. He was peddling doped females and recreational drugs. I had just passed the Lieutenant's exam and was hoping to improve my financial standing through bribery, and kickbacks. Kemp, not wanting to risk another term behind bars, quickly became my easiest touch. In return, my warnings kept him out of jail.

"As we piss toward the close of this week's services, brothers and sisters," said God's latest mail-order lament, "I want you to keep in mind that it's a jab-up-the-ass if we cut-out, or cut-in, when it ain't polite — like you lowlife bastards bad-mouthin' me to kith and kin."

Kemp's chiseled face displayed little emotion. His black eyes were wide and level beneath bushy brown eyebrows. His tawny hair was parted in the center and carefully combed back along top and sides. His bony nose ran like a ridge between flattened cheeks down to a long philtrum. In the right light, perhaps even a flash from heaven, he could be taken for a howling Collie.

"Now, brothers and sisters" said Kemp, "I want to close with this reminder: If I catch you sorry bastards and bitches flippin' off 'bout the money I'm payin' you, the heavens are gonna' open and your maker's gonna' come down and kick your spotty backsides." Then, he extended one hand and dramatically made the sign of the cross. "Can I get an Amen, on that?"

The congregation muttered slurred unintelligibles.

Walter Osgood Kemp was not one to run a charity, let alone a religious gig. Not unless it could twist his verbal tar into golden pocket-lining. But, as far as I could see, the Church of Hidden Salvation offered no profit angle. Each and every one of Kemp's followers appeared to be financially desolate. What had he said about paying *them*?

"That's it, shit-bags!" he shouted. "Back on the bus."

I moved away from the door to facilitate what would be a very fragrant exodus.

Like robots, the congregation rose from the pews and staggered out in a disarrayed procession, except a little guy crowded by a crutch and a skateboard. There had been no attempt to make a collection. Unusual, I thought. While it had been decades since last I attended services, my recollections of church-ritual included passing the plate. Even criminal clerics had to eat.

"Bishop," Kemp said. "Thanks for coming."

"Hallelujah," I returned.

In spite of my current financial shortcomings, I was quickly losing interest in Walter Osgood Kemp's need for a private investigator. Whatever he had in mind doubtlessly included this makeshift church. Although I was not of a religious bent, I was uncomfortable with the idea of someone getting an unholy screwing in the name of God. That being said, the lingering parishioner intrigued me.

I moved down the aisle to get closer to him.

He was a tiny fellow who looked to be about forty years of age. His face was gaunt and white. One of his small hands reached up and pushed aside a tuft of long, brown hair. The errant lock had straggled from beneath his dusty, black fedora. The broad brimmed hat was too large for his brain-case. It came down over his ears, riding atop his neck and the tufts of brown eyebrows. He had swathed a black raincoat about his narrow shoulders. The shabby garment's sleeves, tied at the cuffs, were gathered around his neck. This left the remainder of the coat draped down his back, in cape-fashion. Beneath this makeshift cloak I saw a t-shirt with white and blue horizontal stripes. Farther down, I noticed shabby dark trousers. These had been rolled to his knees, presumably as an aid in skateboarding.

He noticed my interest and grinned. One of his sockless feet began to kick, like that of a dreaming dog. The opposite appendage dangled as if paralyzed. Both were encased within mismatched shoes.

"Meatball," said Kemp, pointing at the little man. "Hang loose."

The fedora flopped up and down in eager agreement.

"Me and the private dick got things to kick around, in my office," Kemp added. "When we're done, I'll jerk your chain. Get me?"

Again, the fedora flopped.

The expensively adorned preacher left the pulpit with a flurry of robes, quickly crossed to the closed door, opened it, and disappeared into the room beyond.

"I'm Deacon Bishop," I told the fellow in the pew. "I'm the private dick."

From the looks of him, he was a hapless soul; innocent of sin, bereft of guile. Which nagged at my curiosity. Why would such a wretched creature be part of Kemp's desire for a P-I?

"What's your name?" I asked.

"Shadow," the little man chirped, excitedly.

His voice was shrill like he suffered from undescended testicles.

"Shadow?" I echoed.

Had the little guy actually been graced by such a curious name? Then a flash of memory brought me understanding. I smiled. His name was not Shadow. Based upon the little fellow's makeshift garb he believed he was Lamont Cranston, alias *the* Shadow of radio and movie fame.

"Don't worry, Mr. Cranston," I said. "I won't disclose your

secret identity."

He offered me a toothless grin, his hollow eyes all but concealed by the big hat, his empty gums glistening with thick saliva. I could not help but wonder what the Shadow knew that made him so important to Kemp's operation.

A thirty-second walk brought me into the pastor's office.

"God will get you for this, Ozzie," I warned, closing the door.

"Take a seat," he returned.

Walter Osgood Kemp stood in front of an open armoire, clothed in a white shirt, black slacks and slip-ons. While I watched, he secreted his religious trappings into the furnishing. From the pleased look upon his face, Kemp was enjoying his role as God's last hope for salvation.

"Who's the little guy?" I asked.

"The Meatball."

"Meatball?"

"It's complicated," Kemp said.

"Complicated makes me nervous, Ozzie."

He closed the armoire and faced me.

"Relax and I'll lay the groundwork," Kemp explained. "After we gab, the Meatball will give you the details."

"Ozzie, I spoke to the little guy. So, you'll forgive me if I don't bet my life on anything he might say."

The office was shallow and wide, about the size of a delivery van. There were no windows. The only door was the one I had used. There were two desks. Each was topped by half a dozen telephones. There were two customer chairs. These wooden constructs did little to dress-up the dingy, linoleum. Resting on the edge of one desk was Charlene Holland, that special patient of Dr. Firth's. Was there a connection between Kemp and Firth? Was that interaction limited to Charlene, Roxy and the Firth, with Kemp holding the camera? I smiled as my dirty mind considered lurid possibilities. Then, my grin faded. Was Firth behind Kemp's desire for my services?

"I admit, the Meatball's a little weird around the edges," Kemp said. "But, he's got the straight skinny, this time."

"This time?" I came back.

"That bigfoot sighting, on Anderson Avenue, was due to a

mix-up in his meds."

"Was he the one with the piss gun?"

Kemp's arms rose and fell.

"That was unfortunate," he said. "But, on the plus side, nobody got hurt."

"He spritzed three cops with urine before they tackled him."

Kemp looked around his office as if he had lost something but couldn't place it.

"Wet noses and nobody pressed charges." The paper preacher made an impatient gesture. "What's the big deal?"

We faced each other. His eyes locked on mine and then wavered before darting across the room and back. Kemp was hiding something. And, considering the presence of Charlene Holland, I had a feeling it involved the missing Connie Firth.

"I'm sort of on a case, right now," I said. "Missing woman. Her name's Connie Firth. You know her, Ozzie?"

His eyes jerked away.

"Don't know the woman," Kemp said.

He was lying. I looked over at Charlene. Her body language indicated a lack of concern.

"Running numbers or nags?" I asked, pointing to the phones.

"Stop being suspicious," he said.

"A symptom of our relationship."

"Them phones keep me in touch with my faithful."

"And I'm Cardinal Woolsey."

Walter Osgood Kemp shut the armoire and went over to the blonde.

"This is private, baby," he told Charlene, in an offhanded way. "Go keep the Meatball busy."

"Reggie smells," she complained, not moving.

"Who's Reggie?" I asked.

"The meatball," Kemp returned.

"His real name's Reggie Shepherd," Charlene explained.

Kemp returned his attention to her.

"You don't like the Meatball's smell, splash him with perfume."

"At three hundred smackers an ounce?" she demanded.

"Damn it, Charlene!" Kemp thrust a finger back toward the

door. "Get out there and keep the Meatball from wanderin' off."

"Ozzie, I'm not your slave!"

"If he gets on that damn skateboard, we won't see him 'til next Sunday."

Although we recognized each other from Dr. Firth's office, I assumed Charlene did not know my relationship with Firth. But, she could be forming assumptions, based upon Kemp's desire for a private investigator.

"Aren't you going to introduce us, Ozzie?" I cut in.

Walter Osgood Kemp blinked several times, my question having taken him by surprise. The usual niceties were always the exception to Kemp's rules.

"Bishop," he said, "this is Charlene Holland, my fiancée. Baby, this is Deacon Bishop. He's a private detective." The introduction was fast and furious, much like my licentious plans for Charlene. Then, Kemp warned her, "Whatever you do, don't lend him money."

The busty blonde smiled at me. The same smile I got at Firth's office. A nonverbal communication which would keep me up nights, pondering ropes and handcuffs, for weeks to come.

"Nice to meet you, Mr. Bishop," Charlene cooed.

"I'm in the book, Charlene," I said, "in case you need a friendly ear, or someone with a warm heart — and no aversions to offering IOU's."

"Anything she needs she'll get it from me, Bishop," Kemp snapped. Then, he returned his attention to her. "Why aren't you out there keeping an eye on the Meatball?"

I walked over and settled into one of the customer chairs.

"Reggie stares," Charlene complained.

"Every man stares." Then, Kemp grinned. "Why do you think I paid for them headlights?"

"It's like Reggie's got x-ray vision, Ozzie." Charlene Holland made a disgusted face. "I think he wanks-off thinking about me."

Walter Osgood Kemp jabbed a thumb in my direction.

"Me and Bishop won't be long," he promised.

"But, Reggie doesn't talk unless I ask questions."

"Then ask questions."

"Not when I'm alone with him." Charlene made a pleading

gesture. "I never know the answers I'm gonna' get." She shuddered. "Those hands, of his, are always going in and out of his pants."

"So, the Meatball's got an interest in body parts." The paper preacher gave another jab in the direction of the door. "So, let him have a look at your tits. Or better yet…" Kemp, then, made a pumping motion with both hands. "Let him juggle 'em."

"Ozzie!"

"Baby, you ain't in no position to critique my style." Kemp clenched his fists and glared at her while sweat gathered in beads on his livid face. "Now, move!"

With whimpers of protest, Charlene slipped the nail-file into her purse. Then she slid off the desk. Her face showed a mix of revulsion and frustration. She was nearing the end of her tolerance for Walter Osgood Kemp. I liked that idea. What that woman needed was an experienced private detective who was devoted to his personal toys. One who would demonstrate his dedication by using her base functionality as frequently as his heart, and supply of blue pills, could manage. One, who would not mind suffocating beneath her bloated mammaries. One, who would…

"You treat me like I'm a cheap slut, Ozzie," Charlene cried, when she reached the door.

"That I flatly deny," Kemp disputed. He raised a long forefinger solemnly overhead. "Anybody who knows anything about you, has the bills to prove that cheap ain't part of your personality."

From the wink Charlene tossed me on her way out, she was definitely ready to move on. That put my fantasies into high gear. The trick from my end would be to convince her a fold-away bed offered far better sheet tag opportunities than the soft-top mattress she was probably used to. Scotch would help. Morphine could be a plus. Maybe steel shackles?

"Private stock, Bishop," Kemp warned, noticing my glazed-eyes.

"A guy could die in Charlene's arms," I observed.

"Well, it won't be you."

Walter Osgood Kemp settled into a swivel behind one of the desks, his face showing contempt. That suited me. Because I had plenty of the same for him. I smirked, wondering if he knew about Charlene's visit to Dr. Paisley Firth, and Firth's view of special handling.

"Charlene's out of your league," I told him.

"Not, according to her."

"Maybe she's not the complaining type."

"There are three reasons for that woman's mouth," he snorted. "Eatin', suckin', and bitchin'. The last bit I get in spades."

I lit a cigarette, resuming my fantasies for Charlene. A swing, dangling from the ceiling above my bed, might be the ticket. I could lay there, look up and watch everything and anything swooping back and forth. Maybe floodlights and strobes to enhance the view? A video camera could put things over the top.

"What d'you think of my church?" Kemp asked, cagily.

"Knowing you, as I do, it has to be a scam," I replied.

"Bishop, you're cutting me to the quick."

"What I don't get is the money angle." I poked a finger back toward the Chancel. "Your parishioners have no cash, so you're not bilking them. They're not reliable enough to peddle dope. As for prostitution, there's little call for tricks by the unbathed." I paused to regard him, for a long string of seconds. "Which leaves me completely bewildered by your motivation."

"Can't a guy lend a helping hand?"

"A guy could," I replied, caustically. "But, not a parasite." I made another jab toward the phones. "What're you really doing with the ring-a-ding-dings?"

He made noise sucking his teeth.

"They're hotlines to the main dog and horse tracks," Kemps replied.

"Why a church to front a bookie operation?"

"It's more than that." Kemp glanced around as if worried about being overheard. Then his voice dropped to a murmur. "I'm runnin' the entire shebang through here. Nags, gambling, drugs, whores — the whole nine yards."

That little warning bell in my head began another dour jangle.

"That doesn't explain the church as opposed to a fry shop," I said.

"Churches don't pay taxes," he said. "I'm surprised you didn't know."

I did know. The tax angle had been worked many times by many people, the latest could be found on radio and television. But few of these electronic preachers had made it a long-term success. Invariably, power took control and zippers dropped. And when the photos of the fun hit the internet, the action imploded.

"Who's in this with you?" I asked.

He puffed up his chest, proudly.

"This baby's all mine," Kemp said. "I own the land, the building, the whole show."

"You, like me, are always short of cash. Which means, somebody else financed this expedition into heaven's hell."

"Okay. Maybe I got some help."

"From who?"

He grimaced.

"Let's just say, I have the right connections."

"Those connections also dreamed up this scam?"

"Charlene's more than body beautiful," Kemp said.

That was a small strike against the young woman. The smart ones were always deadly. Case in point: Rita Portello. She had a genius I-Q with the temperament of a Tasmanian devil. Nevertheless, I was determined to make my sexual fantasies for Charlene come true. But, to be on the safe side, I made a mental note to see my doctor for a physical. When submitting to the mother of all carnal Olympians, a man should understand his limitations.

"Smart women don't enjoy being treated like trash, Ozzie," I remarked.

"I don't treat Charlene like trash." He made a dismissing gesture with both hands. "Maybe I get a little rough, now and then. But you gotta' keep women on a leash; don't ya? Otherwise they go off on a power trip."

"You support the barefoot and pregnant ideology?"

"I make sure Charlene knows her place."

I blew a stream of smoke at him.

"How could you and your yellow-sheet qualify for tax-exempt status?" I asked.

"It's a cinch." He tugged at his ear, grinning. "You just fill out the forms in somebody else's name."

Ask a stupid question…

"Like Charlene's?" I pressed.

Kemp considered and then made a noncommittal cock of his head.

"Technically, I'm one of her employees," he said.

"So when the cops raid your unhallowed betting parlor, she'll take the fall?"

"Better Charlene than me."

"You're a sweetheart, Ozzie."

"Relax, Bishop. Charlene's got nothing to worry about." He laughed weakly. "I got the action rigged, like I had with you."

"You better than most should know how payoffs come back to haunt."

He stared at me with bitter loathing.

"I don't need a reminder on how you bled me white," he snapped.

"Who's helping you out?"

"Lt. Charlie Trent."

Trent was a familiar name. He was a police officer of low character and a cousin of Austin's mayor. He had, also, been one of my partners during my time with Austin P-D.

"I wouldn't bet my life on Trent," I warned.

"You know him?" he asked, in surprise.

"Worse than that, I've worked with the bastard."

Kemp abruptly fell silent, his face showing concern.

"You're saying Charlie Trent's running a game on me?" he asked.

"I'm saying you'd better watch your back."

His next words were slow in coming and filled with false confidence.

"Charlie and I have an understanding," Kemp said, with a nervous laugh. "He'd never pull a double-cross."

I gave Kemp more smoke.

"Charlie Trent'll take your money, Ozzie. He'll grin and nod. But, there's no understanding." My lips came back from his teeth. "If things go south, Trent'll cut off your head and shit down your throat."

Walter Osgood Kemp tilted back in the chair, thinking. He was not enjoying my words. He wanted them to be lies. But, deep down, Kemp suspected I had fed him the bitter truth.

"Trent said I'd have nothin' to worry about," Kemp eventually muttered.

"Ask around," I said. "You'll discover you've got plenty of worries."

I took a long draw on my cigarette, mulling over Kemp's church dodge. It had a snowball's chance in hell. The problem was keeping secret the real reason behind Kemp's calling. No matter how clerical the dress, no matter how heavenly the speeches, somebody always uncovered the scam; somebody always talked; somebody always went to jail.

"You're still operating under Salvator Portello's franchise?" I asked.

"No choice," he said. "One way or another Sal takes his cut." He swallowed hard, as if still trying to force down my warning. "But by signing on the dotted line, I get protection."

"What does Sal think of your setup?"

Kemp shifted in the chair as if a spring had suddenly dug into his backside.

"I ain't exactly told him," he replied.

"Not smart, Ozzie."

"Why should Sal care?"

"He's sensitive when it comes to religious scams."

"It ain't like I'm callin' myself the Pope."

I took another pull on my cigarette. Salvator would be furious with Kemp. Dominic Portello, Sal's younger brother, had tried a religious gig. That scam, intended to facilitate cocaine distribution, had worked for about a year. Then, with my discrete help, Dom's world of religious fervor collapsed. It had been an expensive mistake for the Portello clan. As a result, Salvator had refused to get involved in anything remotely tied to sacred convictions.

"How'd you get the bodies polishing your pews?" I asked.

"The first three Sundays, the dump was empty," Kemp replied. "Then Charlene saw the light."

"An angel shined down from heaven?"

"I shouldn't think so. Not with her history." God's latest wail for salvation inhaled deeply, and exhaled through his mouth and nostrils, making soft whistling noises. "But Charlene figured out how to bring in the punters."

"Shanghai? Or, intimidation?"

"None of the above." Kemp's elbows hit the desktop and his hands formed a church steeple, upon which he rested his chin. "Each of the shit-bags gets fifty bucks a week for sitting through my sermons."

That clarified Kemp's warnings about loose talk. It also explained why the parishioners were there. If you're living on the street, an easy fifty was a godsend — in spite of its source. What surprised me, was how few had accepted phony preacher's offer. At fifty a head, Sunday services should be standing-room only.

"A little outgo, to wash a lot of income?" I suggested.

"What can I say? Charlene's a financial genius." He chuckled like a young thief with a stolen toy. "I've never known a broad with a brain before."

"Frankly, considering your romantic history, I'm surprised you're still alive."

He wet his lips.

"Which relates to why I sent for you."

"Trust me when I say you're not my type."

"Somebody's been fuckin' my flock."

I tried not to take Kemp's words literally. Worst case, he was complaining about a deranged rapist with a taste for the unwashed. Best case, Kemp was referring to outside pressures designed to intimidate. Something Salvator Portello's franchise would oblige the mobster to resolve. Either way, I was not interested.

"Not my kind of case, Ozzie," I said, getting to my feet.

"Hang on a second," he sputtered. "My livelihood's on the line."

"Next time I pass a church I'll go in and light a candle."

Kemp jumped up, his eyes bugging.

"You can't just walk out," he shouted.

"Watch me."

The Lord's last lease on religious conviction raised his hands and then dropped them to his sides.

"Bishop," he pleaded, "if them IRS snoops show up to count

heads, and I don't have enough butts brushing wood, the Feds'll wonder about the money I'm runnin' through this place."

"You're bringing tears to my eyes, Ozzie."

"Can't you, at least, hear me out?"

I chuckled at the misery in his face. His troubles went far beyond the IRS. Once someone signed with Salvator Portello, it was a lifelong commitment. There was no option for failure. It was meet the minimum franchise fees, or die. Right now, I suspected, Walter Osgood Kemp was as close to looking death in the face as anyone without actually being embalmed. That made me feel all warm and cozy. But, not enough to stick around.

"I've got laundry to do," I said, and headed for the door.

"Damn it, Bishop! Four of my parishioners have been butchered."

I liked the idea of a God who would wreak havoc on the likes of Reverend Kemp. Still, I found it hard to believe the Almighty, at least the one I used to pray to, would lay waste to Kemp by killing vagrants. Morbid curiosity stopped me and I returned to the chair.

"When did this happen?" I asked.

"Last week."

"I didn't hear about four homicides," I told him. "When was this?"

"Last week." Kemp resumed his seat. "Them brain-dead cops labeled 'em accidents."

"Maybe they were."

"All from my church? All living in the same place?"

Kemp fell silent. From the look on his face, his thoughts were galloping down a twisted curve too sharp to pave with words.

"I'm no whiz at math, Bishop," he eventually said. "But the odds of them deaths being accidents has to be higher than Charlene's credit charges."

"Alright," I said. "If they're actually homicides, did you share your concerns with the police?"

"I'm working for the local Mafia Don. Do you really think I'm that stupid?"

Point taken.

"Okay," I said. "Let's say you're right." I lit another smoke. "Who hates your guts enough to do four killings from your flock?"

"Julie 'the Cutie' Caivano."

My brow puckered in confusion. Another Cutie?

"Should I know him?" I asked.

"Nope. He's recently a Portello button-man."

"Caivano works for Sal?"

"One of Dominic's guns."

I knew very few of Dom's people. Dominic Portello was a psychopath. And mental cases were not easy task masters. Sometimes his men left to attend business elsewhere. Sometimes they simply disappeared never to be heard from again. Mostly, they cut and ran to save their own hides.

"What's Caivano got against you?" I asked.

"Charlene was engaged to him before she met me."

"As crazy as Dom is, Ozzie, he's not going to allow one of his torpedo's to make war, on the likes of your parishioners, out of jealousy."

"You don't know Dom as well as you think."

Something began to nag at me. I could not place it. But, it tugged at my brain like a monkey working the strings of a marionette.

"Maybe. Maybe not," I said. "But, I know Sal, inside and out. And the last thing he'd want is mass-murder publicity."

"Sal might be willing to overlook the usual rules in return for a favor."

"You're dreaming, Ozzie."

"I think he would if Caivano killed Sal's wife."

That hit me between the eyes like a turd dropping from an eagle.

"Connie Portello's dead?" I gaped.

"That's what the Meatball, and the dead four, weren't supposed to see," Kemp said. "Which is why the dead four are dead and the meatball is overdue for his funeral."

"Why in hell would Sal order a hit on his own wife?"

"According to my sources, Constance was pretty tight with Julie 'the Cutie' Caivano," Kemp explained. "So tight, she was offering puckers at both ends and sharing belly button lint in between."

"Not a chance."

"Chance." Kemp waggled a finger. "Sal got wise. So, he had Dom handled the family cleanse."

If Constance had been unfaithful I could see Salvator insisting upon the transgressor executing her. And, afterward, having the transgressor murdered. Such a ritual would satisfy the Mafia Don's desire for revenge and it would send a message to the rest of the worker-bees to keep clear of Portello bloodline. What did not work was the idea of Constance Portello straying. She was a nasty piece of work. But, not the type to violate her husband's trust. Further casting doubt on Kemp's theory, was the idea of Dominic Portello overseeing the hits. He was a basket case of problems.

"You've got the wrong end of the stick, Ozzie," I told him.

"You're calling me a liar?"

"When haven't you been?"

"I'm giving it to you straight, this time."

"Ozzie, Caivano would have to be the dimmest bulb on the plant to mess with Constance Portello."

"Smart doesn't enter into Caivano's lifestyle."

"But, Constance wouldn't have reciprocated under any circumstances."

"You never saw Caivano. That pretty boy could've had any woman he wanted."

I flicked cigarette ash onto the floor. The more I heard, the more I wanted to distance myself from Walter Osgood Kemp. Then, I had a eureka moment. Constance Portello was a redhead. So was Connie Firth. She was missing. She had been with someone nicknamed, Cutie. What if the murder Kemp was talking about had actually been Mrs. Firth's? I decided to listen a while longer.

"When was Constance Portello killed?" I asked.

"Couple weeks, or so, back," Kemp replied.

"Nine days, maybe?"

"Maybe. Why?"

"Does this theory of yours include where Dom buried the bodies?" I asked.

"According to the Meatball, Caivano dumped her in the trunk of his car."

"And?"

"And that's as far as I got with him." Kemp shook a finger at me. "But, I'm tellin' you the Meatball's on the right track."

"Did the little guy mention seeing anybody besides Caivano at the shooting?"

"Not so far. But, his brain don't work like yours and mine. He thinks his brother's a butterfly."

"Did Reggie say anything about another shooting?" I asked.

"You gotta' understand, Bishop, he just blurts stuff out."

"Look, Ozzie," I said. "Gad Reggie seen Caivano kill Constance Portello he'd have seen Caivano killed, right afterward. Sal is an equal opportunity killer. He'd have had Caivano hit right afterward. Which means, Reggie would've seen half a dozen other people at the scene, to witness the events."

"Bishop, when it comes to the Meatball, it'll all come out. It just takes time."

"I'm not buying it."

"It don't get any better than an eye-witness."

I did not tell Kemp eye-witnesses get it wrong fifty percent of the time. At least the ones with fully functional brains, and the usual delusions. As for the odds on a valid identification from someone who considers himself a comic book hero, one could only speculate. But, I was fairly certain I would have a better chance of getting intimate with a Saudi harem.

"Tell me about your dead parishioners," I said.

Walter Osgood Kemp held up one hand, the fingers spread. Then, using the forefinger of the other hand, he ticked off digits as he spoke.

"Warren Suppanen, that's who the Meatball calls Bat Man," Kemp said. "Warren skateboarded off the roof of a building. How often does that happen?"

"Depends on the building."

"The Seton Tower. It's thirty-six stories high with twenty-four hour security."

A thirty-six story drop from the roof of a highly secure building was unusual. But, security personnel were not overpaid and often negligent.

"The others?" I asked.

"Norman Chaves," Kemp said. "He was the Green Lantern.

Norman decided to go Bungee jumping off Pennybacker Bridge."

"Nice high spot prone to accidents."

"Only instead of Bungee cords, Norman used a collection of suspenders. The braces snapped. One wrapped around his necked and hanged him."

Dying from a bungee fall I could understand. Hanging because of defective suspenders? That was a stretch. But, it could happen.

"Keep going," I told him.

"Louie Ayres was Captain Marvel," said Kemp. "Louie accidentally got electrocuted."

"He climbed a power pole?"

"Nope. Louie went up on the Anniston Arms Hotel's roof to piss on a pigeon."

"You're telling me the pigeon was hotwired?"

"No. His urine spray wandered to a power pole and hit one of the wires. Knocked out the power for eight square blocks."

That sounded more or less accidental, albeit rare.

"How often did Ayres piss on pigeons?" I asked.

"Louie had unusual ideas about birds."

"It doesn't sound like something staged, Ozzie. What happened to unlucky number four?"

"Henry Herschel. He was Spider Man. Henry drowned in the hotel's fourth floor toilet after his cape got flushed."

"I'm a little hazy on flushed capes."

"Henry was sitting on the crapper takin' a dump. He pushed the flusher as he got off the seat. His cape dropped into the water vortex, and dragged his skinny shoulders through the hole in the seat. This, in turn, sucked his head under."

"That's another hard act to arrange."

"You ain't heard the whole thing." Kemp got up, strode over to the door and jerked it open. "Baby," he growled, "put your boobs back in your bra and drag in the Meatball."

I crushed my cigarette butt under foot. Then, I crossed my arms and legs, trying to get comfortable. It was time for the Shadow.

Chapter 3

Reggie Shepherd hobbled into view. Under his left arm was the skateboard. The crutch supported his body's right side. This allowed the little man to move without his dangling foot touching the floor. The latter did not look injured. But, it flopped limply as though lacked a connection between bone and sinew.

"The Shadow knows!" the little man cried, excitedly.

Charlene Holland strolled in, adjusting her clothes.

"I'll just bet he does," I muttered, enviously.

"Shut the fuck up, Meatball," Kemp shouted.

"Reggie's fingers were sticky, Ozzie," she complained. "God knows what they've been doing." Charlene sniffed audibly and then made a disgusted face. "My cleavage stinks."

"Stop complainin'."

"I need a bath."

"It'll have to wait." Osgood Kemp closed the office door and strode over to the desk, glaring at me. "Baby, get the Meatball talking," he said, before slumping into one of the swivels.

"Tell Mr. Bishop what you saw, Sweetie," Charlene instructed. Her hand went to her forehead, it appeared milky under a shadow from blonde hair. "And no more talk about laser-shooting nipples, okay?" Then she went over to the desk, resumed her perch on its top, and dragged out the nail-file.

The little man crutched his way over to where I sat, his eyes wide and glistening with excitement. He looked like a little boy who knew the world's biggest secret.

"What's the story, Shadow?" I prompted.

"Naked lady," Reggie blurted.

"Tell me about her."

"Red hair. Kitty tattoo."

"In that case, you'd better take a load off." I pointed to the adjacent chair. "Nothing I like better than hearing about naked ladies with red hair and tattoos." I looked over at Kemp. "Not once, Ozzie, have I noticed tattoos on Constance Portello."

"Maybe you wasn't lookin' in the right spots."

I, also, had not noticed a kitty tattoo on Mrs. Firth whose 'spots' I had seen in spades. But, Connie Firth did have a massive rendition of ink art across her back. It displayed a leaping tiger with an enormous erection.

"You'll have to lead Reggie with questions, Mr. Bishop," Charlene said. "After he's been talking to me, he tends to zone out."

"I can't blame him." Then, I returned my attention to the little man. "Was the naked lady a friend of yours?"

The little man's fedora did another vertical dance.

"What was the lady's name?" I asked.

"Connie," Reggie returned.

Reggie Shepherd winced as he planted his backside on the chair. Then he looked over, his fedora twisting crooked on his head, and offered me a sloppy grin. His face gave the impression of someone who had spent a lifetime searching for a friend, without finding. I felt a wave of pity for him. Not so much because of his desperate life. But, I got the impression Reggie Shepherd was betting his hopes of friendship on me.

"Constance Portello?" I prompted.

The fedora made another series of flops.

"Now do you believe me?" Kemp cut in.

"Who else was there?" I asked.

"Cutie."

"Cutie Caivano?"

Still another bout of fedora flops.

"Just Cutie and Constance?" I pressed. "No one else?"

Reggie replied with yet more head bobbing.

"What did Cutie do to Connie?" I asked.

"Bang," the little man replied.

"He shot her?"

His chin move up and down.

"What did Cutie do with her body?" I asked.

"Blanket."

"Caivano bundled Mrs. Portello's body in a blanket," Kemp

explained, "before dumping her in the trunk."

"Reggie, what does Cutie look like?" I asked.

The little man gave me a blank stare.

"Cutie," he eventually said.

"I know he looks like Cutie," I frustrated, with animated hands. "He is Cutie. But, what does Cutie look like?"

"I wouldn't put too much mental pressure on Reggie, Mr. Bishop," Charlene warned. "He'll piss his pants."

"Which ain't no treat 'cause I gotta' clean it up," Walter Osgood Kemp chimed.

"I gotta' tell you, Ozzie, there has to be another explanation for what Reggie saw," I complained.

"He saw what he saw." Then, Kemp thrust a finger at the little man. "Tell Bishop where you and the other freaks were when you saw the killing."

"Warehouse," Reggie told me.

"Which warehouse?" I asked.

"Hillman's," Kemp explained. "They go there to have secret meetings." He snorted. "As if any of 'em could've kept a secret."

"Why secret meetings?" I asked.

"Reggie and the others had a super-hero club," Charlene explained. The upper bulge of her breasts gleamed like quivering alabaster. "They skate-boarded around battling imaginary bad guys." She smiled. "I thought it was kind of cute."

"You've always had a soft-spot for freaks," Kemp complained.

"Reggie and his friends never hurt anybody."

"Why does Hillman's Warehouse sound familiar?" I interrupted.

"Salvator Portello owns it," Kemp replied.

"Sal isn't the type to tolerate spying eyes. He'd have security personnel, to bar outsiders."

"Sal's not the type to tolerate anything. But, the day-guard's a drunk. His name's Fitzroy. Willard Fitzroy." Tiny muscles crinkled the skin at the corners of Kemp's licorice-drop eyes. "Spends most of his time sleeping. So, getting' in and out's no problem."

"But, why choose a warehouse?"

"Originally, Reggie and his friends used the public library for their meetings and the downtown strip for their adventures," Charlene said. "But, the merchants complained." Her head moved negatively from left to right. "Skateboarding was chasing off the customers. So, the city made it illegal to use skateboards in shopping areas." She lifted the hand holding the nail file for emphasis, while her free hand went to her breasts like she was shielding a pair of frightened baby whales. "It was either give up their skateboards or go somewhere else."

"But, why the warehouse district?" I asked.

"Nobody but the teamsters care about the goings on there." Then, Charlene's hands resumed their nail-filing roles. "Well, maybe the police, if there's nothing else going on."

"Bang, bang, bang!" Reggie erupted.

"What's happening?" I asked, staring at Kemp.

"The Meatball's letting you know how Cutie shot at him and the other freaks," the unvenerable vicar replied.

Reggie's hat danced up and down, once more, announcing his agreement with Walter Osgood Kemp.

"Tell him all of it, Meatball!"

The little man squirmed on the chair, grimacing with discomfort.

"Me and Green Lantern and Bat Man and Spider Man and Captain Marvel was there," Reggie said. "We saw."

"This was the day after they got their butts shot full of rock salt for trespassing, at another warehouse," Charlene chimed.

I looked over at her. She was putting her nail-file away. I let my interest dip from Charlene's hands to her dangling legs. They were well-muscled, like a dancer's. It was easy to imagine those long, shapely limbs wrapped around my waist. Or, clamped around my neck. But, Kemp's reference to high-maintenance had created a minor concern. Money was elusive. Of course, there was nothing wrong with tossing fate to the wind and letting Kemp carry the freight while Charlene and I enjoyed a jazzy weekend.

"How do you know about the rock salt?" I asked her.

"Reggie wanted me to take a look at his butt, because it hurt." She made a horror-struck face. "I declined."

"Meatball, get on with what you saw," Kemp barked.

"Run," Reggie quickly returned.

"Run?" I echoed, resuming my stare at the little man.

There was another session of head nodding.

"Cutie chased 'em," Kemp said. "That put the freakish five on their skateboards, cutting wind."

"Which allowed them to escape? Prompting Julie 'the Cutie' Caivano to go hunting amongst your parishioners for the witnesses to his dirty work? After he executed his boss's wife but before Cutie was shot dead? In between body disposals?" I scoffed. "Seriously, Ozzie?"

"Caivano was an animal."

"Ozzie, Cutie was very sweet," Charlene protested.

"Skateboards don't make snappy exits," I said. "If Caivano had sighted in on Reggie, and the others, they'd have been cooling meat within seconds."

"You ain't seen the Meatball in action." Kemp's surveyed me, his eyes blinking dull signals back to his equally dull brain. "Once he gets that crutch in gear, he's a rocket."

"Who knows what evil lurks in the hearts of men?" Reggie shouted. "The Shadow knows!"

"Ozzie," I said, "the Portellos train their shooters. They're all crack shots. As for Caivano whacking your flock, he'd have been dead seconds after Connie's execution." I rubbed a palm across my ache infested forehead. "Which means, if they those accidents were homicides, somebody else is responsible."

"Reggie isn't lying, Mr. Bishop," Charlene insisted.

"I believe that," I said. "But, what actually happened doesn't, necessarily, have to jive with Reggie beliefs."

Kemp frowned as he contemplated my resistance.

"I get it this thing's a bit shaky, Bishop," he eventually said. "But, the Meatball hardly ever hallucinates."

"He thinks he's the Shadow."

"Other than that, I mean."

"Have you got anything to corroborate the little guy's claims?" I asked.

"Just that nobody's seen hide nor hair of Julie 'the Cutie' Caivano and Constance Portello since the date of the killin'."

There could be a hundred reasons for that in Caivano's case.

But, it was not like Constance Portello to hide from the social limelight. She was known for her charity work. She, also, never missed an opportunity to attend gatherings where members of Austin's Social Register rubbed elbows. So, if Constance was missing, and not dead, where was she?

"Which, I'm sure you'll agree, makes a perfect fit to the Meatball's story," said Kemp.

"Question any five witnesses to a crime, Ozzie," I returned, "and you'll get five different stories — each a good fit."

"If you want a different story," Charlene cut in, "take a look at the boil on Reggie's butt." She shuddered. "It's like a puss-oozing snooker ball."

"Wait a sec," Kemp blurted at her. "You said you didn't look at his ass after he was shot."

"Not then. But, later…"

"You were humping him in the pews, for Christ's sake?" Kemp interrupted.

"I didn't do that!"

"Then, how'd you get a gander at his glutes?"

"When you called to come in here, Reggie stood up," Charlene explained. "That caused his suspenders to let go. Which prompted his pants to fall." She made a disgusted face. "Reggie doesn't wear undies."

"Which gave you a magical view of his ass through the meatball's raincoat?"

"Ozzie, he lifted the coat to pull up his pants."

"What doesn't work, Ozzie," I interjected, "is the player's lack of connection."

"What connection?" Kemp snapped, at me. "There ain't no connection."

"Between Reggie, Caivano and Constance Portello."

Walter Osgood Kemp gaped for nearly a minute, apparently dumbstruck.

"Is this one of them trick questions?" he asked, in due course. "'Cause, I gotta' tell you, Bishop, it's bouncin' off my brain."

"How would Constant Portello and Julie 'the Cutie' Caivano meet Reggie Shepherd?" I asked.

"It ain't like there's a law against it."

"I think Mr. Bishop wants you to explain how Reggie would've become acquainted with Mrs. Portello, and Cutie," Charlene put in.

"What difference does it make?"

"It's not like they'd all hang out, Ozzie," I said.

"The Meatball could've seen 'em some place," Kemp said. His eyes climbed across my face like feeding crickets. "Or, somebody told the Meatball who they were. Or, he saw pictures in the newspaper."

"Reggie can't read, Ozzie," Charlene said.

Kemp raised his arms overhead in frustration and let them fall.

"This is why I quit school in the fourth grade," he muttered. "Everybody was talkin' 'bout stuff I knew nothin' about."

"Mobsters, and their families, by necessity, have a limited circle of friends," I said. "The chance of Caivano and Constance Portello — both — entering into an acquaintance with Reggie Shepherd would be like Lassie winning the Triple Crown."

"We agree the Meatball ain't lying, right?" Kemp said. "So why not accept the obvious truth? Caivano killed Constance Portello."

I looked over at Reggie. His eyes twinkled. His foot danced. He was at the center of attention and thrilled beyond his dreams. Someone desperate for fame might lie for this type of consideration. But, not him. He truly believed all he had said.

"Where did you first meet Cutie?" I asked the little man.

"Comic Con," Reggie replied.

Professional killers, like Julie 'the Cutie' Caivano, would never attend such a happening. They're on-call to the mob twenty-four-seven. But, the Cutie from Mrs. Firth's sex life had met Roxy at Comic Con. So, perhaps, the solution to this mystery was far simpler than Kemp, and his entourage, believed. Simple enough to warm up my bank account to the tune of a few days' work.

"Where did you meet Connie, Reggie?" I asked.

"Comic Con," the little man replied.

Wives of Mafia Dons never attend such events. It was an unwritten rule. At least for wives who were ardent social climbers. But, from what Roxy had told me, Connie Firth attended the event. Of course, the kitty tattoo was still an open issue. Unless Connie

Firth had acquired new ink after I memorialized her in film.

"Where did your four friends live, Reggie?" I asked.

"Same as him," Charlene said. "The Anniston Arms Hotel."

I offered Kemp another questioning look.

"It's owned by Minerva and Mortise Anniston," he explained. "A pair of spinsters." He smirked. "Last of the family line since lightning killed their sister, Mariah."

"Lightning?" I echoed, in surprise.

"It's a tradition with the Anniston family," Charlene said. "The Anniston sisters have a nephew. Mariah's son. His name's Drax Ravaillac."

"How in hell do you know that?" Kemp demanded. "Have you been goin' out with him, too?"

"I met the sisters, downtown. Drax was with them."

"Are you goin' out with him behind my back?"

"Of course not."

"Because you've had a lot of headaches, lately."

"Drax Ravaillac lives in town?" I interrupted.

"He does, now," Charlene said. "But, I think he was born in Detroit." Her eyelids flexed, causing her peepers to bulge. "His mother, Mariah, married Frank Ravaillac. A psycho who stabbed his own father."

"Technically, Drax ain't an Anniston," Kemp snorted.

"Anniston or Ravaillac, Drax is as kooky as Reggie." She tilted her head to one side, offering me a coy smile. "Drax thinks he's the Phantom Vampire."

"Whatever," grumbled Kemp.

That, according to Roxy, was the same comic book character favored by her and Mrs. Firth's Cutie. So was it coincidence? Or, had I identified the mystery lover?

"Does Drax Ravaillac have a nickname?" I asked.

"Nobody but nobody," said Kemp, "would give Drax a nickname. He's an idiot."

"Cutie," said Charlene. "Mortise Anniston told me."

"Damn it, Charlene! Where'd you go, earlier today?"

I intervened with, "You have regular dealings with the Anniston sisters, Ozzie?"

"I slip 'em a few bucks each month." His face had colored

with jealous blood. "That way any new arrivals, at the hotel, get tipped to my prayer-for-pay program. Why?"

"Just trying to get a handle on all the players," I said.

"They're a couple of busybodies," Charlene chimed. "I told Ozzie to keep clear of them." Her voice became husky with mocking. "But, Ozzie knows best."

"It ain't like my arrangement with the sister's is illegal," Kemp protested.

"How can Reggie afford hotel rates?" I asked.

"The Anniston's rent one-room flops at weekly rates," Kemp explained. "The occupants are mostly druggies or mental cases."

"That doesn't explain Reggie's finances."

"Reggie collects Disability Social Security," Charlene said.

"If you're a druggie," Kemp said, "you get State Welfare." He sneered. "Our tax dollars at work."

"You said Reggie thinks his brother's a butterfly?" I remarked.

"Gordon Shepherd," she said. "But, he abandoned Reggie years ago. He's some kind of bug expert who works for the State."

"Do you know Gordon?" I asked.

Charlene's head shook.

"Reggie told me about him, last Christmas," she explained. "Reggie was hoping for a gift." Charlene shrugged her shoulders. "Nothing came."

"Reggie has no other family?"

"None who'll admit to him."

It was quite common for families to abandon members with limited social and economic skills. That way embarrassing explanations were unnecessary.

"People like Reggie often overlook their obligations," I said. "So, how can the Anniston's count on being paid?"

"Them payments are direct-deposited into a bank account controlled by Mortise Anniston," Walter Osgood Kemp explained. "She has power of attorney for everybody in that flop-house. In return she gives room, board and laundry service; plus a few bucks for spending." Kemp batted the air with one hand. "It's so legally profitable, it makes me sick."

"Then, why didn't you buy a motel and turn it into a help-house, instead of this religious shack?" I asked.

"You need a doctor on staff to qualify," Charlene explained. "Their services eat up the profits."

"Then, how does the Anniston Arms Hotel succeed?"

"My theory is," said Kemp, "is they've got Dr. Parker by the balls and he works for free."

"Parker?"

"Dr. Nathaniel Parker," Charlene said. "Widower. He's got a practice in Fredericksburg. But, he comes in, every week, to check on the hotel's residents. This makes Parker part of the hotel staff as far as the authorities are concerned."

"You're just full of information, aren't you?" Kemp said, suspiciously.

"Dr. Firth also helps out, there."

"You been screwin' those two, as well?" Kemp shouted.

"He's my optometrist, Ozzie," she said.

"Why were Firth and Parker chosen?" I butted in.

"I don't know about Dr. Parker. But, he and Dr. Firth are brothers-in-law. So, I think that explains how Firth got involved."

"Ain't that just like it?" Kemp complained. "Nepotism up the ass while I'm jumpin' hoops tryin' to stay alive!" He thumped his chest. "When's it my turn? That's what I wanna' know."

I redirected my interest back to Reggie Shepherd.

"Does Connie live at the same hotel as you?" I asked.

The fedora slid back and forth in a negative response.

"See?" said Kemp. "Now, do you believe me? Ask him about Cutie."

"What about Cutie?" I pressed the little man. "Does he live there?"

Once more, the fedora slid back and forth.

"If that don't cinch it," Kemp beamed, "I don't know what does."

"Anything else I should know, Ozzie?" I asked, getting to my feet.

He wagged his head.

"Other than you'd better get a wiggle on, before I run out of parishioners," Kemp said.

"Look, Ozzie," I said, "Reinvestigating four deaths will be

expensive. I'm going to need expense money up front."

Kemp quickly fanned the air in front of him, with both hands.

"I don't want to prove Dom had 'em killed," he quickly said. "That'd get me a death sentence, for Christ's sake!"

"Then, why am I here?"

"After the Meatball told me about Caivano killing Connie, I got in touch with Dominic Portello."

"You didn't try to shake him down?"

"I'm not a complete idiot."

"That's to be seen," Charlene sighed.

"Then what did you do, Ozzie?" I asked.

"I may have suggested he pull his head out of his ass and put a leash on Caivano or I'd do it myself."

"Caivano would've already been dead."

"At the time, I didn't know that." He rolled his eyes. "I still don't know that. Not for sure."

"I'd say that went for Constance Portello, as well."

"The point is, Dom got a little peeved and said he was putting a contract out on me."

"He can't do that without Sal's approval."

"Which is why I need you to speak with Sal on my behalf."

"Sal hates my guts, Ozzie."

"He still listens."

"You're better off talking to him, yourself."

"About that..." Walter Osgood Kemp dragged one hairy paw across his face. "There's a teensy-weensy complication on the Salvator Portello front."

"Teensy-weensy my Aunt Fanny," Charlene cut in, "What Ozzie's not telling you is, he's been skimming."

"Now you're Miss Conscience?" Kemp spat at her.

"Ozzie, you're a dead man," I told him, flatly.

"You think a place like this gets a pass without greasing a few palms?" His paw made another sweep across his face. "I'll have what I owe Sal in another week. Until then, I need protection from Dominic."

"I'll phone Sal, and arrange a meeting. But, don't count on my getting you out of this mess." I held out my hand. "I'll need a grand."

"I'm not made of money."

"What's your life worth, Ozzie?"

He pulled out a wad of bills and counted out my demand.

As I pocketed the cash I pointed to the little man.

"Keep pumping Reggie for information," I said. "The more you can get the better my position when I talk to Sal."

"The Meatball will stay at my house."

"Ozzie!" Charlene blurted in protest. "I'm not having him living under our roof. Reggie stinks."

"I'll put him in the garage."

"I'm not having Reggie sleeping in our car."

"I'll chain him to the old dog house."

"You can't do that! We'll be arrested."

"How can it be illegal? People do it to puppies all the time."

"Reggie's not a puppy."

"I'll be in touch, Ozzie," I said. Then I took a business card from my pocket and handed it to the little man. "Call me if you think of anything I should know."

Reggie grinned as he snatched the card from my grasp. It was like I had given him gold.

I headed for the door when a knock rattled its other side. Before Kemp could respond, the door opened and a dark haired man about thirty years of age, stepped across the threshold. He was slightly built wearing a bus driver's uniform. I stopped, taken by surprise.

"Everybody but Reggie's been paid and on the bus, Mr. Kemp," the fellow announced, his eyes focused upon Charlene. From the way his peepers worked her body, he was very familiar with each curve and crevice. "I need to get 'em back to the Anniston or they'll miss lunch."

"We'll be done in a minute, Leonard. Give the Meatball an extra fifty this time. And tell Buford, at the Anniston, it'll be worth a c-note to keep an eye on him."

"Will do."

After Leonard shut the door, on his way out, I asked Walter Osgood Kemp about him.

"Leonard Morgan's my bus driver," Kemp explained. "Gotta' have somebody with a special driving endorsement to haul the shit-bags."

"Leonard's a member of your church?" I asked.

"Nonbeliever." Kemp made a disgusted face. "As if I ain't tried to convert the bastard."

"You're a saint, Ozzie," I said, dryly. "Has Leonard been with you long?"

"Couple of months. What gives?"

"Just curious. Who did your driving before him?"

"Another guy. Fred something or other. I forget his last name." He squinted. "Do you know Leonard from somewhere?"

I wagged my head.

"Fred Worth," Charlene cut in.

"What happened to Fred?" I asked.

"Died," said Kemp.

"Cut in half by a freight train," she added.

"How'd that happen?" I asked.

"Fred went on a bender and passed out on the tracks." Charlene cringed with revulsion. "The wheels cut him the long way, missing both legs, if you get my meaning."

Instinctively, I tucked my knees.

"Closed casket funeral," she continued. "Not that anybody but me and Ozzie showed." Charlene swallowed thickly as if being flooded with frightening memories. "We decided against a reception."

"Any connection between Fred and the dead four?" I asked.

"Anniston Arms Hotel. Fred lived there. Leonard lives there, too."

"Why does Leonard live there?" I said. "He's employed. He's too healthy to be on drugs."

"I pick up the tab," Kemp returned. "Special dispensation by the Anniston sisters. And it's convenient for Sunday pickups what with most of my flock living at the Anniston." He tilted forward looking worried. "D'you think Leonard's in on the killings?"

"Let's hope not."

"Buford's another who lives at the hotel but he isn't under social services," Charlene said.

"Tell me about Buford."

"He's the hotel manager."

"Bishop, you know him," Kemp said impatiently. "Buford Reese. You busted his ass for murder, just before you retired from Austin P-D."

Buford Reese, in his prime, had been a high-flyer. Pushing dope and women, he had earned and spent millions. But, at the height of his career, his life crumbled thanks to me. I had asked for a cut of his action, in my usual cop-on-the-take fashion. He had refused. As a result, I felt rejected. This prompted me to paint Buford Reese into a corner from which there was no escape. That had not been easy. Buford was clever and well-organized. Lucky for me, he was blindly vindictive. So, after I spread rumors of a mole in his organization by the name of Chili Zumba, Reese got it into his head to kill Zumba. Which, after massaging evidence and manipulating witnesses, allowed me to net Reese in a murder charge.

"Buford should still have time to serve," I said.

"Not with bleeding heart liberals in Texas politics," Kemp said. "Every time some dirt-bag gets religion, they let him out."

"Thank god we had a more conservative government when you were behind bars," I said, dryly.

"Buford's good behavior qualified him for early parole," Charlene explained. "It's a new program for prisoners thought to be rehabilitated."

While the news about the release of Buford Reese was unexpected, I understood the reasoning. Texas prisons were overcrowded. Crime was rampant. So prisoners demonstrating contrition, especially those convicted on questionable evidence, were often paroled.

"How long has Buford been out?" I asked.

"Few months."

"How's he doing?"

"I'm not sayin' he's reformed," said Kemp. "But, the Annistons are noted for keepin' people on the straight and narrow." His brows abruptly met over his nose, as if his less than nimble brain was confronted by a surprising thought. Then, he opened his mouth, paused, and closed it before adding, "Sort of like marriage."

"Religious types, the Annistons?" I pressed.

"They're close enough to quoting chapter and verse."

"When it suits them," Charlene put in. "They can also curse like lumberjacks."

I dropped my cigarette butt to the floor and crushed it under foot.

"Okay," I said. "I'll let you know what happens with Sal."

On the drive back to my office, I telephoned Salvator Portello. We argued for several minutes, him ringing off repeatedly. Finally, after I mentioned rumors concerning Constance's murder, the Mafia Don agreed to see me. His first open appointment was on Friday. I told him to pencil me in. This was followed by his usual vow to fit me for cement overshoes, and take me for a swim in the ocean. There was nothing like the devotion of an old enemy.

Chapter 4

The next morning, while having breakfast at Manuel's Taco Bar, a Tex-Mex joint on Wilson Boulevard, Lt. Herby Mann appeared at my table. He was short, stocky, and pokerfaced with a drooping moustache. In spite of living a dieting marathon Mann's waistline had continued to expand, since last we met. He was wearing his favorite suit, a snuggly fitting brown herringbone with terminal wrinkles. Mann looked his usual unhappy self. I pointed to the vacant chair, across the table. He sat down, his jaw muscles rippling, his stomach rumbling.

"What's your business with Walter Osgood Kemp?" Lt. Mann growled.

"Order something, Herbie," I told him. "You'll feel better with a quiet stomach."

"Answer me, Deke."

"I can recommend the rattlesnake and eggs. But, tell 'em to go heavy on the onions. It'll cut the sweetness of the venom."

"Damn it, Deke!" he snapped. "I'm in no mood for your lame humor."

I took a bite of rubbery meat while I pondered possibilities. Herby Mann had a habit of baiting with seemingly irrelevant questions in order to garner unwary admissions. Which made me assume something, involving Kemp, had gone south. And my foot was buried in the stink right up to my ass.

"You know I visited Kemp," I told him. "So, it follows, you know why."

Lt. Mann angrily shifted his chair. Then, he tilted across the table.

"The Feds are using RICO to take another flier at Salvator Portello," he confided. "Kemp'll be their key witness."

That sounded ridiculously optimistic, even for the FBI.

"Does Kemp know?" I asked. "Or, are the Feds planning to spring it on him just before one of Sal's button men pulls the trigger?"

"Deke, this time the Portellos are history. They just don't know it.""

"In your dreams, Herby. Because one way or another Kemp won't make it to court."

"By the end of this month, the Attorney General will be charging Kemp with a laundry list of felonies. He'll testify, because he'll have no choice. Then, Kemp'll disappear into witness protection."

"Kemp'll disappear, all right. But, witness protection will have nothing to do with it."

Mann fanned the air dismissively.

"The Feds'll surround him with a ring of steel," the Lieutenant countered.

"And Mother Teresa was a great lay."

"Never mind your sick fantasies." Herby Mann's eyes narrowed to chocolate slits. "Let's get back to your relationship with Kemp."

I grabbed a tortilla and loaded it with breakfast fixings. Then I topped off the pile with several spoons of Salsa Verde.

"Kemp asked to see me," I said, taking a bite. Then, I chewed out, "I obliged."

"Asked about what?"

"It's confidential, Herby."

"Talk, or I'll arrest you for obstructing justice."

"You'll never make that stick."

"Maybe not." Mann's wide mouth twisted into a taunting sneer. "But, while I spend the next month doing the paperwork, you'll be in locked-up wondering if your attorney's gonna' catch on before your cellmate gets romantic."

Mann's innate distrust was beginning to irritate me. But, from the pulsing vein in his forehead, the threat of arrest was genuine. Unusual, for Herby. Something had him by the short hairs.

"If you must know," I said, setting down my meal, "Kemp and I got together for old time's sake. We tipped a few. Reminisced a lot. Afterward, I hit the bricks."

"You'd never visit a slime-ball like Kemp without a dollar being in it."

There was nothing worse than a smart cop. So, I decided to further aggravate his mood with more ill-considered humor.

"If the truth be told," I said, "I went to Ozzie for an intervention."

"Intervention?" Mann scoffed. "You?"

"You might not know this, Herby, but I've got a gambling addiction."

"Which you're going to cure with the help of God's last gamble with redemption?"

"It works on TV."

Lt. Mann laughed harshly.

"Come on," he gritted, between clenched teeth. "We'll continue this at the station."

So much for breakfast, wit and wile. But, I was not about to admit being Kemp's pipeline to Salvator Portello. So, I offered a 'mostly' truth.

"All right," I conceded. "Four members of Kemp's parish died. He thinks they were murdered. I agreed to look into the deaths. That's it, I swear."

"There hasn't been a multiple murder, in Austin, for over a year."

"Louie Ayres, Norman Chaves, Warren Suppanen, and Henry Herschel."

Mann hesitated a beat, evaluating the names.

"I remember them," he said. "Accidents, the lot."

"From what Kemp described, I pretty much agree. But, he's insistent."

"Assistant Coroner Sheldon Fields doesn't make mistakes. If he ruled those deaths accidental, they were."

"Then, why's Kemp paying my rates?"

Again, Mann fell silent.

"Kemp doesn't know his ass from a hole in the ground," he said.

"That being the case, then it must be his nurturing nature covering my time and expenses."

"If a phony preacher like Kemp hires you because of concerns for his fellow-man," he said, "then somebody's getting fucked during the litany."

As usual, Herby Mann's observation was sound. But, just as I was about to hand him a snappy of not demoralizing comeback, I experienced a revelation. Charlene Holland might be Kemp's fiancée but she was not in love with him. The goddess of my dreams was the informant fueling the RICO investigation.

"How much have the Feds told you about their plans for the Portellos?" I asked.

"Only that the prosecution will succeed," he returned.

"I think they've got somebody working from the inside."

His left eye twitched as his mind worked.

"Could be," Mann said. He eased back in his chair, and crossed his arms. "But, I doubt it. The Portellos run a tight ship. Getting a spy under their radar would require a miracle."

"I think the snitch is Charlene Holland."

Lt. Mann's brown eyes took on the look of hot molasses, his arms dropped and a grin spread his face.

"I remember her," he murmured. "Tits the size of basketballs."

"Who better than Kemp's fiancé to get him talking?"

"Charlene's his fiancée?"

"That's what he told me and she didn't argue."

He jerked his chair forward and rested his chubby forearms atop the table, the grin still wide.

"Those tits would get at my secrets," Mann said. "Can you imagine spreading her out on black satin sheets?"

"Every moment since I first saw her."

"What I wouldn't give to bury my face between her milkers."

"My prayers from your lips, Herby," I said. "A shame, really, considering you're married to one of the most beautiful women in the world."

My dig at this marital status returned Herby Mann's stoic personae.

"Have you got any proof Charlene Holland's a Federal source?" he snapped.

Would you like to put money against it?"

He slumped back in his chair.

"Not the way my luck's running," Mann said.

Usually my offering of a wager would put him into a betting frenzy. Mainly because in all the years I'd known him, Herby had never lost a bet. So, something was out of kilter in Herby Mann's life. Something he was unable to control. Something that had him walking on eggshells.

"What's happened?" I asked.

"Nothing."

"You're not yourself, Herby. If there's something I can do to help..."

"I'm going to retire," Mann cut in.

That was not good news for me. In fact, it was catastrophic. Without Mann as my police contact, I would go out of business.

"With you gone, what am I supposed to do?" I demanded.

"It's all about you, isn't it?" he gritted.

"Herby, I'd been counting on you making Chief."

"Well, it ain't gonna' happen."

"Not if you retire."

Mann's knuckles dimpled as he made two fists.

"I was passed over for promotion," he said.

I pushed my plate off to one side. Herby man was a clever cop. He was one of the few carrying a badge entitled to every step up the career ladder.

"You passed the Captain's exam with flying colors," I said. "You've got a sterling conviction record. How in hell could this happen to *us*?"

"Local politics bit me in the ass."

That meant Austin's mayor had a relation, or friend, who was short on qualifications, but big on plans.

"Who's the new homicide Captain?" I asked.

"Charlie Trent."

Charlie Trent, Kemp's current partner in crime, was dead from the neck up. But, as the mayor's cousin, he was politically connected. I considered letting Mann in on the Kemp-Trent partnership. But, I changed my mind. Herby would confront Trent with threats of exposure. Trent would counter with an insubordination write up. Herby would lose his temper and shoot the brain-dead bastard.

"Stay the course," I advised.

"I'm tired of swimming upstream," Herby Mann grumbled.

"I refuse to take this lying down, Herby."

"Which is one of my recurring nightmares."

From the determination in his voice, Lt. Mann was not ready to accept my involvement. So I decided to put his future on hold, for the time being.

"How about helping me with a small matter?" I asked.

"Like what?"

"What do you have on Julie 'the Cutie' Caivano."

"He's new to the Portellos." Mann gathered his thoughts, for a moment, before continuing. "Caivano came from the Manavati mob, in Chicago. Last I heard, he was Dominic Portello's bodyguard." He squinted at me. "Has he done something I should know about?"

"Charlene Holland used to be Caivano's lover," I said.

"Since when did that become a crime?"

"Actually it supports my theory of her being the information source, behind the RICO investigation. You see, she can supply information from both Caivano and Kemp."

Mann wrinkled his forehead.

"If that's true," he mused, "why'd she leave Caivano for Kemp?"

"Because the Feds gave Charlene no choice." I picked up my tortilla, and took another bite. "Any recent corpses on your Jane Doe blotter?"

Lt. Herby Mann abruptly pushed back, eyeing me with surprise.

"One," he said. "We recovered the body, from Lake Travis, last night."

"My guess is, she was shot," I said.

"Now, you're psychic?"

"Redhead?"

Mann nodded.

"I'm getting worried, Deke," he said. "What've you done?"

"Tattoos?"

"A tiger across her back. Did you do something stupid?"

My heart sank. I felt no affection for Dr. Firth, or his wife. But, anytime someone known to you dies, there's a feeling of loss.

"I'm guessing your floater's Connie Firth," I said. "How long was she in the lake?"

"Eight to ten days."

"Naked?"

"As a newborn. What was her relationship to you?"

"Nine days ago, I spent an unbelievable evening taking snapshots of Connie Firth being ravaged by one of her lovers."

Mann made a disgusted face.

"What kind of a sicko have you become?" he demanded.

"Connie's husband, Dr. Paisley Firth, hired me. Her in-and-outs are sort of his hobby."

"Meaning, if the dead woman is Connie Firth, the guy in your snapshots could be her killer?"

"That's one theory," I said, and took a sip of coffee.

"What's his name?"

"All I was given was his nickname: Cutie."

"Caivano?"

"The description I was given of Caivano doesn't fit the guy I photographed."

Mann took out his notebook and made several entries.

"I'll want those photos," he said.

"Send somebody to my office." I glanced around. "Was there another tattoo on the dead woman?"

"Nothing but the tiger." He put his notebook away. "You know Mrs. Firth well enough to make an identification?"

"I could draw you a map of her moles."

"Come on," Mann said, getting to his feet. "Let's go to the morgue."

"I haven't finished breakfast."

"After you see her, you won't be hungry."

"Get her husband to do the honors."

Lt. Mann smiled a little, showing the tip of his tongue between his incisors.

"What's the matter, Deke?" he taunted. "Gone squeamish?"

"Fine. I'll do it," I told him. "But, I get something in return."

"Like what?"

"The investigation files on Louie Ayres, Norman Chaves, Warren Suppanen, and Henry Herschel."

"All right," he said. "We'll go over them together. Now, if you don't mind, we've got a body-box show to go attend."

I stacked cash and coins on top of the café's receipt. Then, I followed Lt. Mann outside.

When we got to his unmarked cruiser, I stopped to light a cigarette. He shoved his hands into his pockets and looked around, like a man afraid of being seen with me. Something I had become accustomed to, during our years of hot and cold friendship.

"Have you turned in your retirement papers, yet?" I asked, blowing smoke to the breeze.

"I'm waiting until the end of the month."

"Why not hang loose for a while?"

"Work for Trent? Not on your life."

"The idiot'll screw up, like he always does, and be demoted."

"And like he always does, he'll dump the blame onto somebody else and they'll get demoted. That somebody being me." Mann ground his teeth for a moment. "When I think back to all the times I covered for that asshole, I could kick myself." He pointed at the cruiser's passenger door. "Get in the damn car."

Chapter 5

After identifying the remains of Connie Firth, I drove to Dr. Paisley Firth's offices. When I arrived, Roxy greeted me with a wink and a smile.

"Back so soon?" she asked.

"I need to see him," I told her.

She glanced around at the full waiting room.

"Paisley's booked," Roxy said.

"It's about his wife."

She wet her lips.

"Good news or bad?" Roxy asked.

"It'll take but a few minutes."

"Definitely not good news," she said.

Roxy picked up the telephone and dialed an intercom number. After getting Dr. Paisley Firth on the line, she told him there was an emergency and I would be waiting for him in the other exam room. Then she rang off and pointed toward the door where Firth had met me, on my previous visits.

"Last door on the left," she said. "Do you think I should reschedule his patients?"

"Might be a good idea."

I followed her instructions and found myself in an empty room about the size of a large closet. Optical equipment was expensive. So, I could understand why it lacked furnishings. Still, Firth had a thriving practice. From the body count in the reception area, he could easily support a partner. Why not fit out this space and hire a second optometrist? Perhaps his libido forbade any competition.

The door burst open and Dr. Paisley Firth rushed in.

He blurted, "You found my wife?"

I moved past him and closed the door.

"I have bad news," I said.

"Jesus!" Firth exclaimed. "Don't tell me Connie's not coming back."

"She's dead," I told him.

His legs buckled. I rushed forward to catch him. But Firth got control of his legs before hitting the floor.

"That can't be," he whimpered.

"I saw her body," I returned. "I'm very sorry."

"For the love of God, what happened?"

"She was murdered."

"By who?"

"Her friend, Cutie, comes to mind."

"Cutie? Never."

"How can you be certain? It's not like you knew the guy."

Dr. Firth showed me some teeth.

"Cutie and Connie had something special," he insisted.

"Loyalties governed by sex are fleeting," I countered.

"You don't understand. Had Cutie frightened Connie she'd have said something."

I put some distance between us and lit a cigarette.

"You didn't mention you'd heard from your wife when I was last here," I said.

"I hadn't," Firth bleated. "But, if there'd been problems during any of their dates, my wife would've mentioned it." He dragged his hands through his hair, locking his fingers at the back of his neck. "I warned her. I told Connie to keep her mouth shut."

"About what?"

"The Anniston Arms Hotel."

That came out of the blue.

"Do you know Walter Osgood Kemp?" I asked.

"No. Do you think he killed my wife?"

"A number of people he's involved with live at the Anniston Arms Hotel." I took a deep drag on my cigarette and blew smoke at the ceiling. "What's going on there?"

"I don't know." His hands dropped. "But, the Anniston sisters are up to something."

"We're all up to something," I told him. "Look, Dr. Firth, you hired me to find your wife. I did that. So, our business is done."

"But, you have to help me."

"Let the police deal with it."

He reached out and grabbed my arm. A glistening tear floated in each of his eyes.

"They could be involved," Firth whimpered.

"In what?" I demanded, impatiently.

"Whatever it is, the sisters are making payoffs," Firth said, releasing his grip. "That much I do know."

"If you don't know what they're up to, how do you know they're making payoffs?"

"Connie told me. But, she clammed up when I asked for details."

He grabbed for my arm again. This time I dodged his effort.

"Was your wife involved?" I asked.

"Cutie told her about it."

"Unusual for pillow talk."

"Connie had a way of delving into a man's deepest secrets."

"I noticed her doing plenty of delving. But, nothing in the way of secrets came to light. Did your wife share her payoff ideas with anyone else?"

"I overheard Connie on the telephone, talking to Nathaniel about it."

"Dr. Nathaniel Parker?"

Firth nodded.

"Our brother-in-law," he said. "She asked if he was receiving payoffs."

"And?"

"From the bits and pieces she said, Nathaniel denied it."

"Did you confront your brother-in-law about it?"

Firth shook his head.

"After Connie went missing," he choked. "I went to Hillcrest. I told Nathaniel to send her home. But, he said he didn't know where she was."

"Why would you think she was with him?"

"They had an affair, a while back. I thought Connie was going to leave me." He licked the corners of her mouth with the tip of his tongue. "That's when I suggested she interest herself in outside activities."

"Like Cutie?"

"I thought a hobby might help her relax."

"Did Dr. Parker have any suggestions as to where your wife

might have gone?"

"No. Nothing."

"You should've told me about this."

"It's not something a man brags about."

"Anybody else get a call from your wife about payoffs?"

"Not that I know of. But, after I left Nathaniel's office at Hillcrest, I lingered outside his door. He telephoned a friend on the police force. Lt. Trent. Nathaniel warned him I was asking questions."

"Lt. Charlie Trent?" I asked, in surprise.

Firth's eyebrows shot up into worried arches.

"You know him?" he asked.

"I'm not on Charlie's Christmas list. But, yeah, I know him." I flicked the ash from my cigarette onto the floor. Surprisingly, Firth never said a word. "Did your wife have a connection to the Anniston sisters?"

"Not that I'm aware of." He shook his head vigorously. "Mr. Bishop, can't you do this for me?"

"Legally and ethically, yes," I said. "The problem is, I'll have to share anything I discover with the police." I jabbed a finger through the air between us. "Including any involvement you might have in your wife's death."

His eyes bugged.

"I didn't do it!" Firth cried.

"And I believe you," I said. "But, as the spouse, the police will consider you their primary suspect until you can be cleared from their investigation. Are you sure you want me involved?"

"Do what you have to do to find Connie's killer." He from a pocket within his suit Firth pulled out his checkbook. "How much to get you started?"

I quoted him an amount which should have curled what remained of his hair. But, without hesitation, Dr. Firth filled out a draft in my favor.

"When you need more, let me know," he said.

Chapter 6

It rained all the next day. The drops spattered knee-high off the asphalt and concrete. From time to time, thunder rumbled so loud it shook the windows in my office. I hunkered down in my swivel chair, smoked and pondered my prospects. I still had an obligation to speak with Salvator Portello on behalf of Walter Osgood Kemp. Then there was Reggie Shepherd's claims concerning Connie Portello and Julie 'the Cutie' Caivano. Reggie might be a kook. But, there was no denying Connie Portello's abrupt disappearance.

That evening, as the rain continued, there was an unexpected knock on my apartment door. I got up from the kitchen table expecting to see Dr. Paisley Firth in a state of uncontrolled mourning over his wife's death. But, when I responded, I was greeted by Rita Portello's lusty smile. Immediately, parts of me jumped to attention with the usual anatomical salute. It had been nearly a year, since her last visit. I looked past Rita's svelte figure hoping to see my son, Diacono. But, to my disappointment, he was not with her.

"Bishop, you bastard," Rita said.

"I love you, too, Rita," I returned.

Her beautiful face was flush with anticipation, her dark eyes glittered. She drew a deep breath, arching her breasts. Thank you, God — or whoever — for wicked blessings. I backed out of Rita's way, trying not to clatter like a tripod. She swayed across the threshold, grinning at my eager anticipation.

"Slumming?" I asked.

"Considering how you live, an affirmation should come as no surprise."

"I admit my lodgings could use an upgrade. But, it's hard to beat the innate character of its atmosphere."

"Atmosphere?" she gaped. "Character?"

"As one matures, one learns to appreciate the sophisticated elements in apartment living — at the poverty level."

"There's a rat, in the hallway, doing the Fandango."

"What can I say? The fuzzy little guy has rhythm."

Rita slipped off her coat and handed it to me, providing a view of sexy female encased in a clingy black dress. My zipper nearly ruptured itself trying to contain my eagerness.

"Last I heard, you were in Sicily," I remarked.

"Momma wanted Diacono to meet the rest of the family."

"What does our son think of his relatives?"

"Thanks to them, your son plans to be a goat herder."

From the look in her eyes, and the rapidity of her breathing, Rita had something besides catching up in mind. That made me smile to the point my face hurt.

"Goats are good," I said.

"Have you smelled one?" she returned.

"It's on my bucket list."

Rita Portello glanced around.

"You alone?" she asked.

"Aren't I always?"

"You keep claiming that. But, I've always suspected you're guilty of chasing anything in a skirt — number of legs up to six."

"Nonsense. I live like a monk, except when you're around."

"Let's not complicate things with what a monk's life could entail."

She traversed the kitchen, through the archway to the front room. I closed the door, set the lock, and dropped her coat onto the table. Then, I headed after her like a horny Basset Hound.

"How's your brother, Dom, these days?" I asked, entering the room.

"Fix me a drink, will you?"

Her lithe figure and throaty voice had always enchanted me. Qualities, I believed, she reserved only for me. Outwardly, Rita Portello was cool and aristocratic. Her willowy body was exquisitely dressed, her dark hair coiffed in the manner of a goddess.

"That sounds like an evasion," I said. "What's he done wrong, this time?"

"Nothing."

Rita was sitting on my pull-out bed, unbuttoning her blouse.

Her hair glistening like morning dew on crow's wing. Her large, dark eyes smoldered. She was the type of woman a man would die for. She was the type of woman who would help that idea along if a man crossed her.

"Has Dom had another psychotic blowout?" I pressed. "You know… Ghost spotting? Little Green Man glimpsing? Dreams of naked sirens writhing in agony, under the crack of his whip?"

"Did you hear me ask for a drink?" she said, impatiently.

I went to the bureau where I kept my underwear and liquor. Then, from the top drawer, I took a couple of scruffy jam glasses and a bottle of Jack Daniels. After pouring two inches in each container, I hurried over to where she sat.

Rita grabbed one and took a hefty pull. Then, she set the makeshift beverage container on the floor.

"I wouldn't have mentioned Dom," I said, over the rim of my glass, "but I've heard rumors."

"He had an incident, okay?"

"Something terminal for brother Dom, I hope?"

She gave me a scowling glance.

"Dom thought he saw daddy's ghost," Rita explained.

Not what I expected. Not what I would have wished on Dominic Portello. He deserved a far more painful experience. But, frightfully satisfying, just the same.

"Old Frank out of his coffin," I mused. "That must've shaken family values."

"My brother and daddy never got along."

"Does Dom get along with anybody?"

"Because of that, Dom feels guilty. And his guilt gives him delusions."

"From what I've observed, Dom feels guilt about nothing. Fear, however, he feels aplenty." I lit a cigarette. "Old Frank's ghost would be something to fear. That idea even gives me the shivers."

"My brother's not a coward, Bishop," she snapped.

"Of course he is. All psychopaths are."

"Dom simply has difficulties in social situations."

"Like explaining why he took a hooker to a motel and skinned her alive?"

Rita gave me another scathing look.

"You're no saint," she snapped.

"But, so far, I've never had the urge to dice body-parts." I filled my lungs with smoke and breathed out slowly. "Maybe it's a rollback to when Dom was a kid."

"Since when are you a therapist?"

"You must remember when Old Frank even called Bishop Tegan and asked for an exorcism? And, Tegan sent Father Drapula to cure Dom's evil infestation?"

"Why do you revel in the misery of others?"

"Not others, Rita. Just Dom's."

"You're a sadist."

"Tell me true," I coaxed. "Did Old Frank's ghost threaten to kill Dom?"

She turned her head lazily away from me.

"Dom said daddy's ghost pointed a gun," Rita said.

"Old Frank was never one to leave unfinished business."

"Whatever unfinished business daddy had died with him."

"Then why did Old Frank crawl out of his cozy coffin to pay your brother a visit?"

Rita Portello fell silent, her jaw muscles working.

"When Dom was a kid, he hijacked one of daddy's liquor trucks," she said.

"You mean the one where the driver was found hung upside down, and hacked to death?"

"Dom didn't do that."

"Then why is Old Frank's ghost making house-calls?"

Her blouse dropped to the floor.

"Dom said it was so real," she murmured. "Like daddy was really there. Dom could even smell daddy's cologne."

My lusting eyes focused upon the cups of her bra.

"Old Frank always put the scent on, heavy," I said. "But he was the type of mobster who could carry it off."

"Dom grabbed his gun and emptied a clip at the ghost," she said, more to herself than me.

"There's nothing like a son's devotion."

"The bullets went through the wall."

"Bullets tend to do that."

"Woke poor Momma from a sound sleep."

"That's why silencers were invented."

"It wasn't the noise, it was the bullets," she said. "Sixteen of them. They sent shattered glass and porcelain, all over Momma's room."

My heart jumped to my throat, with worry.

"Is Momma okay?" I asked.

"Physically, yes. But, she hasn't slept well since." Rita, absently, ran one hand across the rough bed spread. "Momma wakes up screaming for Daddy."

"How'd Sal take the incident?"

"He made Dom move out."

"That's the safest approach."

"But, he's treating Dom like a madman."

"Which, in all fairness to your eldest brother Sal, is not far off the mark."

"Damn you, Bishop!" Rita's forehead suddenly wrinkled in suspicion. "You're asking a lot of questions about people you care nothing about."

"I care about Momma, you and Diacono."

"Only when it suits you." Her head went down, slightly, but her gaze slanted over to my face. "Sal's got a duodenal ulcer. He blames you, for it."

"What have I done?"

She shrugged.

"But, he's planning to have you packed in cement if he goes in for surgery."

"Lovely," I said, dryly. "Constance is well?"

"Damned if I know."

"You, two aren't talking?"

She picked her glass up and took a swig.

"Connie was gone when I got back from Sicily," Rita said.

"Gone where?"

Her eyes flashed to mine.

"What's with you and these damn questions?" she demanded.

"You don't have to get defensive. I'm merely trying to catch up on what's happening in my son's life."

"Between you and my family, I'm always on the defensive."

"Not that's totally unfair."

"Connie's at a fat farm." She smiled, then. "But, keep that to yourself or she'll cut your balls off."

It was an explanation that made no sense. The last time I had seen Constance Portello, she had been thin enough to do swimwear commercials. Something I had suggested, in my own licentious way, which had gotten me a slap. But Rita's voice indicated truth, in the telling. At least to the extent, she believed it. But, Sal had a history of misleading his family over sensitive issue. Perhaps the fat farm story had been Sal's way of keeping the family unaware of Constance's death?

"Why are women so sensitive about their weight?" I asked.

"Because men judge a woman solely by her looks."

"That's not true."

"Oh, I forgot about your special assessment methodology." Her lids drooped giving her an expression of guarded tolerance. "You rate a woman five stars only if she takes you to bed."

"I flatly deny that." I took another draw on my cigarette. "Bedding me is worth a full ten stars."

She laughed.

"You're the most self-serving bastard I know," Rita said.

"I send you and Momma a card each Christmas, don't I? And don't I buy a Santa gift for Diacono?"

"Only because I telephone to remind you."

Well spotted.

"The point is," I returned, "those efforts represent selfless acts." I took another sip of booze. "Connie's doctor suggested the fat farm?"

Rita's dark tresses rustled on her shoulders, with the shaking of her head.

"Connie's weight issues aren't that serious," Rita said. "Just nervous eating."

"You don't gain weight."

"I'm not nervous," she calmly said.

Rita set down her glass, stood up and began working on her skirt's' zipper. My heart went thudding into overdrive as I fantasized about what lay beneath.

"That's one of the many things I love about you," was my own jumpy response.

Perhaps, the fat farm story was completely legitimate? Nervous eating could pack on the pounds. Factor in the emotional strain of being married to Salvator Portello, the local Mafia Don, and waistline expansion was all but guaranteed.

"Does Constance have a tattoo?" I asked.

The zipper went down under the guidance of thumb and forefinger. Then, her skirt dropped. My eyes widened upon the blue lace exposed by the fallen garment. I took another sip. Tonight was going to be spiritual experience.

"There's a kitten inked on Connie's ass," Rita said. "But, that's another thing you'd better not talk about." She put her hands to her hips and faced me. "Are we, finally, done with family trivia?"

The tattoo's description gave me renewed concerns for Constance Portello's wellbeing.

"Where's Julie 'the Cutie' Caivano?" I asked. "Same fat farm?"

"Again with the questions," she complained. Rita thrust a finger through the air between us. "Tonight, you're going to concentrate on me."

"Already doing so," I said.

Rita gave me a leering wink as her hips rocked and she playfully toyed with her panty's elastic. I dropped my cigarette butt into my glass.

"Ready for action?" she cooed.

I nodded.

"In my last dream, you were naked except for thigh-high boots," I told her.

"You should have warned me about this kink. I'd have come dressed for the occasion."

I bent over and set my glass on the floor. Then I resumed my visual feast of her flesh.

"You were in Sicily when I discovered my sexual calling," I returned.

Her arms crossed as she gave me another look.

"Acquired how, during your time as a monk?" Rita demanded.

"While I was at evening prayers, my elderly neighbor, Mrs.

Forges, stopped by."

"An octogenarian wearing only leather boots, I presume?"

"As I recall, there was also a red satin corset."

"All of which required a neighborly what?"

"The poor dear hand-delivered a misdirected letter."

"Does she often dress like that when delivering your mail?"

"Not usually," I replied. "But, her husband had just been resupplied with blue pills and, while she was waiting for something to happen, Mrs. Forges decided to perform a Christian act. Something about how she was about to sin, like never before, and needed a few points on the plus side of her life's ledger."

Rita rolled her eyes.

"Well, I'm not Mrs. Forges," she said. "So, anything I mete out will have nothing to do with Christian acts."

I did a quick Hail-Mary while praying for the stamina of ten men.

"In case you need some creative incentive," I told her, "in my dream I was chained to the bed."

"Handcuffed and naked?"

"Actually, I was dressed like a rabbit."

Her brows drooped into a confused frown.

"A rabbit?" she asked, in disbelief. "Seriously, Bishop?"

"In my own defense, the bunny suit was crotchless."

Her thumbs hooked behind the elastic of her panties. Then, Rita slid the lacey item across the slight swell of her hips. My eyes followed the wispy garment to the floor.

"There should be laws against that," I choked.

"Wait 'til we get between the sheets and I get down to the nitty-gritty."

"I'm not sure my heart will stand the pressure to perform."

Rita stepped clear of the panty. For several beats, I pondered the value of insisting she hold that pose while I went in search of a camera, and vitamin supplements. But, I decided to hold off until I had finished my investigative business.

"Speaking of dirty dreams," I said, "rumor has it Caivano had an unhealthy interest in Constance."

"Sexual?" she scoffed. "Constance?"

"Considering your family's history, on dealing with

interlopers, what could be unhealthier?"

"Even Cutie's not that stupid."

"You know him?" I asked in surprise.

She curled her hand over each bra-cup and gave her breasts a jiggle.

"Not the way you're worried about," Rita said. "But, yes, I knew him."

"'Knew him'? Past tense?"

Her hands dropped as she turned away, her face going from smile to stiff and guilty concern.

"Life goes on, Bishop," Rita murmured.

I felt a pain in my heart that had nothing to do with naughty thoughts. If Caivano was dead, Kemp had been correct and Constance had been the naked redhead of Reggie's tale.

"When did Caivano die?" I asked.

Her response was slow in coming as if she had shared a hand in the man's demise. As she spoke, she turned back to face me.

"I'm the only friend you've got," Rita said. Her painted fingernails dug at her palms. "Burning your bridges with me, before sex, would not be smart."

"At the moment I can think of nothing more foolish. But, I'm curious as to the how, why and when of Caivano's demise."

"He and Dom had a disagreement. Disagreeing with my brother is not smart. Bad things tend to happen to those who do."

"Was this disagreement over Caivano's interest in you?"

Her mouth pursed up tight.

"Let's leave it that Caivano had to go," she said.

"When did this happen?" I asked.

"What difference does it make?"

"Humor me."

"Back a couple of weeks."

Assuming Rita's dating of the incident was not far off the mark, Caivano's death fell in line with that of Connie Firth. But, Constance Portello had the tattoo Reggie described. Which put me back where I had first started.

"Any chance I could have a peek at his corpse?" I asked.

"I'm standing here naked and you want to look at a dead body? Do you know how insulting I find that?"

"On second consideration, my body viewing pursuits could be delayed."

She hesitated as if trying to decide if I was worthy of what she had in mind. Then her shoulders jumped, as she came to a decision.

"Look, Bishop," Rita said. "I'm not part of the business. I don't want to be part of the business. Now, either we move on or I leave."

"I definitely vote for moving on."

Her fingers reached back and release the brassiere's clasp. Then, she pulled the lacy blue garment from her shoulders, and tossed it across the room. I could not decide which way to look. The floor, where the goody-holder lay. Or directly at the goodies. I decided to focus upon the latter. The milky-white pair jiggled as if they were having a good time beneath her touch.

"I don't suppose I could make a photographic history of this event?"

"Forget it."

So much for artistic expression.

"I never get tired of looking at you," I murmured.

"No news there. You're a dirty old man."

"I was giving you a compliment."

Rita bent over and unhooked the garter belt from her stockings. Then her thumbs slid between flesh and nylon to lower the silky material. The act was similar to a slow, naughty waltz. When the stocking hit the floor she kicked it through the air. I felt a gripping pain in my chest. Instinctively, I sucked in breath. The effort made a funny rasping sound. Sort of like a man gasping his last. At my age, that was a genuine possibility. I went over to the bed and sat down, quivering with expectancy. But, I could not tear my eyes away as the other stocking fell. Then, Rita turned in a full circle, to give my eyes a complete picture of the fun to come.

"I can't decide whether to grab, lunge or wait for you to pounce," I remarked.

"Bishop, a man your age should never be indecisive."

"Vacillation enters this type of fray because a man my age considers it a minor miracle to survive the situation."

"Understandable. But, wavering might cause you to forget

what's expected." She cocked a warning eyebrow. "Trust me when I say, tonight you do not want to disappoint."

Everything I had was trembling with anticipation.

Rita Portello moved forward, roughly shoved me back on the bed. The bedside table lamp, toppled to the floor. For some reason I did not notice the crash. I was too busy trying to loosen my belt.

"Now, I know why old men wear suspenders," she observed.

"Whatever you do," I pleaded, "don't start without me."

She backed away, laughing.

I managed to get trousers and shorts down to my ankles. But, after a short tussle to get cloth over shoes, I gave up and resumed a mixed position; most of me horizontal, part of me vertical. All of me franticly eager.

"I suppose it's to be expected, at your age," she said, scrutinizing my erect member.

"What do you mean?"

"You've shrunk."

"I'm the same size I've always been."

She screwed up her eyes.

"Well, I suppose I'll have to make do with what you've got," Rita said.

"I'm ready. I'm more than ready. I'm bobbing ready." I took a ragged breath. "But don't become alarmed, in the heat of the moment, should I scream for oxygen."

Well, being ready might have been a small brag. No man in his right mind would ever be ready for sex with Rita Portello. Sex with her included wheezing along my throat and the nagging chest pains. Then, there was the throbbing at my temples and pulsing blood pressure. I was about to overcome my feelings of desperation, or I die trying.

"Get me a knife," I instructed.

"I know you're feeling panicky over the shrinkage issue, Bishop. But, you're not thinking clearly."

"I've never been more clearheaded in my life. Get me a knife."

"Do you really want to cut off the one thing you're going to need?"

"I'm talking about my pants."

Rita turned and swayed away, a few paces, to give me an overall view. With each step, her hips moved enticingly, her pert buttocks jiggled, her hip-length hair danced. I made desperate kick, trying at getting clothes past shoes. But, there was no go. I was hobbled by my own apparel.

"You have three choices," she said. Rita stopped, turned and swayed back to the bed. "You can lay there and continue struggling, or you can leave your trousers alone and do something suitably lascivious, or I can take charge and finally get this show on the road." She cocked a questioning eyebrow. "Preferences?"

I sat up, reached out and grabbed her hips. Then, I jerked her toward me and pressed my face to the hollow below the arch of her ribcage. She giggled and embraced my head with her hands.

I moved one hand up to explore the swelling of her breast. Rita cooed something in Sicilian, her fingers intertwining my hair, her hands gripping me harder. My other mitt slid between her legs to probe the coils of hair covering her Mons Venus. She uttered a low grunt, and strained her body forward. Within seconds, I felt the oozing wetness coming from her sex. As determined as I was to consummate our passions, I would have to pace myself. There was nothing worse than a pre-climax coronary.

"Now, you've got the idea," she cooed. "But with your pants locked around your ankles I've got concerns about follow-through."

"I'll manage, if it kills me."

"I'm not interested in a bumpy ride on a dead man."

"Will you stop anticipating the worst? I'm trying to focus on blood-flow."

Rita grabbed both my wrists and pressed me back on the mattress, her lips going to mine; hot and hungry. Her tongue slid into my mouth, digging and teasing and searching. Eventually she reached down and grabbed my pulsing wedding tackle. It was my turn to strain in an effort to line up our respective components.

"This is going to be a night you'll never forget, Bishop."

"So long as I live through it."

Suddenly, I felt a rush of wet heat across the head on my penis. Then came the sensation of velvety, encircling warmth.

"We have lift off," I groaned.

"I've waited way too long for this," Rita whimpered.

She began to gyrate her hips.

"Keep this up," I vowed, "and I'm prepared to take a subscription."

"Promises, promises."

Rita began to breathe hard; her pelvis grinding, her buttocks bouncing. I did my best to keep in rhythm. But, it was not long before she outpaced me. I watched her beautiful face flush with delight, and her eyes close. As her passion increased, the color in her cheeks darkened. Then, her hands gripped my shoulders; the fingernails digging in. I grabbed her breasts and pinched her nipples. She caught her breath, and then accelerated her movements. I wanted to scream. But, a blood curdling cry might kill the mood.

"Oh, God!" Rita gasped.

"I'll be damned if he's getting credit!"

Her fingernails sank deeper, as she reached orgasm. Blood dribbled across my skin. Then, there was another groan. This time it was mine, and pleasure had not fostered it. I reached up and jerked her claws from my bleeding flesh. Then, I lowered my hands to her hips, slid behind, and gripped her bottom. In response, Rita's vagina clamped around my favorite body part like a strap-vice.

"You're killing me," I complained.

"I've just gotten started," she grunted in return.

My mind went into a spin. Between flesh tearing fingernails and tormented tumescence, I had severe doubts about future functionality.

"There's no need to strangle the damn thing," I whimpered.

"Shut up!"

We continued our frantic actions for several more passionate minutes and then I groaned in release. Her vagina flexed several times, before releasing its grip. I collapsed my head to the pillow. Rita let go a contented sigh. My heart was thudding, my lungs were aching. She rolled off and I stared down to perform a post-passion damage assessment. No bruises on my manhood. But, it seemed to be trembling in terror.

"I may have collateral damage," I told her.

"You've gotten old, Bishop."

"Age has nothing to do with injury."

"Ten years ago, you'd be taking a curtain call instead of complaining."

"Ten years ago, I was foolish enough to risk life and limb for sex."

"Relax. Catch your breath. One more session should do it."

I took another look at my flaccid equipment.

"Don't count on anything anytime soon," I muttered. "I think he's trying to hide."

"Nonsense." She shifted to lay on her side, her back to me. "In no time, I'll have you up and romping."

"At my age, repeated romps require restorative interludes." I rose up on one elbow, talking to her naked back. "That's something a truly sensitive woman would understand and accept."

"A truly sensitive woman would have nothing to do with you."

Rita had a less than subtle way of making solid points.

"If we did this two or three times a week," she said, "you'd be in perfect health."

"I'd be a day late for embalming."

"Men a lot older than you are getting it on."

"With you?"

"Shut up."

"Light me."

Rita looked over one shoulder, showing her small white teeth in a grin.

"See what you can do when you really try?" she said.

"I mean, get us a smoke."

"Now, you're claiming I broke both your arms?"

"I can't reach the table drawer from here. And standing up, during afterglow, could be hazardous to my health"

She sat up, opened the drawer and fumbled out a pack of cigarettes, along with a disposable lighter. I let my eyes drift across her nakedness. Rita reminded me of a porcelain doll, smooth and perfectly formed. She lit two cigarettes and passed one over. Then she lay supine, next to me. I flopped back onto the pillow and inhaled the smoke as if it would be my last. Life was good. Scary, but very good.

"I need to speak with Constance," I told her, blowing a stream of smoke toward the ceiling.

"What for?"

"To clear up a small confusing matter."

Rita smoked for many seconds, thinking.

"Is there anything you do tactfully?" she asked.

"What did I do wrong, now?"

She got out of bed, dropped her cigarette into her drink, and then began to dress.

"I thought you had me penciled in for a rematch," I said.

"Talking about another woman after sex kills the mood."

"But, I'm coming back to life. Look. He's smiling."

Her panties paused in their upward lift, dangling from her thumbs like lacy wisps.

"I hope the two of you will be happy in your dreams," she snapped.

I watched her finish dressing. We had frequently argued. It was the nature of our relationship. But, tonight Rita was more impatient than usual.

"What's really bothering you?" I asked.

With a long sigh, she slumped back down on the bed.

"Sal plans to have Diacono run the family business," she said.

"Sal's getting liberal in his old age. Not that I think a five year old couldn't outthink Dom, six days out of seven."

"It's no joke, Bishop. When our kid turns eighteen, Sal's bringing him into the fold." There was a long silence. "That means Diacono fills a murder contract and becomes a made-man."

Sudden rage boiled inside me. No matter what it would take, my son was not going to be a Portello button man.

"Sounds like I should convince Sal to change his mind," I gritted.

"And admit your parenthood? That'd get us both killed." She raised a hand and waggled a finger. "The only way out is for Diacono to become a priest. Even Sal can't object to that."

"What about Diacono? You're taking the best part of life away from him."

"Is sex the only thing you value?"

"I'm partial to cheeseburgers and pepperoni pizza."

She stood up and faced me; her lips slightly parted, her legs splayed. Her face radiating the dull white burn of pent up anger.

"You stay out of this," she said, in a deadpan voice. "Diacono's my son. I'll deal with his future."

"He's my son, too."

"I mean it, Bishop." Rita turned her head slightly to look at me. "Stay clear or I'll kill you."

My smile drooped along with another body part.

Chapter 7

I spent Friday morning at the Jockey Betting Parlor, on Austin's west side.

"Your nag came in last, eh, Bishop?" asked Fillmore Teal.

He was a retired accounting professor with a knack for picking gee-gees, and a habit of betting on the wrong woman. His last romantic entanglement was with a tattooist who had a penchant for drinking blood. Their ding-dong ended when, during a drunken tryst, she attempted to satisfy her vampiristic whims with a toothy circumcision. Unfortunately for Teal, intoxication had altered her aim. This resulted in a fast trip to emergency surgery to repair a penile perforation.

"Picking losers is my specialty," I told him.

Despite its name, the parlor was nowhere near a horse track. It was, actually, an electronic version of the sport. Rows of televisions lined several walls. Through these audio-video feeds horse-racing devotees, like me, could enjoy contests from across the country. Inserted into a wall, near the back, was a row of teller windows. Cash wagers, only.

"You need a system," Teal urged.

"That I got," was my return. "An inner voice speaks. Based upon its information, I place a wager. Unavoidably, the betting parlor wins." I raised my glass in a salute. "Why mess with success?"

"I mean one which works in your favor."

My well-educated companion was sixtyish, short and chunky. He had a pale complexion and white shoulder-length hair. His gray eyes were slightly bloodshot, like those of an insomniac. His voice had a door-hinge squeak.

"What's your secret?" I asked.

"*Margaritomancy*," he replied, confidentially.

Beard-stubble frosted Teal's chin. He wore an eight panel cap, plaid shirt, leather vest and faded denims. There were sandals on his bare feet. Decades earlier, Fillmore Teal would have passed for an aging hippie.

"You've got a computer, huh?" I said.

His long hair swooshed in a head-wag.

"I'm talking about divination by pearl," he said.

"Come again?"

"Near an open fire, I cover a pearl with a vase. Then, I go through the racing form, uttering the entrant's names." Teal sipped his drink. "When the winner is spoken the pearl jumps, rattling the bottom of the vase."

An irritated flush warmed my cheeks.

"Look, Fillmore," I said, "if you don't want to share just say so."

"Deacon, I'm serious."

"Where in hell would you get a pearl," I scoffed, "let alone an open fire to warm a vase?"

"I've had moments."

"You're living in a camper and paying alimony to three ex-wives."

"That's down to bad luck with women."

"Bad luck? That last one tried to eradicate your sense of humor."

Teal scratched the side of his jaw.

"There are worse things, Deacon," he said, "than having to repair one's Tally Wagger."

"If so, I've never faced it."

There was another rustle of head-shaking from my companion.

"Unbeknown to me," he said, "my idiot son's been selling off my collection of portrait miniatures."

"Goodwin?"

"Goodwin's the only son I've got." Teal's false teeth clattered noisily as he grimaced. "Century old ivory, decorated by watercolor, squandered to feed the little deviant's philandering." He took a shuddering breath. "I could wring his neck."

"Deviant, you say?"

"Goodwin likes being whipped."

"Sounds like something from one of my dreams."

"Don't let anyone mislead you with tales of parental bliss,

Deacon. Raising children is like taking a rocket up the ass."

"Is your son going to make good on the loss?"

"Goodwin's a short-order cook at an all-night diner." He rolled his eyes. "A paycheck, for him, barely pays for his condoms."

"Fillmore, considering your educational and professional achievements, are you sure Goodwin *is* your son?"

"Don't think I haven't asked myself that same question dozens of times?"

"Have you considered a DNA comparison?"

"Done years ago. The little shit's mine, all right." Teal rubbed one hand across his face. "If I knew then what I know now, I'd have divorced his mother before getting her pregnant."

"Would you like me to speak with Goodwin? I might be able to straighten him out."

"Only if your offer includes a post-embalming prayer service."

"I gave up religion for Lent." I pointed to his racing form. "But, I know a guy in the business."

"That was just me spouting off. Forget I said anything."

"How 'bout sharing your picks while I consider less obtrusive options for your son's future?"

Following Teal's suggestions, I quickly managed to turn loss into gain. And, by the completion of the day's racing, I was well into solvency. A novelty for me.

"No reflection on your ample form, Fillmore," I said, as we collected our winnings. "But, have you ever stayed at a fat farm?"

"Most of them, at one time or another," Teal returned. "Not that any did me long-term good." He folded cash into a pocket. "Still, each stay provided a satisfactory solution to late-night loneliness."

"Are you talking about what I think you're talking about?"

He tossed me a wink.

"The fairer sex is not unknown to me, Deacon," Teal bragged.

"No argument there. But, how does one succeed at seduction, when the object of lust is starving?"

"Incentives."

"Cash?"

"Chocolates."

I let my eyes drop to his ample middle.

"That's a sure thing, huh?" I asked.

"Smiles all around."

I took a meditative sip of booze turning his words over in my mind. Perhaps I should consider incentives? A new mattress, could work. Air conditioning during summers might be a draw. Or, at least, functional ventilation. I made a mental note to write a letter to my landlord about unsealing the windows.

"During your sexual conquests," I said, "did you seduce anyone with contacts at Texas facilities for the over indulgent?"

He tugged at his belt which created a ripple effect through his overhanging flab.

"What's your interest?" Teal asked, suspiciously.

"I've got a situation."

"I'm not lining you up with another of my female friends."

"There's a kooky little guy who saw a murder," I explained. "He thinks he's the Shadow. But, I believe his story about the killing."

He cocked a disbelieving eyebrow.

"The 'Shadow knows', Shadow?" Teal asked.

"Exactly."

"And I'm worried about Goodwin."

"My problem is, the cops found the remains a woman who almost fits the description given by the Shadow. Same first name: Connie. Same hair color: red. What doesn't fit is the last name and the tattoo."

"How about your witness thinking he's the Shadow?"

"The tattoo the Shadow saw was a kitty. The dead woman, Connie Firth, was inked with a tiger."

"That's some kitty."

"I'm thinking there were two murders. Mrs. Firth, and the one the Shadow witnessed."

"I'm thinking you need to do a rethink."

"The other woman was a match on physical description as well as first and surname, to what the Shadow told me. She's also, missing."

"Then, you've probably identified the victim."

"But, according to a reliable source, she's at a fat farm in

Texas."

"Did you think to ask which farm?"

"My source is a little excitable."

"The Shadow, again?"

"She's sort of a friend of mine and I'm worried about her."

"Sort of a friend?"

"We have a love hate relationship."

"That sounds familiar. How's the missing woman fixed for tattoos?"

"We're not that close. But, with your help, I should be able to verify that she's still alive."

"Why not just introduce the stiff to the Shadow? If he agrees she's the one he saw, the job's done."

"The body was in a lake for about nine days. Not a lot left by which to make an identification."

Fillmore Teal paused to stare at a televised news broadcast concerning the indiscretions of a local politician. The object of the storyline had been caught, flagrante delicto, with a hooker. She claimed they were just good friends. The politician claimed it was mistaken identity. Video expose to follow.

"Let's say I do know someone with the connections you need," Fillmore Teal said, looking back at me. "Who's the missing woman?"

"Constance Portello."

His eyes got the size of saucers, as he turned to face me.

"You think I'm stupid enough to rat-out a mobster's wife?" he gaped. "I wondered why you weren't mentioning her name."

"Fillmore, it's not like Constance would kill you for telling tales out of school."

"Her husband would."

A well-founded observation, considering Salvator Portello's track record.

"Sal's not going to order a hit because of his wife's weight mismanagement program," I said, in my most reassuring tone.

"Deacon, you have no understanding of women," he said.

"I'm not exactly without paramours, Fillmore."

"Then, how is it you don't know about a woman's killer instinct when it comes to keeping the secrets she shares with her scale?"

Not new information. But, well worth hearing again.

"I'll keep you and whoever helps you out of it," I said.

Fillmore Teal gulped the remains of his drink, an ice cube leaving a drip on the end of his nose.

"Don't make promises you might not be able to keep," he said, flicking the wet from his proboscis with a finger.

"Look, Constance won't be alone."

"So I'm helping you expose her as well as her deadly friends?"

"Not friends. Hired help."

"Dear God, man! If she's rented a gigolo, the last thing I want is to uncover it!"

"Constance travels with the family bodyguards: Thomaso and Pietro Fortuna."

He fanned the air with both hands.

"I'm not doing it," Teal insisted. "I don't care who she's with, where she's at or what she's doing."

"The Fortuna brothers are two chunks of Sicilian un-fun with New Jersey accents." I cocked my head to one side, grinning. "At a fat farm in Texas, they'll stand out like walnuts on a pear tree."

"Do these walnuts carry guns?"

"Of course. But, they hardly ever use the hardware."

"Forget it."

I took the folding money from my race proceeds and held it up.

"What if I sweeten the deal with today's winnings?" I asked.

Teal pondered possibilities.

"So I don't have to mention Mrs. Portello's name?" he asked.

"When it comes to names, not so much as a whisper." I reached out and patted his shoulder. "Just ask your contact to search for a pair of squat New Jersey cannolis wearing black suits."

Fillmore Teal bobbed his shoulders before uttering a volley of execrations.

"I'll see what I can do," he grumbled, snatching the cash from my hand. "But, no guarantees."

After leaving my slightly neurotic betting-buddy, I drove

around for two hours before heading over to Salvator Portello's new home in one of Austin's western suburbs. It was a big, slant-roofed place on Kilbourne Street. The construction was white sandstone topped by blue tile. There were four floors, each with numerous windows. The structure's front looked out upon a broad terrace, shaded by a widely projecting trellis. The back stared at several acres of neatly trimmed grass. To one side was a separate garage. Based upon the number of doors, it held half a dozen cars. A tall, sandstone wall, surmounted by razor wire, encircled the Portello homestead. Salvator had never been one for friends.

"Bishop, you bastard," the Mafia Don growled.

"Nice to see you, too, Sal," I returned.

We were in the Mafia Don's home office. It was as big as a ballroom and cluttered with French provincial furniture. Surrounding himself with luxury was the mobster's way of legitimizing his family history. Across one end of the room was a 1930's style mahogany bar. It had a shiny brass rail spanning its base. Fronting this, on the gray carpet floor, was a brass spittoon. The container's numerous dents and dings suggested an extensive pedigree in skull-cracking. Traditional fun for members of the Portello clan.

"Because of you," Salvator Portello complained, "I've had a morning of acid reflux."

"How's your digestive complaint my problem?" I demanded.

"Initially I blamed Momma's breakfast meatballs," he said. The mobster was thin as a reed and short, clothed immaculately in tailored blue. "God knows where she dug up that gastronomical nightmare. But, since your arrival, my stomach acid's been clawing up my throat. So I figure my distress actually relates to the subliminal anticipation of your arrival."

"Throat cutting's a cure for any problem," I chipped.

The Mafia Don gave me a look at a gold-capped canine.

"Don't think I haven't considered that, for you," he returned.

The *Capo di tutti capi*, Boss of all bosses, was handsome in a chiseled way. Even at this mature stage in life he could double for a model.

"Momma's doing well?" I asked.

"She's always doing well," he grunted. "Particularly, when it comes to giving me aggravation."

Salvator Portello sat behind a desk designed for a king. It was collection of oak and brass fitted into something the size of a snooker table. The finished had been buffed to a glassy sheen. He puffed on an expensive smelling cigar. From the looks of it, a *Cuaba Salomónes*.

"What aggravation is Momma up to?" I asked.

He shoved the stogy into one corner of his mouth. From the grimace, spreading his lips, Salvator Portello was not enjoying the nicotine delight.

"She's seeing a psychic, for God's sake," Sal replied. "Jubal Lessingham."

I knew Lessingham. His psychiatric expertise had been used many times by Austin P-D. He knew his stuff. Perhaps, too well where it concerned his zipper. I had become acquainted with him during a missing-person case. In the end, Lessingham was incidental in resolving that investigation. Shortly after, much to his economic and personal embarrassment, he lost his medical and psychiatric licenses. Apparently, his zip had dropped one time too often with a female patient. At that time, he had started a desktop publishing and printing business. As to how he had become a psychic, I could not imagine.

"That doesn't sound like Momma," I told him.

"The lying bastard's convinced my mother to lay out a hundred bucks a week so she can talk to my dead father," Sal complained.

I had a flashback to Rita's remarks concerning Dom's pistol usage. Perhaps he, too, had visited the amoral healer? Perhaps Lessingham had used his skills from psychiatry to instill dreams in Dom's head? Planted memories were possible. Why not nightmares?

"A smart man would want Old Frank to have uninterrupted rest," I remarked.

"Well, smart or not," the Mafia Don vowed, "I'm about to introduce him to my old man's ghost."

I was perched in the room's only visitor chair. It rested directly in front of the desk. While the furnishing accommodated my bulk, its legs had been cut short. This left my lower extremities outstretched, and my backside barely a foot off the floor.

"What prompted Momma's interest in contacting Old Frank?"
I asked

"She says she's lonely."

"Maybe Momma should marry?"

"This is my mother we're talking about," he snapped. "Not
some slut."

"Do you really want her to mourn your father's loss for the
rest of her life?"

Salvator Portello squirmed in his chair, irritated by my
conscience tweaking.

"That's none of your business," he eventually said.

"Would you like me to share your concerns with
Lessingham?" I suggested, trying to lighten his mood. "Nothing
heavy. Just a little nudge in the right direction."

"And have Momma find out?" The mobster pointed at his
groin. "She'd cut off my balls."

That sounded like the Momma Portello I knew and loved.

"She wouldn't if Lessingham explained how Old Frank
wanted to be left in peace."

He considered for several beats.

"There's still the money," Sal returned.

"A few hundred isn't worth quibbling about."

"It's over a thousand."

"Still not worth the aggravation." I lit a cigarette. "How'd
Momma pick Lessingham over the other fortune tellers?"

"Some lunatic who thinks he's the Shadow introduced her,"
Salvator Portello said. "Momma took pity on the nutcase because
he had a bum foot. And to show his appreciation, the idiot took her
to Lessingham."

I had underrated Reggie Shepherd. Not that I would let
Lessingham get away with conning Momma Portello. But, Reggie
had made a powerful friend with her.

"I'll get your money," I told the mobster.

Salvator Portello ground his molars for a few seconds.

"While you're at it," he said, "make sure the bastard
understands how close he came to dying."

I took a long draw on my cigarette.

"You're still seeing Dr. Hernandez for your heart?" I asked.

"He's another quack needing redirection."

"Many would disagree, Sal."

"The man's taken me off red meat." The mobster belched loudly. "I hate fish. And chicken backs up on me."

"Rita and Diacono are doing well?"

"Don't talk to me about my sister."

"What's happened?"

"It's none of your damn business. That's what happened." He shook a finger at me. "But I'll tell you this much for free. Rita's chances for a wedding at the Cathedral of Monreale have gone down the shitter." He paused, as if waiting for me to respond. When I continued my confused, silent gape he gritted out, "Right there on the Sacrarium for God's sake! Her and some lowlife she picked up in the piazza. I'm tellin' you, my sister has no shame."

"If I'm understanding you, Rita was actually in the cathedral, on top of the Sacrarium, doing the…"

"It's none of you damn business what she was doing!" He wheezed for a couple of breaths. "I made a healthy donation to calm fears and stop wagging tongues."

"Much appreciated by the Sicilian Diocese, I'm sure."

"Cardinal Tamera assures me the Pope will never hear about it. He's even quashed Father Marceline's demand for Rita's excommunication." Salvator Portello puffed out his cheeks. "As far as the Catholic Church is concerned, the situation never happened."

"I've always admired your sister's free spirit."

"Rita's certainly free about something!" He made the sign of the cross over his chest. "The only thing worse than what she's been doing would be her hooking up with you."

Not exactly a sideways snub. But, I felt somewhat hurt.

"Rita would never lower herself to my level," I told him.

"Well, what she's been doing is never going to happen again," he growled. "I've seen to that."

"Not the convent Petralia Sottana, again?"

"Of course not. Rita's been banned from there, for life. Instead, I've found my sister a suitable marriage partner."

I blinked several times, completely bewildered. Rita had said nothing to me about marriage plans. Perhaps she didn't know what her oldest brother was up to? If not, Salvator Portello had better buy himself a cast-iron genital cup.

"Does that mean Rita's not yet aware of her future husband?" I asked.

"I make all family decisions."

"Sal, based upon Rita's history, arranged-marriages are not a good idea."

"My sister has to start honoring her family obligations."

To be a fly on the wall during Sal's sharing of Rita's impending marriage would be worth the risk of getting swatted.

"Who's the lucky guy?" I asked.

"A Sicilian widower with four children who owns a pig farm," Sal replied.

"Sounds like the sort who'd put a sparkle into any woman's eyes," I said, dryly.

"So maybe he's not a beauty," Sal said. "So maybe raising pigs in Sicily won't be like nights out in Austin. Rita will get used to it."

"Frankly, Sal, I don't think anybody gets used to pigs."

"The man's hardworking and no-nonsense. Just what my sister needs."

I laughed under my breath. Rita would castrate the pig farmer during their exchange of vows.

"Has Momma heard about this upright member of the pork industry?" I asked.

"Not yet," he returned. "But, Momma will understand."

"What about that chiropractor you fianced to Rita?"

The Mafia Don's eyes hardened. For a long moment, he seemed to be holding his breath.

"Rita was never charged in his shooting," he said.

"That's because the terrified bastard disappeared in an effort to keep his remaining testicle." I took a deep drag on my cigarette. "What about Diacono?"

"What about him?"

"Do you think he's going to enjoy living on a Sicilian pig farm?"

"He'll stay here, with me."

"Away from his mother?"

"Rita spends far too much time with her son. Diacono needs a male influence."

I raised my cigarette making him aware of the long ash. Salvator quickly jerked open a drawer, withdrew a small glass ashtray and tossed it to me. I managed to catch it. Unfortunately, the ash dropped upon my shirt. Carefully, I nudged the clump of incinerated tobacco into the container.

"Momma will never allow that," I told him.

"Let's get down to your business," he snipped, "before I lose my temper and do what I should have done years ago."

"We haven't discussed Dom."

"You've got four minutes, Bishop. Then, I'm packing you in cement."

"Can't you make it five?" I pleaded. "I'm thinking that'll give my talent for irritation, and your bad ticker, enough time to turn you from cyanic blue to toxic purple."

"Damn it! Get to the point of your being here."

I purposely paused to further aggravate his coronary complaint.

"You know how rumors are," I said. "First there was the one about you running for governor on an anti-crime ticket. Then, there was the one about Dominic putting his privates into the porn business." I snuffed out my cigarette in the ashtray. "Now, people are saying Constance is dead: murdered."

His dark eyes narrowed sharply.

"Who's saying?" Salvator Portello demanded.

"Just people. But, if it helps, you ordered the beautiful Connie whacked."

"That's a damn lie!"

"My words to deaf ears. But, you know the fourth estate. Always wagging the dog." I gave another pause to give the mobster's heart more time to percolate. "Uh, where's Constance?"

"None of your damn business!"

"Didn't mean to irritate your sensibilities, Sal," I said. "But, when I arrived, instead of the Fortuna brother's usual pat-down for weapons, rather strange and intrusive hands probed my person. And it was done without your lovely wife cheering the search and seizure. Which makes me wonder what's going on?"

The Mafia Don smirked.

"This is why my wife hates your guts," he said. "You're always sticking your nose where it doesn't belong."

"In spite of the beautiful Connie's resistance to my charms, I am worried about her."

"Not that it's any of your business," Sal said, "but my wife's away on a shopping trip. Tell that to those wagging tongues."

"For over a month?"

"She's having trouble finding what she wants!"

"And the Fortuna brothers?"

"Also away."

"A little variety in their suits would be appreciated."

He stared at me directly for a long moment his scathing glare slicing through me like a razor.

"Are we done?" the Mafia Don snapped.

"Cutie."

Salvator Portello frowned for several moments, trying to analyze my unexpected statement. Failing to understand, the mobster returned a sidelong glare filled with accusatorial and threatening overtones.

"What in hell are you playing at?" he snapped.

"Julie 'the Cutie' Caivano."

I watched his Adams Apple bob twice.

"What about him?" the Mafia Don asked.

"Rumor has it, Caivano's gone off the tracks." I let go my most boyishly lighthearted laugh. "Shot four innocents and a naked redhead who fits the description of your lovely, and missing, wife."

"Constance isn't missing!"

The mobster shifted in his chair, obviously discomforted. Far more upset than he should be if his wife was stropping his plastic. I crossed my ankles. From the color rising up Sal's neck my favorite purple hue would soon appear.

"Who's been feeding you this bull?" he asked, doing a bad job of sounding vaguely interested.

"There's a line of witnesses."

Salvator Portello jumped to his feet.

"Don't be ridiculous," the mobster shouted. "Nobody sees my business."

He snuffed out the cigar in the huge alabaster ashtray on his desk. Then, Sal strolled over to one of the big windows overlooking the back lawn. His hands went into his pockets, and he stared out.

"When did these hits *allegedly* happen?" he asked.

"The redhead died about ten days ago, give or take. The others, were shortly after."

"There's been no wet-work since Caivano went on the payroll."

"Except his own."

Salvator Portello whirled to face me, his narrow shoulders hunching.

"Who in hell told you that?" he demanded.

"The rumor mill never stops grinding."

"It didn't happen," he said. "Do you understand? It *did not happen*." Salvator Portello drew in a long, whistling breath. "Not to my wife. Not to Cutie. Not to witnesses. Am I being clear?"

"I believe you, Sal." I looked at my wrist watch my allocated time had come and gone. "I think the police would, too, if it wasn't for the bodies."

His mouth dropped open in shock.

"There are no bodies!" he sputtered. "There are never any bodies."

"Not Caivano's, maybe. But, somebody got careless with the others."

Salvator Portello strolled back to his desk and took a perch on its edge, offering me a cold stare.

"The Feds put you up to this?" he asked.

So much for Walter Osgood Kemp's chances in hell.

"Of course not," I replied. "But, the witnesses' story about your wife's death is chilling."

"I'd like to talk to your witness."

"He described the tattoo of a kitten on the redhead." It was a second or two before I taunted him with, "Sound romantically familiar?"

Salvator Portello put his eyes on his fingers. But, the

mobster's mouth had dropped open, again, and he was breathing hard. For a long moment there was silence, while he studied the shine on his manicured fingernails. Clearly, the Mafia Don was having trouble putting a nice spin on what he was about to say. I liked that.

"How is it you know Connie's got..." he began.

"I offered to show her mine if she'd show me hers," I cut in. "Purely for artistic comparisons, you understand. Connie said her tattoo was available to your eyes, only."

"Let it drop, Bishop."

"Sure. Anything you say." I paused a moment to study the ash on the end of my cigarette. "But, just so I can quash the street chit-chat, what about a quick word with your wife? A telephone number will do."

The mobster's eyes rose up to mine. But, I no longer saw the dead stare of a killer. Salvator Portello actually looked worried. From the way he was staring, he thought I knew something worth killing to keep quiet. I gave him more smoke while I pondered escape possibilities.

"Keep pushing," the mobster eventually said, in a deadly tone, "and I'll bring in the dip tank."

"No need." I tapped my cigarette on the edge of the ashtray. "What's Dom been up to? He's in good health?"

He stood up and went back to his chair.

"Time for you to leave."

"I take it your brother's making another stab at revolutionizing the cocaine trade?"

"As a matter of fact, the crazy bastard's raising skunks."

That took me by surprise. That would have taken anyone who knew anything about Dominic Portello, by surprise. Well not the 'crazy bastard' part.

"Who in his right mind raises skunks?" I asked.

"He's not in his right mind," Sal snapped. "Complicating matters is his inability to kill the stinking fur balls, to harvest their pelts." He rubbed his nose with the back of his hand. "He's got four hundred of the smelly stripers running around my ranch, all of them breeding like flies. By next Christmas, there'll be nearly five thousand out there."

"You bought a ranch?"

The mobster gave a weary nod.

"In the valley," he said. "Rita called when she first arrived in Sicily. Said it might be nice to raise goats and would I do it for Diacono?"

"Seriously, Sal? Have you ever smelled a goat?"

His voice came out low and firm.

"After Rita's debacle on the sacristan, I let Dom take over the place for his skunks," Salvator Portello said. "I thought, how bad could it get?" He spoke slowly, like he was still trying to convince himself. "Hell, there'll be goats there anyway. Little did I know the horny stripers never get tired of slipping the Willie."

"What brought about Dom's interest in fragrant animal husbandry?"

"His brain's turned to mush."

"Well, in all fairness, mush was pretty much what your brother was born with."

"Dom met a woman who fancies him," the Mobster said. "Can you believe it?"

There had been many women in Dom's life. All bought and paid for. Several of whom disappeared. So, for him to have one who actually wanted the psychopath was completely off the wall. Or, she was.

"No more paying to dip his wick?" I asked. "That could cause an economic downturn in the specialized services industry."

"Her name's Cornelia Wilson," the Mafia Don said. "But, Connie's her stage name."

"She's an actress?"

His dark head shook.

"Nude mud wrestler," Sal said.

Dom's taste had always tilted toward the exotic.

"Professionally, or for Dom's enjoyment?" I asked.

"He's headlining her at the Counting House Bar," the mobster said. "Surprisingly, the punters love that kind of thing."

"The Counting House Bar's one of your places?"

Sal's arms rose and fell.

"When he's not in South Texas tending his skunks," Sal replied, "I have to keep him busy."

"I have to tell you, Sal, I never expected to see the day when Dom found a woman who'd cater to his whims without credit card prequalification," I said. "Are you sure she's not an escapee?"

"Bottled red and tattoos. Has this idea she can save the world. She's asked Dom to set up a business to house street people."

That rattled my cage. Another Connie with red hair and tattoos.

"You mean something like the Anniston Arms Hotel?" I asked.

"Exactly. Do you know what an operation like that would cost me if she marries Dom?"

"Any of her inking a kitten?"

"I saw one on her shoulder."

Bingo.

"When was the last time you saw the love of your brother's life?" I asked.

"A couple of weeks," he replied. "She doesn't come around, since Dom moved out. Momma doesn't like her."

"Probably the shock," I observed. "One minute her baby boy's staggering around in diapers, strangling kittens. Then next he's getting laid on a non-charge basis. Is there any chance Cornelia's dead?"

"Of course not. She's under my protection."

"Dom's been known to do deadly when a lady refuses his advances."

He tilted toward me.

"Since when do you take an interest in my brother's love-life?" the mobster asked.

"No offense intended. I was so stunned by the news, I guess I got carried away with questions." I cleared my throat. "How well do you know the Anniston sisters?"

"The hotel grannies?"

"They do business with you?"

"Aren't you gone, yet?"

"Just going." I got to my feet. "What about Dr. Paisley Firth?"

"He's my wife's optometrist. What's the bastard done?"

"Rumors abound about an association."

The muscles in Salvator Portello's jaw rippled. His face

darkened a shade as his eyes tightened upon me.

"You snooping bastard!" he growled.

"Who, me?"

"Dom met that slut through a runny-nosed shit named Drax Ravaillac. When I found out she was married, I told him to get rid of her."

Dom was prone to mistakes. An order like that, coming from Sal, could have been misconstrued as an instruction to kill Mrs. Firth. Something Dom would have probably handed off to Caivano.

"Sorry, I took so much of your time," I told him, and headed for the door. Then, I stopped and looked back. "Walter Osgood Kemp asked me to extend his apologies."

Salvator Portello jerked forward his fingers becoming claws, raking the desktop.

"You tell that sorry son-of-a-bitch, if I don't have my money within a week I'll cut him into pieces so small his remains will blow away in the wind," the mobster glowered.

That did not sound good. At least for Kemp. But, I had made my pitch. So, should Ozzie face the worst I could devote all my energies into consoling the lovely and desirable Charlene Holland with a clear conscience.

"Do you have one of Dr. Hernandez's business cards?" I asked. "I'm thinking it's time to get my ticker checked."

"Why don't I save you the trouble, and cut it out?"

"Never mind. I'll ask Momma."

"Hold it."

The Mafia Don opened a desk drawer, did a quick rummage, and then threw a card in my direction. I went over and picked it up off the floor. But, as I resumed my exit he called to my back.

"Let's say," he said, "just to silence those wagging tongues, there was a dead female in one of my warehouses."

"A redhead? Someone who looked vaguely familiar, but you're not admitting to anything?"

"Exactly. Now, let's say somebody dragged the sex-crazed bitch in there, whacked the security guard for reasons I still cannot fathom, and then did the same to the bitch."

"This fictional shooter being somebody you don't know?"

"Somebody I don't know — yet." The Mafia Don snickered, uneasily. "The redhead was not Constance. So get that idea out of your damn head."

"Like it was never there."

"Now, let's say this dead redhead bore a striking resemblance to Connie Firth."

"Like they were twins? But you hesitate to speculate?"

"Exactly. Now, let's say somebody gave somebody else orders to get rid of this body."

"Not that you're admitting to anything?"

"Exactly."

"I'm guessing, Caivano was one of the players in this pseudo-fictional drama?"

The mobster made a vague movement with one hand.

"He may have been written into one of the scenes," Salvator said. "But, again, I hesitate to guess."

"Could you give me a hint as to how this woman's remains ended up in Lake Travis?"

"Who in hell do you think I am? Little Mary Sunshine?" The mobster slumped back into his chair, again breathing hard, his coloring nearly a match to my hopes for him. "Now, get out of here."

Chapter 8

The Hillcrest Health Club was a five stories of Texas limestone. It boasted a candy-red roof and two wings, which formed a 'U'. Surrounding the structure, cuddling a bright green border of mowed acreage, was a hurricane fence. This metal surround culminated at a stone arch which embraced an electronically controlled cast-iron gate.

Carrying a scuffed Gladstone bag purchased from a pawn shop, and wielding Dr. Willamette Hernandez's business card, I pressed the call-button on the arch. There was a gap of silence. Then, a muffled voice asked my identity and business. I held the card in front of the security camera and lied through my teeth, about being Hernandez. When asked the reason for my visit, I explained a pressing need to see Constance Portello pursuant to the instructions of her husband.

"Is Mr. Portello ill?" the voice asked.

"It's her husband's situation I wish to discuss with Mrs. Portello," I replied.

More silence.

"A lack of assistance will not please Mr. Portello," I pressed.

The gates swung open.

I strolled into a gravel courtyard, crunched across the span of crushed stone and stepped onto a canopied porch. Although I did not see another camera, I assumed I was being watched. Mounted to the front door's jamb was another call-button. I pressed it.

Moments later, an elderly man opened the door. He was a wisp of a fellow with wavy gray hair. He reminded me of a concert pianist, in his swallow-tail suit.

"You don't look like Dr. Hernandez," the old fellow observed.

My cheeks warmed with the implication of deceit. Not that I took offense. I was used to accusations. But I was embarrassed by his insight. Nevertheless, my bluff would have to continue. Hopefully, without a surgical demonstration.

"I blame my fair complexion on an Irish mother," I told him. "What's your excuse for looking half dead?"

"A reckless youth and the infirmities of old age, Sir."

"Something to look forward to."

He waved me in, moving aside. I stepped onto a tile floor which shined like black onyx. The old fellow shut the door.

"Like working here?" I asked.

"I have no complaints, Sir," he replied.

The space was comfortably cool and smelled of polishing wax. The air conditioner started as he resumed his position in front of me. The cooling device sent a hum through the building. The scent in the air changed to flowers. It was a nice deodorizing touch. But I could not help but wonder what it was masking.

"You are?" I asked.

"Grimsby, Sir."

He had a deeply seamed face, suggesting active pursuits during a long life. There was a murky pallor under his leathery skin, not uncommon to those with a history of chronic malaria. This suggested a traveller's background, possibly the result of military training.

"Your duties?" I asked.

"Whatever Dr. Parker directs."

"Dr. Parker runs the show?"

"He owns this facility, Sir." Grimsby frowned, suspiciously. "Weren't you so advised by Mr. Portello?"

His cold, gray eyes gave the impression of someone hiding a naughty secret. If so, I assume the elderly fellow would have no trouble protecting it. He had the flattened knuckles of a boxer.

"Do you give everyone, in Mr. Portello's employ the third degree?" I asked.

Grimsby's eyes gave my tired suit the once over.

"I'm sorry, Sir," he said. "But, we weren't expecting you." Grimsby paused a beat, his face scowling. "Dressed as you are, I doubt anyone would."

"I'm here to pass a message, not stand as a fashion-statement."

"I can assure you, Sir…"

I cut in with, "If you could direct me to Mrs. Portello's room it would be appreciated."

"That's not possible, Sir."

His refusal rocked me back on my heels. I had assumed the Portello name would carry the ultimate clout. Everywhere else, the mere mention of Salvator Portello resulted in panic and offers of cooperation plus unmitigated ass-kissing. Of course, if Constance Portello was dead and someone was impersonating her, Grimsby would deny visitor access.

"Why in hell not?" I demanded.

"This facility protects the confidentiality of its clients," Grimsby replied.

"Salvator Portello appreciates that," I told him, still playing my bluff. "But, me going back without speaking to his wife will not be well-received."

"I will take you to a place of comfort where you can await Mrs. Portello's pleasure."

"So, long as it provides absolute privacy."

"This way, please."

Four minutes of walking and I was left alone in what looked to be an office.

The furnishings included a desk, a sofa, a couple of chairs and several bookcases filled with leather-bound volumes. The plaster ceiling was high and arched. There was a deep window seat padded with leather cushions. Bamboo tiles covered the floor. My nostrils flexed. Then they caught the lingering scent of pipe smoke. I salivated. Then, I lit a cigarette and waited.

Seven drags later the door opened. But, the intruder was not Constance Portello. Instead a tall gaunt man crossed the threshold. He had a gaunt, lipless face made evil by a long scar on one side, extending from cheekbone to chin. His hair was black. Spread beneath his pinched nose was a salt and pepper mustache. His clothing looked pricey. A blue suit with crimson trappings.

"I'm Dr. Nathaniel Parker," the fellow announced, shutting the door. "This is my health retreat."

"Spiffy," I returned.

I guessed his age to be about fifty. With the exception of the scar, his complexion reminded me of a ripe peach. There was a white streak through his forelock. I could not tell if it was dyed or natural.

"You're not Dr. Willamette Hernandez," he announced.

A queasy feeling crept into my stomach. Why had I decided to impersonate a physician? Why not a mental-case seeking asylum?

"I beg to differ," I told him.

"I know Will," Parker persisted. "We play golf, most weekends." One finger went to his moustache to tease the hairs. "So, who are you?"

"I'm whoever Mr. Portello tells me to be."

Parker paled, by the implied threat.

"In that case," he quivered, "I'm pleased to meet you — Dr. Hernandez."

Like Grimsby, he gave me a visual scraping. Like Grimsby, his face showed revulsion over my shabby appearance. Unlike Grimsby, Dr. Parker did not have the hands of a fighter. He was more the finger-pointing type.

"Mrs. Portello will be here, shortly," he said. "I hope there's nothing serious to her husband's situation."

"Mr. Portello is as well as can be expected," I returned. "How are you holding up since the death of your sister-in-law?"

"As can be expected. Did you know her?"

"I know Dr. Firth."

Dr. Parker walked over and we shook hands. His mitt was limp and sweaty, putting me in mind of a wet dishrag. I dragged my paw across the front of my brown seersucker to dry it.

"Connie's death was a shock," he said.

"More for her than you, I'm sure." I took a final draw on my cigarette. Then I went over to the desk where I snuffed it in an ashtray. "How does a guy get started in this business?"

The door swung inward several inches. Then, from the hallway, came a woman's voice.

"Dr. Parker," she called. "It's Nurse Gilbert, Doctor. Your brother-in-law's on the phone, again. I wouldn't have interrupted, but I can't calm him down."

Parker's face clouded.

"You'll have to excuse me — Dr. Hernandez," he said.

"Paisley's throwing a tantrum?" I asked.

"Something like that."

'Something like that' sounded very much like one man being

afraid of what another might blurt, during an emotional breakdown, to someone else.

Dr. Parker left, pulling the door shut on his exit.

The door opened, almost immediately. This time my visitor was the beautiful, redheaded Constance Portello. She was about thirty-five, heavier than I remembered but still model material. Constance had a high freckled forehead, playful green eyes, prominent cheekbones, delicate nostrils, and a provocative mouth. Many of my leisure hours had been spent contemplating that mouth.

"Bishop, you bastard!" Constance seethed.

So much for Walter Osgood Kemp's theory.

"Long time no see, Connie," I returned.

Trailing behind her were the Portello family bodyguards: Thomaso and Pietro Fortuna. Each looked thirty pounds lighter, than last I saw. Apparently, what was served to the goose, at this tummy-shrinking getaway, was also supplied to the ganders.

"Where's Dr. Hernandez?" Pietro dully asked.

"He couldn't make it," I said, "so I decided to fill in."

"I didn't know you was a doctor, Mr. Bishop," Thomaso chimed.

"He's not, you idiot," Constance Portello snapped. Then she tilted her head toward the door. "You, two, wait outside."

"We should stay, Mrs. Portello," Pietro insisted.

"Mrs. *Salvator Portello*," Thomaso corrected.

"Mr. Bishop sometimes gets miffed, Mrs. Salvator Portello."

"Yeah," agreed Thomaso. "Sometimes Mr. Bishop gets miffed."

"Guys, I'm a pussycat," I intervened.

"If I need you, I'll shout," she told the two Sicilians. "Should that happen, come in shooting."

Pietro lifted his shoulders and spread out his hands.

"At who?" he asked.

"Well not at me!" Constance shouted.

Thomaso came over and gave me a casual frisk which resulted in the temporary confiscation of my Mauser. We looked at each other. From the weariness in his face, he was exhausted.

"Ready to go home?" I whispered.

Thomaso rolled his eyes.

"If you only knew," he whispered back.

Then, with my hardware tucked away in his suit Thomaso, and his brother, departed.

"What prompted you to crawl from under your rock?" Constance demanded.

"Rumors," I replied.

"Texas is a State of rumors because we're rife with corrupt politicians."

"Nonsense. We haven't incarcerated a governor in years."

"No. We just placed felony charges against the previous one and arrested our current Attorney General."

"If you're going to nitpick..."

"What rumors?" she cut in, impatiently.

"You're dead."

Her eyes flashed.

"Are you threatening me?" Constance demanded.

I quickly fanned the air with both hands to placate her temper.

"Rumor has it you've been murdered," I explained. "Shot, in a very unfriendly way."

"I guess that beats being molested."

"You wouldn't say that if you could watch my dreams."

"Stop being repulsive."

Constance Portello came over and held up two fingers. I got out my smokes and sloughed two up from the pack. She took one. I pressed the other between my lips and returned the pack back to its keep. Then I got out my zippo and touched flame to both cancer sticks.

"Why the doctor routine?" she asked.

"Only way to get past the front gate." I pocketed the lighter as my eyes drifted across her body. "You're looking pretty svelte for a place like this."

"Save the bullshit, Bishop."

"I'm serious."

"I've gained thirty pounds."

"All in the right places."

That got me an appreciative smirk.

"My ass looks like the back end of a Holstein," she said in

halfhearted complaint.

I made an obvious show of leaning over to take a peek at her posterior.

"Watch it," Constance Portello warned.

"Just developing a newfound appreciation for bovines," I said.

"You're a dirty old man."

"And damn proud of it."

She took a long draw on her cigarette.

"I'm surprised you never tried it on with Rita," Constance remarked.

"And violate the sanctity of the Portello line? I'd rather cut my own throat."

"Why put yourself out when Sal will do it?"

"I don't like to impose."

"Are you the father of her child?"

That caught me by surprise. Had Rita been indiscrete?

"Absolutely not," I lied.

"Then, why did Rita name the little monster after you?"

"She likes to taunt her brothers."

"The kid's your dead ringer, Bishop."

"There are a lot of kids out there who look like me."

"Which comes as no surprise to anyone who knows you." Constance Portello smoked her cigarette for a long moment. "I've often thought of what could have been. Kids- wise, I mean."

"You mean banging one of the box boys at Ferguson's Market?"

"Have you seen Rita since she got back from Sicily?"

"I had an informative chat with your husband concerning her."

Constance Portello's ruddy eyebrows arched.

"Sal told you about what she did in the church?" she asked.

"We've all made religious *faux pas*."

"On the Sacrarium?"

"Rita was always a little over the top."

Constance laughed under her breath.

"Cardinal Tamera's call brought Momma Portello down a peg."

"I thought you and Momma got along."

"Her cooking's the reason I'm in this hell-hole."

She moved off to stare out the window.

"Not a fun time, here?" I asked her back.

"I haven't had chocolate since I got here," she grumbled. "Tobacco's not allowed. The same for alcohol."

"What about sex?"

Constance tossed me a dirty look.

"It's like going to camp with a vibrator," she said, "but no batteries."

"Why not go home?"

"Not until I'm down another ten pounds."

"But, the Fortuna brothers have become mere shadows of their former selves."

"The food doesn't agree with them." Constance Portello shuddered. "This evening, we're having something with peaches for dessert. It's so disgusting you should stay."

"I've never been one for peaches."

She turned to face me.

"Why in hell would you worry about me?" Constance demanded. "I hate your guts."

"But in a most sympathetic, if condescending manner."

"Tonight's main course is pizza." She dropped the cigarette to the floor, and crushed it into the blue carpet. "Which is so nauseating, even you don't deserve it."

"What do you know about Connie Firth?"

"Are you having an affair with her?"

"She's dead."

Constance Portello whirled to face me, her mouth gaping in shock.

"When in hell did that happen?" the mobster's wife demanded.

"Murdered. Back a week or two. Don't you get the news?"

"I'm damn lucky to get toilet paper." She raised and lowered her arms, in disbelief. "I had breakfast with Connie the day I drove here."

"Connie was shot."

"I thought you said I was shot."

"Her killer dumped the body into Lake Travis."

"Did the cops catch the creep?"

"Her husband hired me to look into it because he's not sure the police weren't involved. You knew her well?"

Constance Portello played with a lock of hair for a few seconds before nodding her head.

"When I first married Sal," she said, "Connie Firth invited me to a gathering of high-status social-hens. Blue-blooded bitches, as far as I was concerned. Connie introduced me as the new wife of a rising star in the business world." There was a short pause while tears puddled in her eyes. "I knew who and what Sal was before I got into bed with him. Who am I kidding? Everybody knows. But, for the sake of my sanity, I pretended his history was a series of unfounded allegations."

"How is he? In the sack, I mean." I jabbed my cigarette through the air between us. "I'll wager, screwing your husband's like slam-dunking a stack of ice cubes."

"Connie Firth treated me like her kid sister," she continued, ignoring my dig. "My introduction, by her to the social elite, sanctified my husband's murderous life." She headed back to where I stood. "Sal instantly went from blood-thirsty thug to entrepreneur." She smiled sadly. "He likes that title. Entrepreneur."

Sal would, considering what most people called him behind his back.

"Do you know Mrs. Firth's husband?" I asked.

"Paisley's a perverted little bastard who should have his balls in a vice, with me on the handle."

Her words knocked my knees together.

"I take it you went to Firth for an eye exam?" I said.

"He had the audacity to leer at my cleavage!"

"Naughty boy." I purposely ogled her fleshy chest. "But I find it odd that Mrs. Firth would be so generous in her compliments of a stranger."

"Connie was sweet." Then she spat, "Damn you, Bishop, stop staring!"

I flashed my eyebrows and stepped away.

"Why would she bother with you?" I said. "Did Mrs. Firth expect something in return?"

"I think she felt sorry for me." Constance Portello studied the ceiling for a beat. "Or perhaps she wanted to add another wheel to her hobby-cart." She smiled, vaguely. "At the time, Connie was at it with a pair of twins who were hung like horses." Her smiled turned into a giggle. "Can you imagine the possibilities?"

"Not much from my angle, but if you had a twin…"

Her amusement abruptly reverted to its usual staid countenance.

"You're a filthy degenerate," she complained. Constance Portello cocked an eyebrow. "Sal's quite romantic."

That I would believe when licorice popsicles came back in vogue.

"I understand your brother-in-law made Mrs. Firth's acquaintance," I said.

"What are you digging for?" she demanded.

"She was murdered. Dom had been involved with Mrs. Firth. Dom's very good at murder. Therefore it follows…"

"Connie wouldn't tolerate his sexual kinks," she cut me short. "So whatever went on, didn't last long."

"But Dominic's a vindictive bastard."

"He'd have no reason to do what you're suggesting."

"Very protective these days, aren't we?"

"Dom's a changed man since meeting Cornelia."

"He's got less going out of pocket, for starters." I went back to the desk to add ash to the butt I had left there. "Considering Mrs. Firth's hobby, there must've been one or two married men among the players."

"Meaning an irate wife went off the deep end?"

"Jealousy makes a good motive."

"Connie never talked about her lovers."

"But, did her lovers know that?"

Constance Portello crossed her arms.

"A worried husband decided to silence her?" she said.

"Sounds intriguing."

Constance Portello dropped her arms and paced for several seconds.

"Actually," she said, "there was someone who hated Connie."

"Who?"

"Charlene Holland."

An abrupt twist.

"What was her beef with Mrs. Firth?" I asked.

"Charlene was dating Julie 'the Cutie' Caivano." Constance Portello stopped and stared down her nose at me. "She thought Cutie was *the* one. He let her believe it. But, while Charlene was working on marriage vows, Cutie was jumping Connie Firth." She made a depreciatory gesture with one hand. "As you can imagine, when Charlene found out, the shit hit the fan."

"It came to blows?"

"No. But, Connie made death threats."

"At Caivano or Mrs. Firth?"

"Connie Firth." She rubbed the back of one hand with the other. "Now, Charlene's dating some creature with big plans and no brains."

"Walter Osgood Kemp."

"That's the lame-o." Constance Portello made a face. "He's another cleavage freak." She made a beseeching gesture with both hands. "What's the fascination men have with boobs?"

"In my case, not being breastfed." I lit a cigarette. "When was Caivano's last fling with Mrs. Firth?"

"It's not like's she'd advertise."

"Your best guess.

Constance Portello shrugged.

"Some time last year," she said. "Dom caught on and laid down the law to his men. No getting involved with married women."

"Was that before or after Dom's shindig with Mrs. Firth?"

"After."

"How'd Caivano take losing Charlene?"

"I doubt he cared." She smiled, dreamily. "Cutie has his pick of women."

"You, too?"

"Don't be ridiculous!"

"I'm glad to hear that," I said. "Because any itch you might be ready to scratch came a little late."

Constance Portello stiffened.

"What are you saying?" she asked, in a trembling voice.

"Cutie's dead."

Her knees buckled, but she caught herself before falling.

"Who killed him?" Constance demanded.

"I'm told it was Dom."

"Why in hell would he do that?"

"Cutie and your brother had a falling out."

She fell silent thinking. After a few seconds, Constance nodded her head, as if coming to a conclusion.

"Rita," she gritted. "I warned her. I told her to quit playing up to Cutie." Connie pulled on an earlobe. "All she had to do was keep her panties up. But, she couldn't leave Cutie alone."

I felt a pang of jealousy. But, there were no rules in our relationship.

"Rita can be seductive," I said. "What's the connection between Firth and Parker, other than being brothers-in-law?"

"I saw them arguing right after I got here."

"When was that?"

"Three weeks."

"Over what?"

"I heard a name, when Firth raised his voice," she replied. "Reggie."

"Reggie Shepherd?"

She shrugged.

"I didn't catch a surname," Constance returned."

"I understand Mrs. Firth and Dr. Parker had a serious fling."

"Connie had a crush on Nathaniel Parker."

"How did they get along after their affair ended?"

"Well enough, I suppose. It was Connie who recommended I go to this place." Constance interlaced her fingers at her waist. "Who's Reggie Shepherd?"

"I think he saw Mrs. Firth's murder. The trouble is, his deck is short a few cards. So, communicating with the Shadow can be confusing."

"The Shadow?"

"That's another wrinkle in need of ironing."

"Who does the Shadow say did it?"

"Cutie."

"Caivano killed Connie?" she gaped.

"Cutie," I said. "Believe it or not there's more than one."

"Did you get a description?"

"Not so far."

There was a long pause as she considered.

"So, whoever this Cutie is, he knows he was seen?" Constance Portello asked.

"The four men who saw the killing with Reggie are now dead. How well do you get along with Dr. Parker?"

She came over to face me.

"Why?" Constance asked.

"If Firth and Parker were discussing Reggie Shepherd, I'd like to know why."

"It might not have been the same Reggie."

"How many Reggies do you know?"

She weighed my question for a beat.

"Okay," Constance conceded. "I admit the odds favor your concerns. But, you're a tough guy. Firth and Parker are a couple of cupcakes. Warn them off."

"If one of them is the killer, he's a step up from soft and spongy. A warning will only prompt him to hire it done. But, if you were to get Sal to send a couple of men to visit the good doctors, I think they'd give up any plans for Reggie."

"You overestimate my power over my husband."

"You've got Sal's ear. Plus his earthier parts." I tossed her a teasing grin. "During pillow-talk, after a passionate intermingling, you could mention your desire to protect the Shadow. Sal, relaxing with heady afterglow, would insist upon helping. Easy-peasy-lemon-squeezy."

"Forget it," Constance said. She went over and sat down on the window seat. "But, you might get the help you need from Precious Heidegger."

I knew Precious. She had assisted me on several occasions when I needed a computer expert. She was not the typical geek. In fact, her professional specialty was hacking computer systems and making a mature private investigator wish he was back in his teens.

"How does Precious fit?" I asked.

"She's Dr. Parker's stepdaughter. And she was out there with them during the argument. So if you ask Precious nicely, she might share what she heard."

"Precious and I have some history."

"That poor woman. Well, it was an idea."

"She gave me the impression of being an orphan."

"Probably because she didn't want you borrowing from her relations."

Some people do not understand the intricacies of my entrepreneurial efforts.

"I'm not a deadbeat," I protested.

"Yes, you are. But, you may get lucky anyway." Constance cocked an eyebrow. "I heard Precious has a thing for older men. Apparently, she got involved with some over-the-hill reprobate and they spent a perversion filled weekend in Chicago."

There was nothing perverse about that weekend. I had been my usual charming self. Precious had been her unusually receptive self. There had been a great deal of physical interaction. Most of which worthy of my memoires.

"How'd Parker get into this racket?" I asked.

"Insurance money."

"Come again?"

"He had a brother. Jerome." She cocked her head to one side and looked at her hands. "Died in some sleazy hotel. Dr. Parker collected nearly a million as his brother's insurance beneficiary."

"Do you know Jerome's cause of death?"

She turned her thoughts over in her mind. It seemed to soothe her.

"Electrocuted on the hotel roof trying to piss on a pigeon." Her mouth twisted into a confused grimace as her eyes rose to mine. "Who pisses on a pigeon?"

"It's more common than people think," I told her. "Let me take a wild guess. The hotel was the Anniston Arms?"

Her eyes widened in surprise.

"Have you become weirdly psychic?" she asked.

One death, at the Anniston, attributed to pigeon pissing I could buy. Two means somebody's helping. But who? A pair of pensioners, like the Anniston sisters, did not seem likely. Sal and Charlene had mentioned a nephew. Drax Ravaillac. He might be young and fit. Then, of course, there was Buford Reese.

Chapter 9

I have always considered myself well-informed. Since grade-school, I have studied racing journals. During my military tour, I subscribed to sporting magazines with pull-out sections. Even today, I caught glimpses of news broadcasts. Mostly while sipping beer during visits to local gambling clubs. But, my skills with a computer have been, and are, completely lacking. It had nothing to do with deficient interest. I had plenty. What I lacked was time to acquire the necessary skills. Consequently, my entire adult life had been spent seeking the assistance of those with computer expertise. People like Precious Heidegger.

"I came to offer condolences on the death of your aunt," I greeted her.

"These days, Bishop, I get a grand an hour," Precious Heidegger declared, as her fingers clattered across a computer keyboard. "And don't think your plastic sympathies will sway me."

"I stand here with my heart aching because of your loss and this is what I get?"

"The only time your heart ached was when Melinda Sings lost the Triple Crown."

We were in Precious Heidegger's temporary office. I say temporary because hackers tend to move around, a lot. This time she had rented a secluded cubicle at the back of Chili's Pool Parlor.

"I had a fortune on that nag," I said.

"On your way out," she returned, "shove your concerns where the sun doesn't shine."

Precious was sitting on a stool in front of a plank and cinderblock desk, cruising through what looked like Moscow's FSB website. I was standing behind her, smoking a cigarette, and wondering who was footing the tab for this bit of international intrigue.

"I sense a certain reticence," I told her. "Possibly due to our time in Chicago?"

"Not only did you stick me for the airfare, but you dinged my credit for the hotel room."

"I can explain that."

"When can't you?" she snorted.

Twenty-something Precious Heidegger had all the attributes of the average single female. A distrust of shady characters. A concern for fashion. And a love of cats. But, she also had an attribute unique to only a few of her sex. She could see through a dirty old man's lies as if they were written on glass.

"Okay," I said, "the truth is, I'm here because I need your help."

"No more credit," she returned. "I don't care if you're investigating your own murder."

My charming ex-lover had short, blue-black hair. It coiled around her tiny ears like ink smears. Her slender, patrician face would never get a movie contract. But, she was in excellent physical condition and had a room-warming smile.

"In case you've forgotten," I said, "I saved your bacon."

"Only because it was incidental in defending your own."

"To protect your virtue, I threw myself in front of three armed maniacs."

"Bishop, after being debauched by you, there was little virtue left."

So much for romantic history and lifesaving valor. I would have to try something unusual, for me. The truth. Or, at least, my version of it.

"Precious," I pleaded, "you're my only friend with computer know-how."

"Stop lying to yourself, Bishop." She became rigid, her eyes opening wide with curiosity, as the computer screen soiled out column after column written in Russian. "You have no friends. Even your enemies deny knowing you."

"My creditors know exactly what I owe."

"Goodbye, Bishop."

"What about a swap?" I suggested. "An hour of your time in exchange for a month of Lone Star Ed's fabulous burrito breakfasts?"

Precious exhaled with contempt.

"I'm a cash kind of girl," she said.

"I'll throw in an equal number of Lone Star Ed's Sombrero Lunches," I coaxed. "Fricasseed Gila Monster on a hard role, with Ed's special Sonora sauce."

"Why do I get the feeling you did a job for Lone Star Ed but didn't get paid?"

Why were mercenary women so prone to making accurate assumptions? It was absolutely irritating. A man of my suave sophistication, extensive experience, and licentious leanings should be able to con the Precious Heidegger's of this world three days out of four.

"I may have done an investigation that exceeded Ed's financial situation," I explained. "In settlement, he offered a few meals."

"How few?"

"Thirty-two hundred."

Precious heaved herself to her feet. Then she went to the wall, turned and leaned back; her arms crossed, her eyes upon me like red-hot needles.

"So, to keep your belly full you tracked down some terrified woman?" Precious asked.

"His wife, actually. And if any terror was involved, it was on her part."

"You're telling me Ed wanted you to give her a going away present?"

"Not exactly. When she left, his wife took nearly three hundred grand." I pulled deeply on my cigarette. "You know what women are like."

"All in a dead heat to get clear of you."

This was going to be tougher than first I imagined. But, I had the feeling Precious was warming to my subtle charm.

"Since reopening," I persisted, "Ed's been called a culinary genius."

Precious returned to her chair.

"Reopening?" she echoed. "Why did he close?"

"There was a slight ptomaine scare," I explained. "His wife

tried to derail Ed in favor of his competition."

Her fingers resumed their clatter across the keyboard.

"Take your botulism infested barter elsewhere," she instructed.

"Not so fast," I returned. "I'll tack on two months of Ed's blue-plate special. It's rattlesnake basted in a molasses sauce, and grilled to crispy perfection."

"That's disgusting."

"Wait 'til you taste it."

Precious drew in a long, deep breath that lifted her firm bosom in the most enticing manner. I sighed, thinking back to Chicago.

"Okay," she sighed, "I'll give you my desperation rate if you promise to go away and never darken my door again,.."

"Which is how much?" I asked.

"Two-Hundred-Fifty an hour."

That was a bit higher than I had hoped. Certainly a great deal less than her regular rate. But, more than my current finances could absorb. So I took another tact, relying upon my innate sexuality, to win the day.

"Why don't we discuss it over drinks… at your apartment?" I suggested.

"I've given up imbibing with men of low caliber," Precious returned.

"So, you're no longer dating that neurosurgeon?"

"I was referring to you, Bishop."

Some days Precious Heidegger had a crass single-mindedness that could scald the fur from a cat. But, if I wanted her assistance, I would have to accept her terms. Afterward, I would finagle something, to ease my financial burden.

"All right," I said. "No trots with meals. No romantic interludes. Straight cash."

"Thank God, for small favors."

"But, I'll need time to pay."

Her hands stopped keying and she looked at me.

"What in hell do you do with your money?" Precious asked.

"There's rent and groceries. Then, I have reserved seating at several gambling establishments. Of course, a single man is entitled to female companionship which, at my age, can be expensive."

"Have you considered switching from two legs to four, on the companionship front?"

"I'm going to pretend I didn't hear that."

"Okay. It's on the cuff, one last time. What's the job?"

"I need a hundred million."

Precious Heidegger fell silent for nearly a full minute. She opened her mouth to speak. Shut it. And then pondered for another minute.

"You want me to steal a hundred million?" she eventually said. "Have you lost your mind?"

"I need it for just a week," I said.

"That kind of money means hacking a noxious spot not far from Moscow."

"Works for me, as long as I end up with dollars."

"Forget it."

"Why not?"

"Bishop, those people have no sense of humor."

"Nobody'll find out."

"Like you promised not to cum in my mouth?"

Why does every woman remember every detail of every point of verbal misrepresentation involving an errant sexual emission?

"This time, I mean it," I told her.

"Bishop, you with a bank account holding a hundred million will start the entire free world talking." Precious Heidegger suddenly smiled. "Why do you need a hundred million?"

"I've got something going," I said. "But, to finalize the deal, I have to prove a net worth of a hundred million."

"You mean there's somebody out there who will believe that?"

"The cash won't be touched."

She waggled a forefinger.

"Something's not right about this," Precious said.

Her words put me in mind of the first time I saw her. I had been on Padre Island, following a wayward florist and his sultry bit of stuff along the beach. Precious had been in a kiosk selling ice-cream. She had offered me a sample. Somehow, I had misinterpreted. This prompted her to utter those same words and hit me with a bucket of water.

"If you're concerned about my veracity I'll open a numbered account in the Cayman's to receive the transfer. But only you will know the access code. That way the money can be deposited but not withdrawn without your involvement."

Precious paused for many seconds to consider.

"You won't know the code?" she asked.

"I'll establish the account, with the exception of the code. Then, you will telephone the bank to complete the arrangement by providing it."

"And after a week, I can return the money?"

"Not only that, but to further assure your peace of mind I'll camp at your place the entire time." I dropped my cigarette butt to the floor, and heeled it. "You still have that king sized bed?"

She flinched, as if I had burned the end of her nose.

"That won't be necessary," Precious snapped. "When do you need this temporary cash influx?"

"Anytime within the next three days."

"That's impossible." She lifted her shoulders and let them drop. "It'll take a month to set up."

"Just give me something quick and dirty."

"I have to establish a series of blinds. That takes time."

"The quicker you do this the quicker I exit your life."

There was another span of silence. The only sounds were her typing, the faint whirring of the computer's cooling fan and the erratic thumping of my heart.

"As tempting as that sounds," she said, "one slip and this thing'll come back to bite us."

"I'll be the only one at risk. Right?"

"Until you spill your guts to save your own hide."

"When have I ever done that?"

"Calm down," Precious returned. "I'll do it. But, when this goes south I want you to remember how hard I worked at trying to talk you out of it."

"You didn't offer sex."

She stopped typing and glared at me.

"You keep me out of it, understand?" Precious warned. "I don't care if they clamp your balls to a flame thrower and shove a red-hot iron up your ass, you stay *shtum*."

"I'll take care of the bank account, this afternoon. And, as I promised, you'll set up the access code. I presume the banker can give you whatever information you'll need to make the transfer?"

"All I'll need is the telephone number — and you out of my life."

I inhaled a cloud of smoke and let it seep out through my nostrils.

"Now, as long as I'm here and you're on the clock, so to speak," I said, "can we spend a few minutes chatting about an argument you overheard between Drs. Firth and Parker?"

Precious Heidegger flopped back into her chair, her eyes on the ceiling.

"You're scamming them?" she demanded. "That's why you need the hundred million?"

"If the truth be told…"

"Like that's ever crossed your lying lips?" She jumped to her feet. "That's it, Bishop. Forget it." Precious Heidegger thrust a finger toward the door. "Now, get the hell out of here!"

"I'm not lying."

"I don't believe you."

"Look, Precious, before you start hacking my genitals with something toothed and tarnished, my only interest, in your family, is an argument concerning Reggie Shepherd. Do you remember it?"

"Who's Reggie to you?" she asked.

"A quirky friend with a Shadow complex."

"Is he involved with Lone Star Ed's problem?"

"Someone's trying to kill Reggie."

"And you think it's Firth and Parker? Don't be ridiculous. They're pussy-cats." Precious mulled her thoughts, for a long moment. Then, she shrugged her shoulders. "They weren't having an argument. It was a disagreement over how to react, should the worst happen."

"Worst in what respect?"

"Reggie had been blabbing God knows what to some insurance agent. Dr. Firth was concerned the investigator would start a witch hunt into their backgrounds. Dr. Parker assured him they had nothing to worry about."

"From my experience, when people say that there's plenty to worry about."

"Uncle Paisley does all the dental work for the Anniston Arms Hotel guests. Cutie provides the remaining medical care. There's nothing illegal going on."

"Dr. Parker's 'Cutie'?" I asked in surprise.

"My mother gave him the nickname."

Now, I had four Cutie's. Firth, Parker, Connie Firth's lover, possibly known as Drax Ravaillac, and the deceased Caivano.

"Do either Dr. Firth or Dr. Parker have an interest in comic books?"

"Bishop, where do you come off with this stuff?" she demanded, irascibly. "Do you sit up nights writing down inane questions?"

"Are comics their thing? Yes, or no."

"Both men were, and I assume still are, huge graphic arts fans. What's the big deal?"

"Do either of them attend Austin's Comic Con?"

"Since getting out on my own I have no way of knowing," Precious snapped. "But, at one time they did. I know, because they took me along." She pointed back the way I had come in. "Now, shouldn't you be contacting a bank in the Cayman Islands?"

Chapter 10

I got up late, the next morning. My sleep had been interrupted by a recurring nightmare. I had never believed in omens or forewarnings. But this dream troubled me. In it, a hit and run driver had killed Reggie Shepherd. The police had refused to investigate because they viewed the death as accidental. So, it fell to me to find the culprit. But, as the portrayal unfolded, the bad guy's identity became apparent. He was me. Doubtlessly, this reverie was a twisted tale based upon decades of mixed memories. Nevertheless, it took until the completion of my morning ablutions to shake the guilty feelings.

Breakfast was homemade, for a change.

While I nibbled on something green and brown, memories of the past few days stumbled through my thoughts. Salvator Portello's admissions had put Connie Firth and Julie 'the Cutie' Caivano at Hillman's Warehouse. But Sal's version of events indicated Caivano was not her killer. That being the case, which Cutie was?

Paisley Firth and Nathaniel Parker wore that nickname. Also, they were known to Reggie. Against either of them being Mrs. Firth's killer was their history. Neither man had a criminal past. Which nudged my suspicions toward the third Cutie on my list of suspects: the man I had photographed with Mrs. Firth. But his antics with her suggested a lack of murderous leanings. He had been completely submissive to her sexual whims.

The telephone rang.

I got up and dragged the handset from its mount on the wall. After offering to shove the communication device into the caller's anal orifice, I heard a familiar voice.

"It's Kemp," he whispered. "I gotta' see you. The shit's…"

"I've talked to Constance Portello, Ozzie," I cut in. "She's alive and as nasty as ever. So her part in your theory is toast."

"Forget her. The dead woman's Connie Firth."

"Now, you tell me?"

"I finally got it from the Meatball."

"How?"

"I showed him a picture of a tiger tattoo. He called it a kitty."

That explained that — probably.

"As for Caivano, being Connie Firth's killer," I said, "it didn't happen."

"I know."

"You showed Reggie another photo?"

"It worked once, so why not try again?"

"You're still getting a bill, Ozzie."

"Somebody's trying to kill me and you're bitchin' about money?"

With Kemp, 'Somebody's trying to kill me' usually meant one of his dirt-ball relations going off the rails.

"Who, this time?" I asked.

"I don't know."

"Ozzie, you must have some idea."

"I haven't ripped off anybody in months."

That was open for debate.

"Where are you?" I asked.

"Church," he said. "We walked outa' my place. The bullets started flyin'. We jumped in the car and burned rubber to get here."

"Who's we?"

"Me, Charlene and the Meatball."

"Can you get to my office?"

"Not a chance. The Meatball says the bastard's outside."

"Reggie saw the guy?"

"Not, exactly."

"Then, how does he know the shooter's outside?"

"He's gone psychic."

A psychic Shadow. Who'd have guessed?

"Call the cops," I told him. "They'll be there in two minutes."

"Are you crazy? I do that and Sal will kill me."

"Have you got a gun?"

"I'm a convicted felon, for Christ's sake," Kemp shouted. "I'm not allowed to have guns."

"Since when do any of you heed that?"

The phone line abruptly went dead.

I returned the handset to its mount and went out to the Buick. Then, I headed for unholy-land. On the way, I used my cell-phone to call 911 and report Kemp's situation.

When I arrived at the Church of Hidden Salvation, the front door was ajar. Kemp's red Cadillac glinted in the parking lot. Near the church entrance, a young police officer was vomiting. That was definitely a worry. A puking cop generally indicated undercooked pork... or murder. Since this was not a diner owned by Lone Star Ed, somebody had made a bloody mess.

I got out of the Buick and strolled over.

"What's happened?" I asked the uniform.

"Murder," he gurgled.

"How many?"

"One."

"Did you secure the building?"

"It's empty," he replied, and resumed upchucking.

I followed a trail of blood drops inside the church.

The pews were empty. But the red drops continued up the aisle. I followed until I came upon the remains of Walter Osgood Kemp. He lay on his right side, near the pulpit, his neck twisted so the back of his head was against the floor and his face looked toward heaven. Not far from the corpse was the butt from a hand-rolled cigarette. Just above Kemp's left ear was a leaking hole. Beneath his head was a thick puddle of brains. From his unblinking stare, God's fourth-class savior was done redeeming souls.

I returned outside.

The cop was all but on his knees, dealing with a case of dry-heaves. First homicides were hard on the digestion. I noticed more blood so I let my eyes follow the drops to the empty spot where, on my previous visit, the school bus had been. The cessation of blood and the missing vehicle suggested an emergency escape. I assumed Charlene had been at the wheel with Reggie riding shotgun. Presumably, one or the other had been hurt in the action which killed Kemp. But, I found it curious she had chosen the bus over the Cadillac.

I went over to the Buick and climbed inside.

Before I could start the engine Lt. Herby Mann's cruiser

stopped, alongside. He got out and strode over. When he leaned in the side window, Mann did not look pleased. Probably because his rumbling stomach was losing the hunger battle.

"Is Kemp dead?" he asked.

"And you thought God had no sense of humor," I returned.

"How is it you're here?"

"I felt the need for prayer."

"One more smart remark and you'll spend a few nights in the drunk tank," he warned.

Drunk tanks were never my idea of fun. Too many drunks. Too many upchucking stomachs. Too many spur of the moment urinations. So, I quickly explained Kemp's telephone-call.

"He didn't tell you who was after him?" Mann asked.

"Herby, that man had half the world chewing his ass," I returned.

"No sign of Reggie Shepherd or Charlene Holland?"

"Just blood drops," I said. "But, the school bus is gone. So, I'm thinking they left in it and one of them is injured."

"Plate number?"

"Seriously, Herby?"

"Description?"

"A forty's vintage, rusty yellow with bald tires."

"I'll get out a BOLO," Mann said. "Other than Salvator Portello, whose ass was Kemp kissing?"

"Ozzie and I were not confidants, Herby."

"Kemp's the type who brags. You're the type who listens with future blackmail in mind."

"I resent that."

"You can take your resentment…"

"But," I cut in, "you may be onto something. Church scams cost a bundle. So, somebody underwrote this operation."

"Then, it had to be the Portello's."

I gave my head a shake.

"Sal's got this thing about staying clear of religious gigs," I told him. "Check with your FBI pals. They've been watching Kemp. They must've seen him with somebody other than me. They may have followed Kemp here. Maybe they saw who killed him."

"The Feds have never been Information-Central."

"Then its time they loosened up."

"Like that's going to happen."

Their only witness against Salvator Portello, is headed for hell. What's the harm in them telling a couple of secrets, now?"

Lt. Herby Mann considered and then grimaced.

"Dominic ran a church, a few years back," he said. "Maybe he's still in the soul saving business?"

"Dom's psychotic not stupid. If he'd financed Kemp, Sal would've done some serious restructuring of little brother's reproductive parts."

"Is Kemp behind on his fees to the Portello's?"

"Yes. But, his murder's not Portello business."

"Maybe. Maybe not."

"Did you talk to Sal about Connie Firth?"

"I did. He admits to being notified, anonymously, of a body in Hillman's warehouse. He claims he instructed Julie 'the Cutie' Caivano, to report the finding to the police."

"Which obviously did not happen or Mrs. Firth's body wouldn't have ended up in Lake Travis."

"Sal blamed that on a miscommunication between him and Caivano. For which Sal fired Caivano."

"Dom did the termination. But it was not limited to employment. Caivano's dead."

"When?"

"A couple of weeks back."

"Over the disposal of a body?"

"Caivano had taken an unhealthy interest in Rita."

"Who told you this?"

"An anonymous source. But, she sounded very sincere." I lit a cigarette. "Did Sal explain how Mrs. Firth's body got to Hillman's warehouse?"

"He thought it may have been the actions of a sexually deranged necrophiliac. I, of course, told him that was an oxymoron."

"A fresh corpse can be a real temptation, Herby."

Lt. Mann made a face.

"You're really sick, d'you know that?" Mann spat. He pushed back from my car. "Get the hell out of here before Charlie Trent shows up."

"How are you and the new captain of homicide getting along?" I asked.

"I'm counting the days to my pension."

"Maybe Charlie's due for a bad accident?"

"Don't even think about going there."

I started the Buick's engine and drove off.

My cellphone rang. Reggie Shepherd, alias the Shadow, was on the other end of the connection. From the tenor of his voice, he was terrified.

"Bang! Bang!" he cried.

"Reggie, where are you?" I asked.

"Hurt lady."

"Tell me where you are."

"Comic Con."

That gathering was not an ongoing event. It was held annually, in October, at Austin Convention Center. But, at the present time, the center was closed having just completed a sporting goods show-and-tell. Which begged the question: How would Reggie, and his hurt lady, get inside that building?

"Is Charlene the hurt lady?" I asked.

There was silence on the connection. During this respite I imagined the little guy making head movements.

"Stay there, Reggie," I told him. "Wait for me."

"The Shadow knows!"

The connection went silent.

I called 911 and requested an ambulance to the Convention Center.

Forty more minutes behind the steering wheel, brought me to a klatch of flashing blue lights, coming from an EMT vehicle and a gaggle of police cruisers. Two street people I recognized from Kemp's congregation stood in front of a police tape. They were passing a bottle, in a paper bag, back and forth. Beyond them was the Convention Center. I let my eyes wander. Further down the block was the school bus I remembered from Kemp's church.

I took a moment to settle my nerves. Whatever had happened, in the Convention Center was more than a Shadow impersonator and a wounded woman squaring off with security. Only a homicide, a very messy one, would warrant a dozen cruisers. And, since Reggie had been with a 'hurt lady', I assumed the deceased was Charlene Holland.

I climbed from the Buick and strode over to the police tape. The uniform, who was logging comings and goings, confronted me. From the wear and tear on in his uniform, the deep lines in his face, and his bloated middle, the cop was nearing mandatory retirement.

"Crime scene, Slick," he declared, in a flat voice.

Considering the average cop's pension, and the poor prospects for post-retirement employment, the reason for the officer's less than receptive manner was understandable. So, I scrounged up my most cooperative smile.

"I was told to come here," I lied. "My name's Deacon Bishop. I'm a private investigator."

The cop checked the clipboard, he carried, and shook his head.

"You're not on the list," he said. "Who called? Sergeant Wells?"

That was not good news. Myron Wells and I went way back. A history which involved venomous hatred, on his part, because of my history with his mother. She had recently remarried. But, Wells's attitude toward me would not have changed. In seducing his mother, I had violated a saint. Little did he know the naughty fun his saintly mother had instigated.

"Yeah, Wells," I replied. "He said I knew the deceased."

"Don't touch anything. No smoking. No spitting. No shedding." The uniform lifted the tape and I stepped under. "Don't wander around. No using the toilet. No pictures."

"Okeydokey."

"Top floor, to the left," the uniform said, making an entry on the log sheet. "I'll radio ahead so you're not hassled."

I thanked the officer and headed for the entrance.

Inside I passed half a dozen uniforms. Everybody looked grim. Nobody batted an eye, at me. A security guard, I knew from my years with Austin P-D, stood behind a desk. He was eyeballing half a dozen monitors. His name was Jason Quill.

I strode over.

"What's happened, Jason?" I asked.

"Depends on who you believe, Deke," he replied.

"Start with the victim."

"A hooker, I think. Biggest tits I've ever seen."

My heart sank.

"Deceased?" I asked.

"Nothing I could've done for her," Quill returned. "She'd been shot more than once."

"Who called the police?"

"Some old lady."

"I thought this place was closed."

"She caught the door, and came in, just after Reggie crutched out."

"You know Reggie Shepherd?" I asked, in surprise.

He laughed.

"Everybody knows the Shadow," Quill replied. "Comic-Con wouldn't be the same, without him."

"I take it you're a graphics arts fan?"

"I got a collection going back to my grandfather."

"Did you get the woman's name?"

"At the time I was expecting gun play. So, I didn't ask."

"Can you give me a description?"

"She was about sixty, maybe older. Blue hair coiled on top of her head. Wore brown slacks, a low-cut yellow blouse and a brown jacket." He groped in a pocket and brought out a small tin. He opened, took out a pinch of tobacco and then returned the tin to his pocket. "Sexy, for an old gal."

"Sexy has no age limit."

"One of her eye-teeth was capped in gold. Left, I think."

"What drew her into the building?"

"She said she'd heard a shot."

"After she got in here, what happened?"

"I told her to leave, for her own safety. That's when she said she'd called the cops and left."

"How did Reggie get in here?"

"Wish I could tell you. There's an exit-lock-release on every door, in case of fire. So getting out's no trick." Quill grabbed his shirtfront with both hands. "But, unless an event is going on, the windows and entrances are secured. There are cameras monitoring all access points. Still, he gets in with nobody the wiser."

"Reggie went out the front doors?"

"He always does. That's the only reason we know he gets in."
Quill gave an almost imperceptible nod. "Because when those
doors open, after hours, the alarms go off." He gestured with one
hand. "By the time I get to the screens, the outside cameras have
Reggie one-legging it down the sidewalk on his skateboard."

"What do you think happened?"

"I think the dead woman was hard up for cash and convinced
Reggie to bring her some place for a quickie."

"Did you tell Wells that?"

Quill took a deep breath.

"I did," he said. "But, Wells insists Reggie's the killer."

"You found her where?"

"In the Blue Room, on the top floor. When I walked in, I
could smell burned gunpowder." Quill grimaced as if the odor was
replaying in his brain. "Which explains the shot I heard. But, I also
saw a blood trail leading in or out of the room. So either she was
wounded somewhere else and dripped on the way in. Or, her killer
didn't get away untouched." He gave his head a mournful shake.
"The round hit her in the face."

"I don't see Reggie as the type to make a head shot."

"If you can convince Wells, of that, you're a better man than
me *Gunga Din*."

"Other than that woman and Reggie, was anybody else in the
building?"

Quill's head wagged.

"But, I heard running feet on the steps. One or two people."
He thought for a moment. "Hard soles and heels."

"Did the cameras catch anybody leaving?"

"Just Reggie. So, maybe the stair-noises were my
imagination."

"Do you believe that?"

"Nope. But, odder things have happened."

I thanked Quill and headed for the elevators.

Standing in front of a doorway, on the top floor, was a
uniform I recognized. His name was Vernon Cobb. He was sipping
coffee from a paper cup and nibbling a pastry. When he spotted

me, Cobb tilted his head toward the entrance. I stopped near him and looked in. Portable spotlights dotted the blue carpeting. Their lavender glow illuminated several suits, and a number of uniforms, a covey of forensic techs and a nude corpse. If the breasts were an indicator, I was looking at the remains of Charlene Holland.

"Has she been identified?" I asked.

"Not yet," Cobb returned. "But, somebody's going to be heartsick over those tits. They must've cost a fortune."

The scene brought back a flood of unpleasant memories. Murder was eternal. Its investigation had been handled in many ways, and would continue to evolve. But, killing would always be the same. A flash of anger. Thick-headed revenge. Uncontrolled lust. The sordid dreams of the deranged. Rarely was homicide the fruit of clever, clearheaded thinking. Stupid people don't understand the difference in killing, and getting away with it.

"Who tops the suspect list?" I asked, feigning ignorance.

"According to the brilliant mind of our dim light in homicide..." began Cobb.

"Myron Wells?"

He nodded.

"Myron says it's a looney-tune named Reggie Shepherd," Cobb said.

"I take it you don't agree?" was my return.

"I know Reggie. His head's in the clouds. But, he wouldn't hurt a fly."

"Then, why is Wells pushing for his arrest?"

"Our new Captain, Charlie 'Fill my Pockets' Trent, is trying to impress his cousin, the mayor, with quick results."

"How quick?"

"Investigators have twenty-four hours to solve each homicide. An impossibility, in most cases; this one included." His eyes glittered as he stared at me for a long moment. "Which is why Reggie's piss-gun incident makes him an easy fit for a fast solution."

"Better a wrong than an unsolved?"

"You got the idea."

The body was lying on the carpet. Neatly piled next to it was female clothing. I assumed Reggie had not done the folding. It seemed equally unlikely Charlene had participated in this pre-murder act. Which left her killer as the neat freak. Not a common male pursuit. But, not completely unknown among the insensitive set.

I cleared my throat noisily to draw attention.

Wells took note of my presence, and came over.

"I heard you'd arrived, Bishop," he said. "But, I didn't send for you."

"Silly me. I was sure the voice was yours." I pointed to the corpse. "She the only victim?"

"That'd be police business."

"Shot?"

"Also police business."

"Have you identified her?"

"Ditto and don't let me keep you."

"Let me help you with ditto," I told him. "Her name's Charlene Holland. She was affianced to Walter Osgood Kemp." I gave him a mocking grin. "Any bells going off?"

Wells stood there, for several beats, his mouth open.

"Are you having me on?" he finally demanded. "Her with Kemp?"

"I'm a detective, Myron. I'm sworn to tell the truth."

"But, Kemp was murdered no more than half an hour ago."

"Talk about coincidence," I said, dryly. "Or, the same killer could be at work."

He tilted his head toward the body.

"What do you know about this?" Wells asked.

"For starters, I know Reggie Shepherd didn't do it."

"He's good for this, at least for the time being."

"Reggie shot her while standing on one leg, holding his crutch and skateboard?"

Wells shifted on his feet, his face flushed with embarrassed.

"My investigation is ongoing," he snapped.

"Reggie saw the shooter kill Connie Firth," I told Wells. "My theory is, the same killer tracked him to Kemp where a less than heroic preacher got in the way, probably trying to hide behind Charlene." When a long moment had gone by, I added, "Then Charlene drove Reggie here, at his maniacal behest. I think the shooter followed and finished her off while Reggie was crutching his way out."

Sgt. Myron Wells pointed at the corpse.

"Why kill her instead of Reggie, if Reggie was the target?" Wells asked.

"I suspect she put herself in harm's way trying to protect Reggie."

Wells fell silent, again.

"Can Reggie identify the killer?" he asked.

"Reggie thinks the shooter is a guy nicknamed Cutie."

"There's gotta' be a thousand guys with that moniker."

"Seriously? In macho Texas?"

"Does Reggie still live at the Anniston Arms Hotel?"

"As far as I know."

My eyes were drawn to Charlene's feet. One was still encased in a sock. The other foot was bare. The nails of her toes had been painted red. My eyes drifted up to her thighs. They were lovely, smooth and rounded. One had a gecko tattoo. The object of my interest went higher to her vulva. It had been shaved. For some reason that both surprised and titillated. I looked further up her figure. Her abdomen showed striations, suggestive of child bearing. I had not considered that. Somewhere a son or daughter did not know mommy was dead. I refocused moving my eyes up to her massive breasts. Despite the surgeon's best efforts I could make out the silhouette of saline filled bags. This was an indication of surgery done some time ago. The weight of the implants having stretched the skin, and pushed aside the fat.

"Sorry to butt in on your party," I told him.

I turned to leave, but Wells grabbed my arm.

"As long as you're here, *detective*, I'd like you to take a look at something." He handed me a pair of latex gloves. "It's a bruise on her back."

He turned and went over to the corpse.

Reluctantly, I slipped fingers into the protection and followed. When I got close enough to see Charlene's face. It was still beautiful, except for the hole in her forehead. There was another hole in her left thigh. Blood was still seeping out of both wounds.

"Whatever sins Charlene may have committed, she didn't

deserve this," I muttered.

Sgt. Wells squatted down and rolled her body onto one side. I immediately noticed the bruise in question. It was on her left shoulder blade. The injury reflected a stack of rings, slightly angled, culminating in a cylinder.

"Any ideas?" he asked.

"What you have, there, Myron," I said, "is a premortem encounter with a tactical baton."

"Considering your version of police methodology I guess you'd know about that," he said, dryly.

"I had a sterling conviction rate for two reasons: One, I was a brilliant police investigator. Two, I filled my baton's end-cap with lead." I fumbled in a pocket for my keys. "Those extra two ounces of weight, bouncing on soft tissue at the speed of sound, made all the difference."

He eased the body back to its prone position and stood erect.

"You're a sadist," Wells said.

"We'll never be friends, Myron. So, stop trying to turn my head."

He groped in his pockets for nothing in particular; his eyes averted from the corpse. I repeatedly wiped my mouth. Neither of us spoke for many seconds. Murder is sickening enough when you are investigating that of a stranger. But, when it is someone you knew it was a thousand times worse.

"I'm thinking, that mark took beef," he said. "More force than a woman could deliver."

"A woman could have done it."

He made a sucking noise with his teeth.

"Do you have a lead on Reggie's Cutie?" Wells asked.

"Have a chat with Dr. Paisley Firth," I said. "He's an optometrist with an eye for the ladies, and a recently murdered wife."

"Connie Firth?"

"Exactly." I sucked breath in. "Charlene was one of Firth's patients. But, I think she may have been more. Cutie's Firth's nickname. He knew Reggie Shepherd." I grinned through tight teeth. "Dr. Nathaniel Parker, from Fredericksburg is another Cutie. He knows Reggie. Charlene knew Parker. Parker is brother-in-law to Firth. Parker had an affair with Connie Firth." My grin widened so he could see my canines. "See how nicely the strings tie together?"

Myron Wells nudged my arm and we walked out into the hallway, down to the elevators. After making certain we were out of earshot, Wells asked what I knew about rumors linking Captain Charles Trent to Walter Osgood Kemp.

"According to Kemp, they're true," I said. "But, I've got nothing to prove it."

"I'm going to bring Charlie to his knees," Wells said.

"You don't like his new investigative directives?"

"I don't like anything about the bastard."

"Take my advice, and let it go," I said. "As long as Charlie's cousin is mayor, Charlie's untouchable."

"If Trent stays," Wells gritted, "I'll never make Lieutenant."

"Getting a paycheck beats the hell out of unemployment."

"Yeah, well, it's about time somebody beat the hell out of Charlie Trent."

Perhaps there was more to Wells than I had thought.

"Just thinking out loud," Myron Wells mused, "a guy getting captain's bars might not want a guy like Kemp in the weeds."

"Just thinking out loud, I agree. And knowing Kemp as I did, I'd wager he shook Charlie down after Charlie's promotion." I gave one hand an expressive wave. "And, knowing Charlie as I do, your less than esteemed new Captain of Homicide would not like being bled white."

"You think Charlie's nicknamed Cutie?"

"Not a moniker I'd give him. But Charlie's a permanent-solution type guy."

Sgt. Myron Wells grinned.

"Meaning a dead Kemp's no problem?" Wells asked.

"Not for Charlie." I pushed the call button for the lift. "Charlene had at least one kid."

"So what?"

"So somewhere there may be a kid waiting for mommy."

The elevator doors opened and I stepped in.

As the sun sank, I stopped at Eggie's Diner. Over a meal of fried potatoes and buffalo steak I read the newspaper. The Globe

News's latest edition devoted its headline to the murders of Kemp and Charlene. Front page photos showed them together at a party. I folded the newspaper and set it aside. Where to go from here?

I counted out cash and change to cover my meal. Then, sucked down the last of my coffee. Technically, I had met my client obligations. That being said, I had not identified Cutie. He was still out there. Probably on the hunt for Reggie Shepherd.

What I could actually do to protect the little guy was up for grabs. He was not family, so forcing Reggie into a safe place was not an option. Demanding he have police protection would only aggravate his situation. As far as Austin politics was concerned, anybody I had concerns for was automatically issued with a bullseye for their back. I guess, for the time being, I could tolerate a roomie and helpmate. At least until I identified Cutie. But, keeping the Shadow under my wing had its own challenges. I had never been one for skateboarding.

Chapter 11

The next morning I drove to the Anniston Arms Hotel, a residential guesthouse in East Austin.

The first Argyle Anniston built his namesake in five stories of Texas red brick. The year was 1844. After his death, in 1898, due to a lightning strike on the hotel's roof, Argyle Anniston II took charge of the hotel. In an effort to modernize the family business, he added green shutters to the hotel's windows. In 1932 Argyle Anniston II was electrocuted while installing a sump pump in the hotel's basement. His son, Argyle Anniston III, inherited the hotel and began a remodeling frenzy. This included a red canopy over the front entrance and downsizing the hotel's thirty guest-rooms to provide each floor with an indoor bath. In 1978 Argyle Anniston III died, while bathing, when a portable television fell into the tub. His death passed the hotel to his son, Argyle Anniston IV. At this time, the Anniston clan purchased the adjacent property; a five story warehouse. The Hotel Annex, as it came to be called, was turned it into a worker's fleabag. Bed to bed space provided nearly four hundred accommodations. Two years later an arsonist was blamed on a fire which destroyed the annex, killing over three hundred people. Although Argyle Anniston IV was not held culpable for the blaze, he razed the gutted structure with no immediate plans for rebuilding. Currently, the vacant lot provided additional hotel parking.

In 1987, during a lightning strike, while attempting to place a satellite dish on the hotel's roof, Argyle Anniston IV met his maker. Because had not produced a male heir, the Anniston Arms Hotel passed to his daughters: Mariah, Minerva and Mortise. The sisters, it was alleged, lacked the necessary business acumen to make a success of the hotel. This opinion seemed justified when, a short time later, the trio converted the Anniston Arms into a haven for street people.

Last year, death cut the Anniston sistership by one with the passing of Mariah. She succumbed in circumstances strikingly similar to her father's. Mariah and her son, Drax Ravaillac, had been on the hotel roof during a thunder storm. According to reports, they had been attempting adjustments to the satellite dish when lightning dealt the fatal blow. Later, during a police inquiry, Ravaillac could not explain his own miraculous survival. But, there were whispers suggesting his involvement in Mariah's demise.

I parked the Buick out front, climbed from behind the steering wheel and entered the venerated lodging.

The dim lobby was overdue for renovation. Its sole Casablanca fan dangled from the ceiling on a length of pipe, the wooden blades wobbling half-heartedly. Their feeble attempt at air recirculation mixed over a century of stale tobacco smoke with the fresh exudations from two men sitting on a tired davenport. Flowered paper covered the walls in blister-pack fashion. More flowers inlaid the blue carpet, complemented by an assortment of vines. The floor-covering's nap was so thin the fibers from the jute sub-pad sprouted through like porcupine quills. At the room's center was an expansive mahogany reception desk complimented by a back-structure of pigeon holes for guest keys and messages. Behind the desk, stood Buford Reese.

I quickened my pace.

"How's tricks, Buford?" I hailed when I reached him.

"Listen at me, Bishop," he growled. "You ain't no cop no more."

I leaned my forearms on the desktop and grinned.

"Considering your history," I told him, "that should improve our relationship."

"Don't gotta' say shit at you."

Reese's face was long, brown and gaunt. A Mexican-bandit moustache grew thick and white below his broad nose. He was about fifty pounds lighter than last I saw him. I attributed this weight-loss to prison fare. The meals, at Huntsville, often disagree with those who prefer a rich man's diet.

"No need to strain your liver," I said.

"Already done last time I got shived," Reese gritted.

"Information is all I'm after."

"Like hell," he spat. "You'd shake down your own mother for

savin' orphans.''

"Where's Reggie Shepherd?''

Reese blinked twice in surprise.

"What's that crazy to you?'' he asked, suspiciously.

"When did you last see Reggie?'' I returned.

"Few days.''

"He didn't come home, last night?''

"Not that I saw.''

"You don't do bed-checks?''

"They's in or they's out.''

In his day, Buford Reese wore nothing but tailor-made from the skin out. At the moment his ensemble consisted of a shabby brown suit, a wrinkled shirt, and a grease-stained necktie. I assumed his underwear was of a similar, serviceable quality. However, when it came to ex-cons there was no guarantee.

"Where would Reggie stay, if not here?'' I asked. "His brother?''

"As far as Gordon Shepherd goes, that crazy's nothin' but ass-wipe.''

Nothing like the protection of a loving family member.

"Walter Osgood Kemp paid you to keep a protective eye on Reggie,'' I said.

His tongue made a dance across his brown lips.

"They's a difference between promisin' and payin','' Reese said.

"Whatever's been promised, by Kemp, won't be coming. He's dead.''

"I heard.'' Buford Reese blandly inclined his head "Listen at me, Bishop. No amount a money in hand would've made any difference. Reggie don't pay no mind. Not to me. Not to nobody.'' His shoulders bobbed. "That crazy just comes and goes, like there a worry in the world. And ever-time he go he shoutin': 'The Shadow knows. The Shadow knows.''' Reese's arms went up and then down, in a frustrated movement. "What's the Shadow knows, that's what I wanna' know?''

"Any strangers sniffing after Reggie?'' I asked.

"Not lately.'' Buford Reese squinted. "What's goin' on?''

"The police are looking for him.''

"His piss gun, again?"

"Reggie's a material witness in Kemp's murder, maybe two others."

Buford Reese pondered possibilities for a beat.

"Maybe Reggie's dead," he suggested. "Folks what see murders get dead."

"I'm thinking you could help prevent that."

"What's in it for me?"

"I'm hoping you'd do this out of the goodness of your heart."

"They's hope. And then, they's hope." He tapped the desktop with the long middle finger of his right hand. In so doing, the forefinger on that hand flopped up and down like a brown worm. "But, no matter which, I ain't in it."

"What've you got against Reggie?"

"The crazy thinks he's the Shadow. Ain't that enough?"

"Then, it follows, you also hated Norman, Louie, Henry, and Warren."

"I don't hate nobody."

"Somebody hated them. The fantasizing four are dead."

His tongue flicked out like a pink bug and wet his lips.

"Them crazies got what they got," Reese muttered. "But, they deaths ain't on me."

"I'd like to think that, Buford. But we both know, from painful experience, all that counts is what a jury believes."

"Cops say they was accidents."

"The cops are doing a rethink."

"Look, man, Reggie probably run off. He always runnin' off. Hell, even when he's in his room he's runnin' off."

"What's Reggie's room number?"

"Four-ten." Reese dragged his hands across his face. "Gordon, Reggie's brother, hired you?"

"You know Gordon?"

Reese's head wagged.

"Gordon come by, once or twice," he said.

"Nice guy?"

"Ain't what I'd call vanilla puddin'."

"Gordon's visited because he was concerned for Reggie?"

"From what I seen, that white boy don't worry 'bout nobody,

'cept hisself." Buford Reese chuckled. "Which makes him related to you."

"Where does Reggie hang out?"

"Don't know. Don't care." Again, he squinted. "Which makes me wonder why you do?"

"I have reasons."

"Reasons hell! You don't do shit lessen' there's a dollar in it." He cocked an eyebrow. "Some to share?"

"Depends on what you know."

Buford Reese mulled his thoughts for a long moment.

"S'pose I heard about an insurance man," he said.

"Know his name?"

"Maybe." He sniffed, wetly. "What's it worth?"

"Twenty."

"Not much for a name."

"Twenty more than you have now."

Again he considered.

"Mortise caught that boy talkin' to Reggie," he said. "She lost it. Told him to haul ass." Reese clucked his tongue. "I'd say a name to that's worth more than twenty."

"Why would Mortise object to Reggie buying insurance?"

"Reggie wadn't byin' shit."

"Then, what was going on?"

"Mortise Anniston don't like Nosey Parkers."

The implication was clear. The insurance agent had been asking Reggie questions. But, about what?"

"Why would Mortise care?" I asked.

Reese laughed, softly.

"They's secrets and then they's secrets," he replied. "This hotel's full of 'em." He gave me a crooked grin. "I'm thinkin' that name's worth a C-note."

From the look on his haggard face, Buford Reese was not enjoying parole. I chalked it up to bad food, worse drugs, and reluctant women. Well, that and the last ten years spent in Huntsville Prison dodging psychopaths carrying sharp and pointies'.

"Do the Anniston sisters carry life insurance on Reggie?" I asked.

"There's that and then there's that."

"Big policy?"

His shoulders heaved in a shrug.

"Burial's what I heard," Reese said. "Now if you're ready to scratch my palm with something gree, I'll give you somethin' big for free."

I took out my money clip.

"Like what?" I asked.

"Gordon Shepherd's bettin' a bundle on Reggie dyin' real soon."

"How big a bundle?"

"Hundred grand."

"How'd you find out?"

"I heard him talkin' at Mortise on the Q-T."

"She's keeping her sister in the dark?"

"I can't speak to that," Reese said. "But, every time Gordon Shepherd comes 'round Mortise shows up without Minerva and I get sent me for supplies." Buford Reese studied me for a beat, his mouth a closed purse. "One time, after I come back, Gordon Shepherd was still here. Him and her was huddled together yappin' and growlin' like hungry wolves." He winked. "So, I hung outa' sight, and got an earful."

"About what?"

"Mortise was pissed 'cause Gordon Shepherd had fitted that crazy with a hundred grand life insurance." Reese grinned with special pride and held out a hand, palm up, forefinger curled in paralytic fashion. "My money?"

I pulled five twenties from my money-clip, and slapped them into his mitt.

"Insurance guy's name is Eddie Walton," Reese said.

"Mortise has burial policies on all hotel guests?"

"She got 'em on ever-body."

"Including you?"

"Includin' me."

"Did Reggie hang out with anybody besides Norman, Louie, Henry and Warren?"

"Nobody but them would have him."

I lit a cigarette and blew smoke at Buford Reese.

"You mentioned secrets," I said.

"That gonna' cost you a whole lot more," he said.

My eyes drifted to a string of fresh scabs along his left forearm. Smack was an expensive hobby for a guy on a limited budget. So, how was Reese funding his illicit fun? Maybe blackmail was an employee benefit?

"Parole officer treating you okay?" I asked.

"I follow the rules," Reese murmured.

"You lucked out, getting parole."

"They cut me loose 'cause you framed my ass."

"Buford, we both know you killed Chili Zumba."

"Sure, I killed that cheatin' bastard. But, that didn't give you the right to fit me up for it."

There was nothing like the reasoning of a narcissistic killer.

"From the looks of those tracks," I said, flicking ash toward the injuries, "you've been flying high. Who's footing the tab?"

Reese's right hand quickly covered the needle marks. Then, his Adam's apple bobbed.

"I gave blood," he mumbled.

"Sure you did."

That pink bug took another wild turn around the perimeter of his mouth.

"Since I done my time, I like to help folks," Reese said.

"By my count you've helped eight times. And from the condition of those scabs all that help's come about in less than a week."

"They like my blood."

"Feeling light-headed?"

His head shook back and forth.

"Feel fine," he returned.

"Buford, selling eight pints of blood would've left you dead." I jabbed my cigarette toward his left arm. "Of course, we both know you were pumpin' in instead of out."

"Why're you always tryin' to hack me off at the knees?"

"We could talk about secrets. Or, we could let your parole officer demand a drug test."

Reese's chin dipped, his voice going soft.

"I talk and I'm dead," he whimpered.

"I like Reggie, Buford. I'm willing to do whatever it takes to keep him safe. Including fitting you for these murders, if I don't get the answers I'm after."

"Drax Ravaillac," Buford Reese blurted.

"How does he fit?"

"That white boy's psycho."

I lit a fresh cigarette.

"He threatened you?" I asked.

"He got hisself hooked up with a married woman," he said.

"That's doesn't make him psycho."

"It does when that woman got herself abruptly dead in some warehouse."

"Connie Firth?"

"She was another one who come snoopin' 'round 'til Mortise sent her away."

"You think Mortise or Drax had something to do with Mrs. Firth's murder?"

"Mortise snaps and Drax jumps."

"Far enough to kill?"

"I got nothin' what says so. But Drax sure as hell ain't my idea of tapioca goodness."

"Tell me about the resident's welfare and social security benefits," I said.

"Nothin' to tell." Reese slapped his open palm on the desktop for emphasis. "They gets direct deposited into a special bank account."

"How much do the residents get for spending money?"

"Varies. Most get ten bucks."

"For an entire month?"

He nodded.

"Give 'em too much and they buy somethin' they shouldn't," Reese said.

"How is the money disbursed?" I asked.

"Drax comes by. He gives me a list of who gets what." His lips pulled back tight to show chipped teeth. "Then, he hands me the bundle. I gives it out."

"What about medications?"

"Drax comes with another list. Then, I sees to it."

"Do the meds change from one time to the next?"

"Some times. Why?"

"Any of those changes have to do with Norman, Louie, Henry, or Warren?"

Reese fell silent, thinking.

"Now that you mention it, yeah," he replied.

"Parker prescribes the meds?"

"That's all down to him. You think he done something to those crazies?"

"What happened to Fred Worth?"

Buford Reese gaped for several beats.

"What you wanna' know 'bout him for?" he asked.

"Call me curious about a dead man."

"Nothin' to do with me."

"Anybody from here besides Fred die on a railroad track?"

"What a man do in his own time is his business."

"What about Leonard Morgan?"

"Leonard don't like me."

"Has he expressed an interest in Reggie?"

He stroked his chin meditatively.

"That white boy had an interest in all the crazies," Reese said. "He slipped me a couple hundred a week, to report where they went and what they did."

"You followed Reggie and his pals?"

"No. I just made up stuff to report."

"When he's not driving Kemp's school bus, where does Leonard work?"

"I think he works for Mortise doin' whatever."

"Is Leonard here, now?"

"He cleared out when Kemp got plugged."

"How'd you got this job?"

"Them two biddies come by the prison," he said. "Wanted to talk at us cons, gettin' probation." There was a gap of silence, then Buford Reese added, his voice sounding emotional. "They liked what I said."

"What happened to the guy who had the job before you?"

He shrugged.

"Dead," Buford returned.

"Accident?"

"Fell off the roof."

"What was he doing on the roof?"

"Raisin' pigeons. The coup's gone. But, them birds is still up there." He scratched the back of his neck. "They leaves shit all over the stoop."

That could explain the reason behind the pissing incident. If the feather heads had crapped on me, I might feel the need to wet down one or two. But, two men being killed during these incidents still smacked of murder.

"I want to see Norman, Louie, Henry, Warren and Reggie's rooms," I told him.

"What for?"

"I'm planning a séance."

"Other than Reggie's, new folks livin' in them rooms."

"Fast turnover."

"Them biddies don't tolerate no dust gatherin'."

"Do you have a passkey?"

Reese backed away a step, in a defensive retreat.

"You can't go snoopin', man," he said. His gray eyebrows shot up like curly rockets. "Them people got rights."

"I'll limit my poking to Reggie's room," I told him.

"You need a search warrant."

"You're absolutely right," I said. "Which, as a private investigator, I would never get."

He grinned, rocking back and forth on his heels, pleased with his point of order.

"Of course," I said, "Lt. Herby Mann could get one. And while he's here, taking particulars from me, I'll point out your personal blood drive history." I took another drag, and blew smoke. "You'll like it back in Huntsville, Buford. They've upgraded the intensive care ward. You'll get express treatment next time you're shived."

Reese's smile drooped. Then he dug a ring of keys from his pocket and set it on the desktop. One had a splash of red nail polish on it. He tapped that key, and then crossed his arms. I picked up the lock-ticklers, wondering why there would be a need for so many if a master key unlocked the resident's rooms.

"Reggie complains, Bishop," Reese said, "and I'm layin' it on you."

I rode the elevator up to the fourth floor and walked down a dark hallway studded with even darker doors. Each portal had brass number identifiers. I found 410 near the end.

The door was ajar.

With a push on wood I followed it into a cubicle the size of a walk-in closet. The furnishings were simple. A single bed, a small bureau, and a folding chair. There was also a tiny alcove. This served as a closet. Within, dangling on hangers, were several striped t-shirts. Pieces of paper, decorated by crayon drawings, dotted the painted walls. Each childish sketch was of the Shadow conquering one sort of evil, or another.

Usually families exchanged photographs, even when they could not visit. But, there were none in Reggie's flop. Apparently, his family had forgotten him.

I tossed the bed and found nothing but dirty sheets. I went over to the bureau and rummaged through its drawers. Most contained dog-eared comic books portraying imaginary crime fighters. One had a collection of faded trousers. Another contained an assortment of hole-spotted underpants. Beneath these was a business card from Eddie Walton, of Walton Insurance Agency. I stuffed the card into a pocket, and was about to leave when I noticed the drawer was about an inch shallower than the others. I pulled the drawer clear from the bureau and dumped it out on the bed. The contents hit the bedding along with a rectangle of plywood and a ledger that had been hidden beneath it. I opened the journal. It contained dated financial transactions going back nearly fifteen years, covering a period of five years. The handwriting was distinctly female. One column contained names. The remainder contained dates and numeric entries, presumably money.

When the lift doors opened on my return to the main floor, I hurried back to the reception desk. Buford Reese was leaning on the reception desk, smoking a cigarette. Reese looked like a man who had experienced an epiphany. One by which he expected to profit. Had it been something I said? Or, had he notified Mortise of my presence and a reward was heading his way?

I slapped the keys down, in front of him. Then, I set the ledger on the desktop.

"When somebody dies," I asked, "who clears out the room?"

Reese blinked, momentarily dumbstruck.

You sayin' I stole somethin'?" he demanded.

"Answer my question, Buford."

"I'm done talkin'," he said.

I reached out and tapped the ledger.

"Recognize this?" I asked.

"Never seen it before." His lips twisted as he spoke. "You find it in Reggie's room?"

Chapter 12

That evening, when I got back to the office, I was beat.

The day's temperature had reached summertime broil, with the humidity approaching soggy-rag levels. But, in spite of the strain on my deodorant, I had hit every place a vagrant — or someone like Reggie Shepherd — could find shelter. Nearly everyone I spoke with knew him. Unfortunately, no one had seen the little guy in several days.

I dropped my suitcoat onto a rack-hook, went over to the safe and deposited the ledger. Then, I went behind the desk and flopped into the swivel chair. Outside, I could hear the squeal of rubber tires on steaming asphalt. I leaned back, plopped my feet on the desktop and closed my eyes trying to evoke a vision of snow collecting around a case of beer. But, just as my fantasy was focusing upon ice-coated cans, I heard two people enter my outer office. My feet hit the floor and I sat up, preparing to make what I hoped would be a lucrative impression. Then came the sound of long and short strides.

A tall scrawny guy come into view. He had a nose large enough to hoover the Vatican. Big-Nose looked to be about thirty years of age. He had dirty-brown, shoulder-length hair and wore desert camouflage. On his oddly small feet were pink sneakers. The sight of him collapsed my hopes for a money-making contract.

"You, Bishop, Pops?" Big Nose asked.

The sweat trickling down the center of my back made me frivolous enough to quip, "Either that or I'm sweating up his chair."

"Smart ass, huh?"

"How 'bout you ask which way is out?"

Big Nose stopped, making a stab at looking tough. He stood splay-legged; cross-armed, locked jaw. He put me in mind of a marionette with a stick up its ass.

"Don't piss-off Mr. Bishop, Alfie," a vaguely familiar voice uttered.

I looked past Big Nose. Behind him approached George Percy, a private investigator with a reputation more dubious than mine.

"Look what the cat dragged in," I said. "Georgie-Porgie."

"How's it hangin', Deke?" Percy returned.

George Percy was short, slightly over five feet tall. He stood nearly as wide. His attire was green: Suit, shirt, tie, shoes. He reminded me of a rumpled pistachio.

"My left testicle is lower than my right. Other than that, no complaints," I returned. "Who's your boy-toy, George?"

"Alfie Baker."

"What dragged you and Alfie from the asylum?"

George Percy was the only offspring of a local doctor and stripper. As a child, Percy had enjoyed the benefits of private schools and expensive toys, not to mention dancing lessons from a nanny. After completing high school with honors, Percy spent several years at Harvard University. But, despite his best intentions, his innate abilities and extensive family finances, Percy never acquired the coveted sheepskin. His varsity years ended abruptly after a quarrel with his father. Georgie-Porgy had disposed of the family's jade collection, for reasons never explained. A transgression his father never forgave.

"Deke, you've got something that doesn't belong to you," Percy announced, as he waddled toward my desk.

"Your wife's dead, George," I taunted.

"You know what I mean."

Percy slumped into one of the customer chairs, in front of my desk. He twisted back and forth, for a few moments, as if trying to screw his ample backside into a jar. Then, after getting comfortable, he sighed and leaned back.

"Nice new digs," he said, glancing around. "I'm surprised you don't have a receptionist."

"I can't find one who'll work for love."

"Get the damn ledger, George," Big nose said, impatiently.

I looked over at the younger man.

"Now, you're giving orders?" I said.

A wave of color crimsoned Big Nose's face.

Percy cut in with, "You were at the Anniston Arms Hotel,

Deke."

"Doing a slow waltz with an old friend," I said, returning my gaze to George Percy.

He crossed his outstretched legs, at the ankles.

"Since when is Buford Reese anybody's friend?" Percy asked.

"Perhaps, acquaintance is closer to the mark."

"Acquaintance, hell! The bastard vowed to kill you."

"That's been tossed out so many times I stopped noticing. What'd your boyfriend mean by a ledger, George?"

Big Nose moved closer. That warning bell in my head went off. So, I crossed left leg over right knee and silently pulled out the snub-nose I kept in an ankle holster. Percy scraped his chin with a thumbnail, thinking.

"You lifted a ledger from Reggie Shepherd's room," George Percy replied.

Buford Reese had been talking. Nothing unexpected. But, the interest in reclaiming the ledger was unusual. Unless those entries, from years ago, had some hidden meaning. Reese had eluded to secrets.

"Who hired you?" I asked.

"That's confidential," Percy returned. "Who's Reggie Shepherd to you?"

"Right back at you, Georgie," I snapped.

"Is the ledger here?"

"Why's an old ledger so important?"

"It's not. The issue is right of ownership."

"It belongs to Reggie."

"He wants it back," he said.

I studied George Percy for a long moment. I assumed he was lying. But, there was a slim chance Reggie had surfaced. Nevertheless, at ten bucks a month for spending, the little guy's cash flow would not cover George Percy's rates.

"Where's Reggie, now?" I asked.

"Around."

"Around where?"

"Hand back the ledger, old man, and everything'll be Jake," Big Nose growled.

"Your boy-toy's beginning to irritate me, George," I said.

"Alfie's advice is well-founded, Deke."

"The ledger stays put until I talk to Reggie."

"You're putting me in an untenable position."

"I'm not interested in your problems."

"I can't go back to my client empty handed."

"Then, point me to Reggie. I'll have my chat. If he okay's it, I'll hand over the ledger."

George Percy took out a leather cigar case and extracted something big and green. From the look on his fat face he was considering unpleasantries.

"That's problematic, Deke," he said. "I don't know where Reggie is."

"Then, don't let me delay you and your monkey's exit," I returned.

"The old bastard just insulted me, George," Big Nose said.

"No," I said. "I insulted the simians."

"Was that another shot?"

"Careful, Alfie," George Percy warned. "Bishop, used to be a cop."

The younger man squinted at me in disbelief.

"You shoulda' told me, George," Big Nose growled. "I hate cops."

"You hate everybody, Alphie."

"Because everybody hates me."

"These days Bishop's a gumshoe, like us."

"I hate him, anyway, George."

"Come closer," I urged Big Nose. "I'd like to whisper sweet nothings in your ear."

George Percy made a frantic wave of warning.

"Don't do it, Alfie." he said. "All you'll get in your ear is his fist."

"I say we take him out, George," Big Nose urged.

"Stop, please." I cocked the snub-nose, as I spoke, to conceal the revolver's distinctive clicks. "Georgy-Porgy I gotta' tell you, all this talk of violence is getting me excited."

"Alfie's overreacting, Deke," Percy said. "Let's not do likewise."

"That old man don't scare me, George," said Big Nose.

I lit a cigarette and blew a stream of smoke at the younger man.

"Obviously, George," I said, "your playmate hasn't seen my credentials."

"Wouldn't help, Deke," Percy said. "Alfie can't read."

"Ah, you've hooked up with an intellectual."

Big Nose took a menacing step.

"Is that another buzz, Pops?" he demanded.

"Come closer, Peach Fuzz," I coaxed. "I'll explain it in detail."

George Percy jumped up and fanned his hands.

"Stay put, Alfie," he shouted. "Don't go anywhere near Bishop if you value your life."

"You're gumming my game, George," I complained. "Red Rover, Red Rover, let Alfie come over."

George Percy settled back into the chair, his eyes on me.

"Taking that ledger made my client nervous, Deke," he said. "Why not, for old time's sake, put this behind us by giving it to me?"

"The ledger covers a five year period starting fifteen years back," I said. "Why would outdated financial transactions worry your client?"

"She's eccentric."

"Mortise Anniston?"

"I can't say either way."

Big Nose began shuffling his hands, from pocket to pocket, in what looked like an endless search for something missing. I kept the snub-nose pointed in his direction, just in case he found what he was looking for. But, I returned my stare to George Percy.

"Your boyfriend couldn't find his ass with both hands, George," I observed. "Have you considered putting him out of your misery?"

"Every day. Unfortunately, he's family."

I could not help but frown in surprise.

"I didn't know you had a son," I said.

"Please. Don't insult me."

"Nephew?"

"Now, you're insulting my sister." Percy stuffed the cigar into his mouth and lit it. "Alfie Baker's my son-in-law."

"Vera's husband? Seriously?"

"I've got only one daughter, Deke."

"Gotta' tell you, George, Vera should've done better than him."

"As you can imagine, he wasn't my first choice."

I tilted my head toward Big Nose. "Even with a bag covering his mug, George, Alfie's got to be every woman's nightmare." I sniffed audibly, and then winced at the rancid odor coming from the younger man. "Has anybody told him the benefits of bathing?"

"Been there. Done that. Unfortunately, Alfie's easily confused."

"Soap and water's not complicated."

"It is when dealing with Alfie." Percy called to Big Nose, "Stop scratching, Alfie. You act like you got worms."

"I know it's here somewhere, George," said Big Nose, still shuffling through his pockets.

"I assume Alfie came from a family with money?" I asked.

"The Baker clan's not known for having financial prowess."

"From the looks of your son-in-law, they're short on prowess all around."

George Percy paused for a pregnant moment.

"That's not the worst of it," he said.

"How much worse can it get?"

"Alfie's a crack-head."

"Shade me slightly stunned." I took another long draw on my smoke. "But, on the plus side, George, I know a cure for addiction."

"Unfortunately, suicide's against Alfie's religion."

"I had a something a little more proactive, in mind."

"Can't let you do it, Deke. Not that your efforts wouldn't be appreciated by me."

"I am Vera's godfather."

"No, you're not."

"Well, I could have been. So, let me take a fatherly stand on her behalf."

"You don't think I haven't urged Vera to divorce him?"

"In cases like Alphie, George, reactions must be focused with lethal intent."

"I've tried. But, every time I get my hands around his greasy throat my daughter wakes up and asks why I'm choking the life out of him."

"Next time try an icepick. It's over with only a drop or two of blood."

George Percy smiled faintly.

"Miracles happen, as do murders, when none but God is looking," he mused. Then, Percy leaned back in the chair and took a long draw on the cigar. "Show Mr. Bishop what's next on God's agenda, Alfie."

I looked over at Big Nose. He was no longer searching his pockets. Instead, my body was the object of Alfie's interest, along with the Lugar he was aiming.

"The ledger, Pops," Alfie threatened, doing a bad impression of Bogart. "Or I'll drill ya."

"Scoot a little closer?" I coaxed. "You don't want to miss during your first rodeo."

"Stay put, Alfie," Percy warned. "Bishop's not a man to encourage without extracting a pain filled benefit."

From beneath the desk, I snugged my finger around the snubby's trigger. Big Nose was about fifteen feet away. The Luger's first round would probably go wide, due to his inexperience. I would have him before he fired a second shot. Of course, that was a moot point if he got lucky.

"Right now, George," I said, "I've got a .38 Special pointed at your big belly." I shifted the snub-nose toward George Percy, my thumb on the hammer. "I'm holding the hammer back with my thumb. My finger's pulled the trigger to the frame. Think of me holding a revolver version of a dead man's switch." I took a surreptitious look, at Big Nose, then returned my gaze to George Percy. "No matter what Alfie does, the snubby fires. No matter what happens to me, your big belly's gonna get a big hole."

"Don't let him scare ya, George," Big Nose cried.

Percy wetted his lips, his eyes getting very large.

"Put the gun away, Alfie," he quivered.

"I got him dead on, George!"

"Bishop's not bluffing, you idiot! Put the damn gun away."

"All this nerve wracking pressure's making my thumb sweat, George," I warned. "If it cramp's you're as good as dead."

"Damn it, Alphie!" Percy shouted. "Put that gun away before I ring your goddamn neck."

"This ain't fair, George," Big Nose whined as he slid the pistol behind his belt. "I get the drop on the asshole and you call it off."

I tilted back bringing the revolver into view, toward Big Nose.

"Here's the deal, George," I said, letting the revolver's mechanics return to normal. "You give me the name of your client, or I'll make Vera a widow and an orphan in one fell swoop."

"As appealing as I find the widow idea," Percy returned, "I'm not too keen on orphans." Again he wet his lips. "Mortise Anniston hired me."

The 'who' was a foregone conclusion. The 'why' was another matter.

"What makes an old ledger worth your rate?" I asked.

"She didn't say."

I lowered the gun to my lap, still watching Big Nose. He was back to going through his pockets.

"The Anniston sisters must be rich," I remarked.

"Depends on who you talk to," George Percy said. "According to Mortise, they're living hand to mouth." He studied me carefully with wide, worried eyes. "Can you put the damn gun away?"

"I hate to disappoint, George. But Alphie might get another itch for his Lugar." With my free hand I took out a pack of cigarettes and sloughed one up. I caught it with my lips, tossed the pack onto the desk and took out my Zippo. "I think we can work a deal on the ledger." I put fire to the cigarette, and inhaled deeply. Then I tossed the lighter next to the cigarette pack. "You give me a few days to have a financial whiz look it over. If it's just part of the hotel's ancient history, I'll hand it over. In the meantime, you find out why Mortise wants it."

George Percy considered for several clicks of a second hand. Then, his thick eyebrows arched.

"A little cash would be nice," he said.

"Things are tight, at the moment."

"I'll carry you. Shall we say, three hundred?"

"Toss in a timeline of the deaths at the Anniston Arms Hotel, going back to when Argyle Anniston IV ran it, we have a deal."

"What else could an old ledger be but history?" he asked.

"I'm thinking Walter Osgood Kemp used a little guy with fluff for brains in a blackmail scam."

George Percy put his fleshy hands on the desktop and got up.

"I'll be back," he said.

"Next time, leave your ringtail at home," I told him.

"Time to leave, Alfie," George said.

"Alfie, this! Alfie, that!" whined Big Nose. "You treat me like shit, George."

"Just get on your horse."

"Uh, George," I called out. "If you decide you'll be needing instructions in icepick usage, let me know. I was taught by the best."

"I'll keep that in mind."

George Percy strolled out of the office, his trousers a shapeless sag across his departing posterior, with Alfie sulking on his heels.

The outer door opened and closed. Then I heard two sets of footfalls along the corridor. This was followed by silence. I slid the revolver back into its holster and dropped my foot to the floor. Things were getting interesting.

I pushed back from my desk, and headed out intending to go home. But, as I reached the Buick, a cruiser with flashing lights jerked to a stop. I strolled over wondering who, among the important, I had offended.

"You Bishop?" the uniform behind the steering wheel asked.

I nodded.

"What's up?" I returned.

"Lt. Mann wants to see you."

"I'll call him tomorrow."

"He wants you now."

Something had gone sour.

I climbed into the cruiser's back seat and failed to get comfortable. There was something about bars on windows and a cage across the top of the front seat that made me uneasy. Perhaps, it was too much like the bedroom of my childhood.

"Whenever you're ready, officer," I said.

Thirty minutes of siren got me to the Travis Country Morgue.

The entrance was locked when I arrived. I knocked. A gaunt man with a death-mask face responded. It was easy to picture him in an old vampire film as the virgin's chief blood-sucker. He was wearing a white smock over a white uniform. His nametag read, 'Harvey'.

"You Bishop?" he asked in a rumbling voice.

I nodded, wondering how he was fixed for fangs.

"Who are you?" I asked.

"Harvey Pagan."

He backed up and motioned me in. I complied.

"Where's Abby Childers?" I asked, as he shut the door.

Abby, a longtime acquaintance and information source, had been the morgue attendant for many years.

"Fired," Harvey replied.

That was a crushing disappointment.

"For what?" I demanded.

"Unofficial tours."

"No chance he'll be reinstated?"

"Not unless God pisses upwind."

"What happened?"

"Got caught red-dicked having it off in a corpse-drawer with a broad dressed like a nun."

That sounded like Abby.

"How are you fixed for extra cash, Harvey?" I asked.

"I don't take bribes."

"Think of assisting me as an advance on your pension," I suggested.

"I'll think about it," he said, tilting his head down the hallway. "Mann's waiting in the cutting room."

"Alive, dead or still draining?"

"The usual post-autopsy stomach-roll issues."

Herby had the queasiest stomach in Texas law enforcement. Back, when he and I partnered, I attended all autopsies resulting from our cases.

"Any idea who's dead?" I asked.

"Nobody I knew," Harvey replied.

I walked down a hallway of glazed brick, pushing through a pair of swinging doors into a room fitted with three stainless-steel tables. On one was the shriveled corpse of a naked male. I recognized him immediately. It was Reggie Shepherd.

"What happened?" I asked, of no one in particular.

The sound of vomiting drew my eyes toward the wash sink. Herby Mann was there, hanging his head into one end of it. The Assistant Coroner, Dr. Sheldon Fields, was at the other end washing his hands; looking calm and collected.

"Single round to the head," Mann gurgled. ".22 caliber." He stood up and looked over at me, his face displaying a greenish countenance. "Match to the round pulled from Kemp, and the others."

The little guy's torso had been opened with the usual 'Y' incision and then stapled closed. I do not know how long I stared at Reggie's remains. But, during the entire time, the rage in me skyrocketed.

"Death was instantaneous?" I asked.

"He didn't suffer," Dr. Fields said.

"Where'd it happen?"

"In the vacant lot behind the Anniston Arms Hotel," Mann said. "Wells had a BOLO out on him, for Charlene Holland's homicide. A couple of uniforms saw him slumped behind an oil drum." The police lieutenant's Adam's apple bobbed as he tried to retain what was left in his stomach. "Who, among his super hero cronies, carries a gun?"

"When did Reggie die?"

"Yesterday around 10:00 p.m.," Fields said.

"That'd be the 25th."

Mann took a notebook from his pocket and flip past several pages. Then he withdrew a pen.

"I need official identification," he said.

I did so and moved away from the autopsy table, sick at heart. Kemp had been absolutely right. Somebody was fucking his flock. Probably Kemp.

"Lieutenant," Fields said, "you'll have my report, tomorrow."

The Assistant Coroner was short and slightly built. His thrapple hung loose from chin to sternum. I guessed his age to be pushing seventy. In spite of his advanced years, Fields was the best in the business.

"Thanks, Doc." Herby tilted his head toward the sink. "Sorry about the mess."

Fields dried his hands on a towel and then strolled out.

"Good night all," he said, over one shoulder.

"The Annistons still own that property?"

"Gravel, weeds and cinders. Why did Reggie have your card?"

"I gave it to him when I met with Kemp." I glanced back at the shrunken body. "I think Kemp was playing me from the git go. I think he was blackmailing the Anniston sisters. I think there were a number of players involved. I think Reggie Shepherd somehow got his hands on information which gave Kemp the leverage he needed to bleed the sisters white."

Mann shrugged.

"The blackmail angle I buy," he said. "But, Reggie didn't have the brains to play spy. He was killed because he could identify the perp in multiple homicides." Lt. Herby Mann belched and then moaned as his face took on a darker shade of green. "Let's get out of here before I marry that damn sink."

We went across the street to Malone's Diner. It was a converted Pullman Car. Portieres of plastic beads decorated the train-windows. Against the aluminum walls, and bolted to the floor, were booths. The service counter was opposite. It had been wrapped in aluminum and topped by maroon laminate. Herby was still wearing a greenish pallor, so I suggested the booth closest to the restrooms. We sat down, avoiding each other's gaze.

"Why do you attend autopsies when you can't handle them?" I eventually asked Mann.

"Somebody has to witness the proceedings."

"But, it doesn't have to be you."

A waitress swayed over. She was plump and blonde. Her nametag read, 'Molly'. She suggested the beef-gravy special. Mann belched and ordered coffee. I told her to bring me a cup of Joe plus a slice of pecan pie. She asked if I wanted it warmed. I told her I was ready for anything she had to offer.

"What could the Anniston sisters be up to?" Mann asked.

"I think a more pertinent question is, what could they be up to that an optometrist's wife could uncover?"

"Is it possible Kemp was involved with her?"

A television set mounted at the corner of one wall was droning weather reports. The monotone voice emanating from the boob-box promised rain for tonight, with the promise of sunshine tomorrow. That meant a rise in humidity with more heat.

"Connie Firth was a liberal in every sense of the word," I told Lt. Mann. "But, I don't see her taking an interest in Kemp."

"An offer of money?"

"An offer of a young stud, maybe. Reggie Shepherd's brother, Gordon, according to Buford Reese, has a hundred thousand dollar life insurance policy on Reggie."

The waitress delivered our order and hurried away. Herby looked at his mug, belched, again, and then took a sip. I dug into the pie with relish.

"I talked to Gordon," Mann said. "But, he didn't say squat about insurance."

"Buford could have it wrong," I chewed.

"Did Reese mention any insurance on Reggie held by the Anniston's?" he returned.

"He said there were burial policies on each hotel guest and employee?"

"So the State of Texas won't be paying for Buford's funeral?"

"Did you check the police database for Cutie monikers?"

"There are six, surprisingly. But all are incarcerated."

Chapter 13

After placing the ledger under the scrutiny of Prof. Fillmore Teal, I drove to Walton's Insurance Agency. It was in an old frame house on Addams Street, in Leander. There were elms lining both sides of the byway. Tree branches dangled over the road, like the embracing limbs of green ghosts. The leaves intertwined, shrouding the drive in a protective canopy. This cover was so thick, the morning rain had to work at reaching the pavement.

I parked out front, turned up the collar on my trench coat, and climbed out. From the missing shingles on the roof of Eddie Walton's office, paint peeling from the siding, and cracked window panes, he operated on a shoestring.

I strode up the walkway went in the front door.

There was no reception area. I stood in a room decorated with sun-bleached wallpaper; ugly furniture, and worn floor tiles. On the wall directly ahead dangled two art prints in pressboard frames. One looked like something from Van Gogh's schizophrenic mind. The other reminded me of a Klimt.

I let my eyes drift.

There were two other men in there. One was standing, sucking the end of a bourbon bottle. He was scrawny and pale, dressed in a wrinkled blue suit, white shirt, and red tie. The other man sat in a swivel chair behind an army-surplus desk. He wore a salt and pepper sport coat and a gray shirt. From where I stood, I could just see black trouser loops over his leather belt. The second man's hands dangled casually from the chair-arms. His eyes were closed. I thought he was napping until I noticed the small bullet-hole just above his hairline.

"A Blue Whale's penis is ten feet long," the bottle-tipper blurted.

That tidbit of sparkling information was not a gem I would cherish. But, it drew my interest from the corpse to the speaker. He was still holding the bottle. But, now, there was a widening puddle of urine around his shoes.

"If you shake something like that at a woman," he quivered, "it'd give her pause."

"Among other things," I returned. Then I jabbed a finger at the dead guy behind the desk. "Considering the stiff, aren't you the least bit curious about me?"

He took another nip.

"I figure you're the guy who killed him," the drinker gurgled.

I was taken aback. Not that murder accusations had never been levelled. Some people insisted upon taking a narrow stance when it came to retribution. But, this was the first time the allegation had related to my ill-timed arrival. Nevertheless, it explained the puddle of piss.

"You cater to the theory of killers returning to the scene?" I asked, in morbid curiosity.

His head made a sloppy wag.

"You realized your mistake, and came back to correct it," he returned.

"What mistake?" I asked.

"You didn't kill Eddie Walton."

Failing to murder the intended target would have been a regrettable mistake. Especially for the dead guy. Then, of course, one had to consider the killer's embarrassment. In a mistaken-shooting situation, those in the profession would have to reduce rates to restore confidence. Of course if an amateur had made the mistake, then no amount of price cutting would warrant paying for another try.

"The deceased is an imposter?" I asked.

"Not intentionally," he said. "Not if he had any sense."

"Come again?"

"My wife's a bitch of the first water. Every moment of every day would've put him balls up on her chopping block." He shivered. "Just thinking about her verbal axe swinging through the air tightens my scrotum."

"I take it, you're Eddie Walton?"

He took another deep draw on the bottle.

"Depends on your interest," the drinker returned.

"Today I didn't make any mistakes."

"Then, I'm Eddie Walton."

I jabbed a thumb toward the corpse.

"Who's sleeping beauty, when he isn't you?" I asked.

"Not a clue. But, I'm open to suggestions."

"A thought or two on who killed him?"

"My father-in-law comes to mind."

"Any idea as to when this happened?"

"Nothing definitive. Although lunch, while I was out, works for me."

A drunk with a logical mind.

"Did you call the police?" I asked.

"Working up to that," Walton said.

"You don't think they'd be interested?"

"First I need a rational explanation. Corpses wearing bullet holes tend to raise questions."

"This is a common occurrence?"

"Never happened before. But, I watch plenty of TV. I know how the cops work." He took another swig from the bottle. "You're new to the murder game?"

"I've sent more than one on his way."

"Something personal, I hope?"

"It was for me."

I went around the desk to the body, and touched it. The flesh was warm, the facial muscles soft. I lifted an eyelid. The cornea was clear. This suggested a very recent death; less than an hour prior. On the dead man's feet were snakeskin boots. In the ashtray on the desktop was the remains of a roll-your-own cigarette.

"Why's he sitting in your chair?" I asked, glancing over at Walton.

"My question to him when I walked in."

"He was alive?" I asked, in disbelief.

"Nope."

"You questioned a dead man?"

"I felt the enquiry was justified, regardless of circumstance."

"You smoke?"

"It's bad for my health."

I took out my handkerchief and, using it to conceal my tampering, I rummaged through the dead man's pockets. His wallet contained thirty-seven dollars in cash, numerous credit cards and a driving license under the name of Gordon Shepherd. The address on the license matched the telephone directory listing for Reggie's brother.

"Have you seen Mr. Shepherd, before?" I asked.

"Shepherd?" Eddie Walton echoed.

"Your lunchtime pretender." I pointed at the body. "The late Gordon Shepherd. Too late for introductions, but feel free to shake hands."

"I've never been one for cold and clammy," Walton said. "That's why my wife and I have separate bedrooms." He took a bleary moment to stare at Shepherd. "An African elephant's dick is over four feet long."

"I'll tuck that trifle away for my next cocktail party."

There was a ring of keys in one of Shepherd's pockets and a collection of coins in another. I saw no resemblance between the deceased and Reggie. But, they may have had different parentage.

"It's got its own brain," Walton continued.

Something the pickled speaker seemed to be lacking.

"You need to get out more, Mr. Walton," I suggested. "Maybe change hobbies to something less involved with animal genitalia."

"The bull climbs on the cow, the dick shoots out and starts searching for some place warm and wet," he said, drunkenly. "Once located, it plows in and starts thrashing about like there's no tomorrow. The bull doesn't move an inch." He paused to squint at me. "Gives a whole new prospective on thinking with your dick."

"Or, how to hit the sweet spot."

I returned the decedent's property to its respective places. Then I went back to the desk-front.

"You a cop?" Walton asked. "You remind me of a cop. Not that I hold any grudges from my antiwar demonstration days."

"How long were you at lunch?"

Eddie Walton staggered over to one of the customer chairs, and slumped down. He pressed the bottle to his forehead and let out a sob.

"About an hour, give or take," he whimpered. "If I'd only been here..."

"You'd be dead," I cut in. "Is an hour absence typical?"

"Sometimes an hour. Sometimes two." His head rocked, like a door with sloppy hinges. "On a really tough Wednesday, I'm up for an afternoon skip-eroo." He took another pull from the bottle. "R & R demands flexibility."

"Today's Thursday."

"You're sure?"

"Where'd you have lunch?"

"Gina's Diner, across the street." His tongue slathered his lips. "Can't beat the Blue-Plate Special."

I went over to the front window and looked across. Walton could not have been sitting more than a hundred feet away when Shepherd died. Even a .22 caliber's report should have been audible.

"You didn't hear a shot?" I asked.

"In this neighborhood it would be a miracle not to," he replied.

"While you were out," I said, "you left your office open?"

"How the dead bastard got in was my second question when I found him."

"You didn't think to ask who'd shot him?"

"I don't like to pry." Walton blinked several times, his pickled brain trying to assess. "What makes you think I was the intended target? It's not like I'm worth much dead."

I lit a cigarette. There was actually logic in Walton's reasoning.

"He's sitting behind your desk," I explained. "The wound lacks powder stippling, so the shooter was several yards away. There's a shell casing on the floor next to the entrance. So, my guess is the killer walked in, fired, and walked out."

"You should be a detective."

"How much life insurance do you carry?"

"None. With my in-laws it's best to run naked and empty handed." Several beats passed while Eddie Walton silently mouthed air. "Are you in need of life insurance?"

"I'm here to talk to you about your connection to the Anniston Arms Hotel."

His eyes widened and then darted from side to side.

"Never heard of the place," Walton said.

"Eddie, you've got a dead guy killed in the same manner as

Walter Osgood Kemp, Charlene Holland, Reggie Shepherd, Connie firth and one other person. Lying, now is not going to be good for your future. Because the evening news will identify Gordon Shepherd, instead of you, as the victim."

Eddie Walton thumped his chest with his free hand.

"Kemp said we'd make millions," Walton bellowed.

"Millions, how?"

"He said the Anniston's had been scamming the government for years, and we were going to cut ourselves in. Nobody was supposed to get killed. Especially, me."

"Scamming, how?"

"All I know is, Kemp said we needed a ledger." His narrow shoulders bobbed. "He said it was red with a big blue stripe. All I had to do was get my hands on it and I could count myself in on twenty-five percent of the action."

"Only, you didn't trust Kemp?"

"Nobody in their right mind would."

"How did Reggie Shepherd fit into the plan?"

"Kemp and I convinced Reggie to filch the ledger next time Buford Reese had the hotel safe open."

"How did you convince Reggie to do that?"

"We told him it was a secret code needed by our government." Walton shook the liquor bottle, angrily. "That looney was supposed to bring it to me. But, what with those crossed wires in his head, Reggie decided to decipher it himself." His head waggled like a plumb on a twig in a high wind. "For weeks I tried to get it from him. But, every time I went to see Reggie, he just shouted 'the Shadow knows', and ran off."

"Who besides Kemp was involved in this blackmail?"

"The broad with the big tits."

"Charlene Holland."

"Every time I saw her, I wanted to kill myself for marrying my wife. Then, there was that bus driver."

"Leonard Morgan?"

"That ex-con was as twisted as Kemp."

"Leonard served time for what?"

"Murder. Got off with manslaughter. But, the truth is, he killed his own wife. Maybe he's behind the killings?"

"Maybe. Who else was to share in the spoils?"

"Just me. We each were to get an equal cut."

"How did Kemp latch onto you?"

"I had my own suspicions about the Anniston Arms Hotel. So, I started asking questions. That's how I met Reggie. Mortise Anniston read me the riot act and threatened to sue. Kemp got wind of my digging and offered to share information."

"I take it you shared and he didn't?"

"I never liked that man." He paused to take another pull on the bottle. "You think I should leave town until this thing blows over?"

I flicked the ash from my cigarette onto the floor.

"You said you had your own suspicions concerning the Anniston Arms Hotel?" I asked.

"My theory was mass murder."

"With the profit coming from where?"

He cocked a questioning eyebrow.

"Did you see the film, 'Double Indemnity'?" Walton asked.

"One of my favorites. An insurance agent gets conned into helping a beautiful woman kill her husband for the life insurance."

"Not once in twenty years of selling life insurance has a broad offered me a deal like that." He leaned back in the chair, his face flushed with alcohol. "And do you know why?"

"You're a straight arrow with an aversion to killing?"

"Nope." His head did a waggle-dance. Then, Walton burst into a volley of laughter. "Because I'm not Fred MacMurray."

"How many people do you suspect died during this film plot revisit?" I asked.

"Hundreds, over the past fifty or so years." He pointed a finger at me and then himself. "Have you caught my attention?"

"I'm on tenterhooks."

"Only trouble was, I couldn't prove it unless I got a look at the hotel's books." Walton drew in a long, deep breath. "Now this is where it gets interesting. Kemp said I had the right idea about the hotel's ledgers. But, I was off the mark on the killings. All the deaths at the hotel related to a fire in the hotel's annex about thirty years ago. But, he said they did have a gig running." He sloppily tapped the side of his nose. "And if I could get a particular ledger book, about which Buford Reese had told him, I could get rich enough to leave my wife."

"Why wasn't Buford Reese involved?"

"Kemp didn't trust him." He winked. "Would you?"

"Why didn't Kemp bribe Reese into handing over this mysterious ledger?"

"He tried. But, Reese refused. Personally, I think he was not about to queer the arrangement he had with the Anniston sisters." Eddie Walton finished the bottle and tossed it into the waste basket next to his desk. "He might even be getting a cut of the action Kemp was after. Might. But I can't prove it either way."

"I was told that Mr. Gordon Shepherd, here, purchased a hundred grand policy on Reggie Shepherd. Is there any way you can verify that?"

Walton rose from his chair and staggered back to the file cabinets. After digging around for several minutes, in a drawer, he withdrew a folder. He opened it, thumbed past several pages, and then let his eyes scan.

"Roughly speaking," Eddie Walton said, closing the file, "I wrote that policy six months ago."

I picked up the telephone handset and handed it to Walton.

"Time to let the cops in on the late Gordon Shepherd."

"What do I tell them?"

"We got back from lunch," I explained. "We're both shocked by the body." I glanced over at his wet trousers. "You, slightly more than me."

Chapter 14

I spent the next day with Fillmore Teal. We went through the ledger. Teal suggested the entries tracked social services payments. But, as he pointed out, a thirty room hotel would not be receiving Welfare and Social Security disbursements for over three hundred people. That being said, the tally amounted to millions. Perhaps the millions Eddie Walton claimed had been in the sights of Walter Osgood Kemp? I thanked Fillmore and asked him to deliver the ledger to George Percy. Then I drove to the apartment building housing Mortise and Minerva Anniston.

A petite, pasty-faced woman wearing black slacks and a blue sweater answered my knock. Her white hair curled back from a wrinkled face. The stiff locks framed suspicious blue eyes, a carrot nose and a receding chin. Her age, I pegged at seventy. When her stare locked on mine, White-hair's red-paint lips spread into a sloppy sneer.

"Listen, Bo," she warned, "if you're selling I'm not buying."

I introduced myself.

When White-Hair failed to indicate recognition, I offered one of my business cards. She grimaced before taking possession, like evil had printed the miniature placard. That may have been the case. Jubal Lessingham, medium to the gullible and desk-top publisher to the frugal, had supplied my printed business needs.

"Who is it, Minerva?" a tinny sounding female called, from within the flat.

"Shamus," White-hair shouted back. "Name's Bishop."

I heard footsteps.

Another woman appeared. She was shapely, about fifty-five or sixty, with dyed blue hair coiled atop her head. She smiled fleetingly, give me a golden wink from a capped tooth.

"I'm Mortise Anniston," Blue-hair told me. She took my card from White-Hair and used one corner to scratch the end of her nose. "This is my sister Minerva. What can we do for you?"

"I'd like a few minutes of your time," I told her.

Mortise's ensemble was sexy. It consisted of a low-cut blouse and tight shorts; both red. In her day, she had been a looker with fashion-model features.

"I'm investigating the death of Connie Firth," I said.

She gave a telling start.

"I don't know the woman," Mortise said. "Do you, Minerva?"

"Never heard of her," White-Hair replied.

"But, you do know Reggie Shepherd," I pressed.

Their eyes met, briefly.

"What's it to ya, Bo?" Minerva demanded.

"Reggie witnessed Mrs. Firth's murder," I explained. "I was hoping your knowledge of him, and his activities, might lead me to Mrs. Firth's killer."

"The cops know you're sniffing around that case, Bo?"

"They know all about me."

"I don't see how Reggie's acquaintances or pursuits could help you," Mortise said.

"Reggie was murdered with the gun that killed Mrs. Firth," I explained. "It is likely, therefore, her killer was his." I quickly added, "I understand you hold a life insurance policy on Reggie."

Mortise Anniston pulled the door wide and backed away, forcing Minerva aside. I stepped into a cozy foyer. The air smelled of lemon oil and lavender. There were oak slats covering the floor, plaster on ceiling and walls. Mortise shut the door. Then, she went back to her sister.

"You're the Bo who talked to Buford," Minerva Anniston observed.

"He and I go way back," I returned.

"Where's the ledger?"

"George Percy has it."

"Surely the police don't suspect us in those murders," Mortise cut in.

"They're not going to confide in me."

Mortise indicated a doorway, with a pointing finger.

"Why don't we go into the sitting room?" she suggested. "It'll be more comfortable."

"Guess that leaves me to pour lemonade," Minerva muttered,

and wandered off.

Mortise Anniston encircled my left arm with her right, and escorted me into an airy corner room. There was a window seat, overlooking a rose garden. The furnishings were meager: an armchair, a davenport, a coffee table and an old fashioned loveseat. Framed comic book covers of the Cutie Pie character from the fifties dotted the walls. Everything was polished and dust-free.

"Most men prefer the chair, Mr. Bishop," Mortise urged.

I went over and settled onto it. She positioned herself atop a davenport cushion. Mortise studied me like I was slice of cornbread with too much jalapeno as she crossed her legs. She was intrigued, but did not enjoy being challenged.

"I'm sorry about sending Mr. Percy," she told me. Mortise stuffed my card into her bra. "But, when we heard about the missing ledger we didn't know what else to do."

"I didn't take offense," I returned. "But, a phone call would've saved you George Percy's fees."

Mortise Anniston hesitated, wetting her lips.

"If Reggie saw who killed Mrs. Firth, it follows you know who killed him," she said.

"Sort of," I said. "Reggie knew the killer only as 'Cutie.' Did he mention such a person?"

"Reggie had no grip on reality. He was always babbling about something or somebody. But, I don't recall that name."

"You should be talking to Gordon Shepherd," observed Minerva, as she returned.

The elder Anniston sister was holding a tray. On it were three glasses of ice and a pitcher of lemonade. Minerva moved past the davenport, placing the tray on the coffee-table. Then, she settled down next to her sister. Minerva's cheeks carried a heavy flush. Her breathing was rapid. Had she been thirty years younger, those indicators might suggest recent sexual activity. But, at her age, the symptoms were probably from a struggling heart.

"You know Mr. Shepherd well?" I asked the pair.

"We spoke with him merely once or twice," Mortise said. "Hardly what I would call knowing."

"The man was worried, Bo," Minerva said, as she poured lemonade. "You got something against brotherly love?"

"Is George Percy linked to your hotel?" I asked.

"Why?"

"Considering all the detectives in Texas, you hired him to tag me."

"Scared ya, did he?"

"Not much."

"We were introduced to Mr. Percy through his son-in-law Alfie," Mortise said.

"You're related to Alfie?" I asked, picking up a glass.

"He was a guest at our hotel for a time."

"Crack-head," Minerva chimed, setting the pitcher down.

"Alfie was a lost soul."

The two women picked up glasses. I took a sip. It tasted like fresh lemons, with just a hint of mint.

"I understand, you found the ledger in Reggie's room," Mortise said.

"At the time I was looking for Reggie," I said.

"How did he come into possess of it?"

"Only, Reggie knew that." I set down my glass. "George Percy had done work for you, before?"

"First time."

"Did Reggie talk about people who frightened him?" I asked.

"He was the Shadow," Minerva snorted. "Nobody scared him. Or, so he said."

"From my chat with Buford, he had it in for Reggie. Why?"

"Buford wouldn't say," Mortise said. "But, I refuse to believe he's the killer you're after."

"Why not? Murder is what sent him to Huntsville."

"The Shamus has you with that, Mortise," Minerva chuckled.

"How many hotel residents carry life insurance?" I asked.

"That's none of your business, Bo."

"Most of them," Mortise said.

"Insurance you pay for?" I pressed.

Both women jutted back, as if offended by an unexpected stink.

"What's wrong with a little something to cover burials?" Minerva demanded. "Street people don't live long. And, since they're with us, we're stuck with the funeral."

"The State of Texas will take care of that," I said.

"Unclaimed bodies are cremated," Mortise said. She offered a twisted smile. "Some religions preclude that."

Male footfalls approached from the direction I had come.

I looked toward the doorway expectantly. A moment later a young man, entered the room. He was tall and bony with wavy brown hair, sharp cheekbones and watchful dark eyes. His attire was casual: a leather jacket, sweatshirt, denims and black boots. I stood up, when he stopped. But, I had trouble controlling a smile. I had seen him before, through my telephoto lens. Naked.

"Drax," Mortise addressed him, "this is Mr. Bishop. He's a private investigator." She offered me a withering smile. "This is our nephew Drax Ravaillac."

I went over to him and we shook hands.

"Mr. Bishop's investigating the murder of Mrs. Firth," Minerva said. "He says the same killer did both Mrs. Firth and Reggie."

"That doesn't sound good," Ravaillac said, grimly.

"Did you know Mrs. Firth?" I asked him.

He flushed crimson.

"Don't recognize the name," Drax replied.

"You live here?" I asked.

"Drax is staying in our guest room, until he finds an apartment," Mortise cut in.

The young man nodded, his eyes going over my shoulder to the women on the sofa, as if seeking guidance.

"My aunts insisted," he quickly added.

"Nothing wrong with being loved," I said. "You work at the hotel?"

"I help out."

"Minerva and I will be retiring soon. Drax will be taking over the hotel's management," Mortise said.

"Dating anybody special, Mr. Ravaillac?" I asked.

His gaze returned to his aunts, stayed a beat and then went back to me. He was under their thumb. Anything they told him, he would do. Anything he did for them was carefully instructed. But, I was sure, his personal life was still a secret. Like his good times with Connie Firth.

"Drax isn't ready to settle down, yet," Mortise said.

"How does Comic Con grab you, Mr. Ravaillac," I baited.

"It's real cool," he said, calmly. "Why?"

"Did you see Reggie Shepherd, there?"

"Yeah, sure." Then his eyes wavered back to his aunts during a hesitation. "Everybody knows the Shadow."

"How about Cutie?"

"Cutie?"

"You should be talking to Buford Reese," Minerva cut in. "He hated Reggie."

"Minerva, please!" Mortise gritted.

"You hired him. I told you he was bad news. But, would you listen?"

"Everyone deserves a second chance."

"Mr. Ravaillac," I said, "did you see Buford getting violent with Reggie?"

"Not me," he replied. "But, Bufford's a junkie. No telling what a junkie'll do, when nobody's around. Something sets 'em off and whack-a-do!"

"Drax, dear, we mustn't hold the past against people," scolded Mortise.

"No past about it," Minerva intervened. "Buford's arms are covered in fresh scabs."

"Mrs. Firth was with a guy who fits your description, Mr. Ravaillac," I said. "Just before she turned up dead."

His face went white.

"I read about Mrs. Firth's death," Ravaillac choked. "But, I've never met the woman."

"You're certain?" I asked.

His tongue darted across his lips, like he had just come off a desert. But, I decided not to push him further until his aunts were out of earshot.

"Our nephew doesn't know the woman, Bo," Minerva chided. "Cut him some slack."

"Go into the kitchen, Drax, and have your lunch," Mortise instructed.

"Yeah, sure, Aunty."

Ravaillac started to leave, but I grabbed his arm and pulled him to a stop. Then, I handed the young man one of my business cards. He gave a flickering glance, at the two women. I looked over and caught them nodding at him. Ravaillac pocketed the card, and then moved off.

I returned to the chair.

"Drax isn't a killer," Minerva insisted.

"I know for a fact Mrs. Firth knew your nephew," I said.

"You got it wrong, Bo."

"I have intimate photos of them, if you'd like to browse."

There was a heavy silence.

"There must be some mistake," Mortise said, protectively.

Minerva rolled her eyes.

"I warned you that kid was thinking with his balls," she grumbled.

"Gordon Shepherd was murdered yesterday, at Eddie Walton's offices," I said. "Where was Drax?"

Mortise swallowed thickly.

"He was here, with us," she whispered.

"The whole day?"

"I told you Drax would be trouble," Minerva said to her sister. "But, you never listen to me. No. You had to help the son of our dead sister."

"Shut up."

"The cops haven't tripped to him, yet," I said. "But there are rules to keeping my license. I'll have to let them know about Drax and Mrs. Firth. So, if he's involved in these killings, lying to protect him won't play well in front of a jury."

"Zip a lip, Mortise," Minerva cautioned.

"We've nothing to hide, Minerva," Mortise Anniston responded. "Mr. Bishop, Drax was here all day." She clasped her hands together. "Considering Gordon Shepherd's unscrupulousness, there must be a hundred people who wanted him dead."

"A hundred who also wanted Mrs. Firth and the others?" I asked.

"That bastard offered a bundle if we'd whack Reggie," Minerva snapped.

"Mr. Shepherd didn't actually suggest murder," Mortise,

corrected. "But, the implication was there."

"Why would he assume you'd do such a thing?"

There a very pregnant pause, while the two women did another round of mutual eyeballing.

"What, exactly, did he say?" I asked.

"That he would reward us when Reggie passed," Mortise said.

"Do you, or Minerva, own a gun?"

"First Drax, now we're the killer?" Minerva ejaculated.

"Our father owned a pistol," Mortise said. "But, it disappeared years ago."

"Daddy was always losing things. His mind, in the end."

"The hotel provides each guest with medical care?" I asked.

"We provide limited care," Mortise said. "Medicines. Eye glasses. If something more serious comes up, we take the resident to the county hospital. At that point State and Federal services come into play."

"Do either of you know Walter Osgood Kemp or Charlene Holland?" I asked.

The two women stared blankly at me. Then, after a couple of beats, both shook their heads.

"They're dead," I explained. "Murdered. That was on the news. You didn't hear about it?"

"Murder isn't a hobby, Bo."

"Mortise, you were at the Civic Center when Charlene Holland was murdered," I said.

"You're talking about the gunshot?"

"It's quite a drive from here and the hotel."

"Shopping," Mortise replied. "There was a sale on sheets at one of the stores. We need to replenish the hotel's sheets every three months. I was walking past, on my way to the sale, and heard a gunshot."

"But, you went inside," I said. "Most people, upon hearing gunfire, duck and cover."

"I did what any responsible citizen would do. I went in to see if I could help."

Minerva got to her feet.

"Start rollin', Bo," she growled. "The dog and pony show's over."

Chapter 15

After leaving the Anniston sisters, I drove off like a man on a mission. Then I looped back, and parked down the block. If the sisters were involved in the killings, my visit should have rattled their nerves. And, if I was any judge of characters, the two women would lay whatever had to be done on their nephew.

I did not have long to wait.

Drax Ravaillac stepped onto the building's front stoop. He looked around as if wary of danger. Probably at the suggestion of Minerva. As I watched, he unwrapped a stick of gum and stuffed it into his mouth. He chewed for a few seconds, his head moving back and forth as his eyes took in the scenery. Then, apparently satisfied the boogey-man was nowhere around, Ravaillac headed into the adjacent parking lot. He had a meandering gait. Every few steps his head rotated, like a gate in a high wind, seemingly to aid his searching eyes. Eventually, he stopped next to a red convertible. The vehicle looked new and expensive. Considering Ravaillac's lack of employment, the fancy car must have been a gift. He climbed into the vehicle, dropped the top, and drove off.

I followed.

At the first opportunity, Drax Ravaillac caught the I-35 onramp. I gave him space and tailed him onto the freeway. We drove several miles, with me changing lanes in order to conceal my intentions. At the Lipton Avenue exit, Ravaillac took the off-ramp. I kept pace as we floated onto a frontage road.

For several minutes, we followed the winding asphalt. It passed several residential areas and a number of small businesses. At a small strip mall, Ravaillac pulled in. He snaked through the parking lot until he found a parking spot in front of Margot's pawn shop. I rolled past, stopping two stores down. When he entered Margot's, I got out and strolled back.

The front window provided a clear view of the pawn shop's sales area. Drax Ravaillac stood at a counter talking to an elderly man. Since the old guy wore a ratty sweater, plaid shirt and wrinkled slacks, I did not figure him for Margot. But, from the greedy look on the shopkeeper's face, he was probably doing a good imitation. I could see only Ravaillac's back side. But, his body language suggested equal eagerness.

The older man suddenly held out a hand, palm up. From the pocket of Ravaillac's jacket, the young man produced a pistol. The shopkeeper gave the weapon a careful examination. Then there was more discussion. Eventually, the old boy set the gun on the counter and pulled out a rubber-band wrapped roll of money. Carefully, he peeled off several bills setting them on the counter next to the gun. Then he returned the bundle to a pocket. Drax Ravaillac snatched the cash. Then he turned and headed out.

I stepped into the adjacent business and feigned an interest in the front window's panties display. Ravaillac came out of the pawn shop and climbed into the convertible. As he drove off, there was a satisfied smile on his face.

"Something for your wife?" a shop girl asked my back.

"I like the lace," I said, turning to face her. "But, I can't decide between pink and purple. I don't suppose you'd model prior to purchase?"

The sales clerk offered the look most dirty old men, like me, get from a young woman. I winked back.

"I'm sorry, Sir," she said. "But, you'll have to use your imagination."

"Same thing the wife says."

I left the lingerie store and strode into Margot's Pawn Shop.

"Something special in mind?" the old man asked.

The pawned pistol was still laying there. I walked over and pointed at the weapon, drawing the shopkeeper's eyes. From the diameter of the barrel, the gun was a .22 caliber.

"I'm interested in this," I told him.

"Sorry," he returned. "Not for sale."

He reached for the gun. I grabbed his wrist. The old man gaped at me as if the devil had him by the throat.

"Not so fast," I said. "I have reason to believe it was used in several homicides."

"Cop?" he asked, with dread in his voice.

"I've been following the seller all morning, waiting for him to shed this."

I released my grip. He shifted uneasily.

"Listen, Bub, I'm just a businessman. People bring me stuff. If it's something I'm interested in, I accept the pawn."

"You buy what other people steal."

"That guy said the gun was his."

"And gullible you saw profits?"

The shopkeeper's arms rose and fell in despair.

"What did I ever do to you?" he demanded.

"I've got a long list of nothing. But, you can start making amends by handing over that gun."

"I paid two hundred, for it."

"Think of this as an opportunity to honor your civic duty."

His hands hit the counter top, taking the weight of his shoulders, his head drooping.

"Civic duty means getting it up the ass," he groaned.

"Lucky for you, I'm a sympathetic type," I said.

"Meaning you're offering a kiss before the screwing?"

"You get your two hundred."

The shopkeeper looked up, expectant but still irritated.

"I'd have made twice that," he complained.

"Four people are dead."

"Not my problem."

"It could be if some nosey nelly from homicide division comes around to check your inventory for other guns."

"You're bleeding me white."

"My heart aches."

"You want heartache? Try having a wife who doesn't understand budgets and a kid who thinks I'm made of money." His hands moved in a flurry. "And don't get me started on my live-in sister."

" But, if you prefer, I could work my magic with Margot."

"My mother was Margot."

"Was?"

"She died over the rising cost of doing business."

I took out my money-clip and counted out cash.

"I don't suppose you could make it three hundred?" he

pressed.

"You'll make up the loss on your next sale," I said, and stuffed the money into his shirt pocket.

After I got out to the Buick, I sniffed the pistol's breach. It smelled of burned gunpowder. I stuffed the weapon into the glove box. Then, I made a cell-phone call to an aging forensic tech by the name of Kenneth Miller. Miller had a young wife. She was a spendthrift, and he was working three jobs to keep her happy. After getting him on the phone, I explained my situation. Miller agreed to examine the gun and compare a round fired from it to the bullets pulled from Connie Firth. When I asked him to keep it on the Q-T, he agreed provided I paid a sum not normally discussed except with IRS auditors. Since, I had no other option, I agreed.

I checked my watch. There was just enough time drop the pistol at Miller's house in West Austin and then swing by Jubal Lessingham's office on Pearl Street in Leander.

Ninety minutes after finalizing my instructions with Miller, I took the stairs from the Pearl Street sidewalk up to the Jubal Lessingham's reception area. The furnishings amounted to a desk and a few customer chairs. A woman I had not seen before sat behind the desk. Lessingham had problems keeping help. So new faces were not uncommon. The nameplate on the desktop read: *Scheherazade*. She was pink-haired and straight-figured, dressed in jade silk and blue denim. She must have been expecting me. As soon as I mentioned my name, Scheherazade grabbed her purse from the floor and locked it in the desk.

"I don't have any money," she blurted.

"I borrow only from my closest friends," I assured her.

"So, I was told, Mr. Bishop. But just so we're clear, you are not my friend."

"Not yet. But, I think we've got a good start."

"It's not going to happen." She made an impatient motion. "Not on my salary." Scheherazade pointed toward the customer chairs. "Take a seat. There's about twenty minutes left on the Doc's clock."

I went over and settled into a chair that had a good shine to the seat.

"How's tricks?" I said, just making conversation.

"There's a sucker on every corner."

Obviously Shahrazad was not drawn to Lessingham's psychic charms.

"You don't believe in foreseeing the future?" I asked.

"I believe in a paycheck."

She was decorated with emerald earrings and a gold necklace from which dangled an emerald solitaire. I would not have considered Shahrazad beautiful. Interesting would be closer to the mark. But, she must have been good at something to somebody with money. Because the stones in her adornments were large and real.

"Who's Jubal's current fish?" I asked.

"A regular. Mrs. Durell." The receptionist's ruddy eyebrows lifted. "She comes every month, like clockwork, to chew out her husband."

"Why doesn't the woman save a buck and do it at home?"

"'Cause Mr. Durell's dead."

I was impressed. Not only was Lessingham a seer, he could raise the dead.

"Lots of regulars?" I asked.

Scheherazade nodded.

"Most come from the retiree set," she explained.

"Jubal's down to plundering pensions?"

"The wrinklies are our bread and butter." She lifted her shoulders, and let them fall. "The older people get, the more they miss loved-ones." She sniffed, without emotion. "Especially the dead ones."

"Got any from the upper crust?"

"A few local blue-bloods drop by, now and then."

"Like who?"

"The mayor." She smiled. "Is he crusty enough?"

Clearly, I had underrated Jubal Lessingham. He was not only bilking the elderly, but screwing the local political machine. The idea of the latter, I liked. But, his business with pensioners troubled me.

"The political polls have, once more, turned our illustrious civic leader into a paranoiac?" I asked.

"Actually," she replied. "The mayor drops in to find out about you." Shahrazad waggled a finger at me. "You're infamous. And not just for who and how much you owe."

I blinked with surprise. Not that she had penciled me as a notorious deadbeat. I was used to that. But for the Mayor to spend taxpayer's money to get me on a spook-line was way over the top.

"I hope you're not inferring amoral intrigue between him and me," I told her.

Shahrazad laughed softly.

"Doc warned me about you," she said. "But nothing he said suggested a romantic interest in men." She twisted her face into a grimace. "Although, any woman within arm's reach was up for grabs."

"How does Jubal fill the mayor's needs?" I asked.

"He hasn't, so far. But, they spend the hour discussing your timeline."

"Timeline?"

"Your predicted death-date."

"Anything I should know about that?"

"You're still alive, aren't you?" she said. Scheherazade hesitated and then tilted toward me, speaking in a confidential tone. "We've also got a gangster on the books."

I assumed she was speaking about Momma Portello. But, I pretended ignorance.

"Sounds scary," I said. "White slavers? Drug dealers? Or, lawyers?"

"The Portellos."

"Who's the player?"

"The old lady."

"Momma Portello? Really?"

"Once the brain hits seventy, it turns to gelatin."

"What's Momma's complaint?"

"No complaints," she replied. "But, every so often, the old lady spends an hour updating her dead husband on family matters." Shahrazad suddenly stopped speaking. "You know them, don't you? Otherwise you wouldn't know she likes being called Momma."

"The brothers and I are no longer close. But, Momma's lasagna is to die for."

"Doc said there are rumors about you and the daughter."

"You know what they say about rumors."

"What?"

"They're only true if you want to believe them." I offered Shahrazad my most reassuring smile. "How's Old Frank taking Momma's news?"

Shahrazad lifted one shoulder.

"I'm told he's the quiet type, since he died."

"That happens after embalming."

"As if Hell hasn't given that poor man enough worries," she said. "Now he's got Doc Lessingham rattling his bones." She shook a finger at me. "It gives a woman pause."

"I hear a whale can do the same thing."

She inhaled deeply and let her breath exhale through her nostrils.

"Do you believe in God?" Shahrazad asked.

"I've said a prayer once or twice."

"I was a lapsed Catholic until Doc told me about the Portellos. Now, I'm at mass every Sunday." She flung out her hands. "What I mean is with a family like them on the loose, going to services is just good common sense."

"I take it you listen in on Jubal's sessions?"

Scheherazade moved her head from side to side.

"That would be unethical," she said.

"Then how did you find out about Momma's problems?"

"Doc is a great one for pillow talk." Shahrazad gave me a sidelong look. "You married?"

I shook my head, but I was grinning. Clearly, things were looking up.

"Harem complex," I told her.

"I know all about that. Every girl knows about that." She moistened her lips. "But, I'm surprised a man your age still has the chronic itch."

Why do young women consider a man who's reached a certain level of experience, old?

"I wouldn't call it chronic," I told her. "Just something I need scratched, now and again." I tried to keep my voice unruffled, reassuring. "What's the latest Portello worry?"

"The grandson's become a pony player."

That was news. I was not sure if it was good, or bad. Nevertheless, my son had an early start on the Bishop tradition.

"How's the kid doing?" I asked.

"According to the old lady, he's a whiz."

I suddenly saw the value in taking an active role in my son's upbringing.

"What kind of family teaches a five year old to play the Gee-Gees?" she asked.

"Disgraceful," I returned. "Personally, I blame the uncles."

"I didn't learn the Trifecta Key 'til I was eight."

"How are you, these days, at picking a winner?" I asked, trying to conceal my greed.

"You have to ask? Seeing where I work?"

Her response was disappointing. But, I found the young woman's honesty refreshing. Shahrazad knew and understood her limitations. Which was more than could be said for most players. Myself, included.

"Considering the issues dogging the Portello clan, a horse playing kindergartner can't be the big story," I remarked, hoping to elicit further indiscretions.

"Clever you," she said.

"So, what is it?"

"I'm not supposed to say."

"I've been known to keep a secret."

Scheherazade grinned and eased back in her chair.

"The old lady thinks the daughter-in-law's having an affair," she said.

"Don't believe everything you hear," I told her. "Constance Portello would never screw Julie 'the Cutie' Caivano."

Her mouth gaped in awe.

"How could you possibly know the guy's name?" Shahrazad gasped. "You should take your act on the road."

"Sometimes, during the throes of sexual bliss, I see things you would not believe."

"Doc says the same thing." She shuddered. "Some nights he's nothing but gasps and drooling." Shahrazad made a purse of her mouth, eying me with curious interest. "Doc said you used to be a cop."

"I had a disillusioning childhood." Since there was a 'No Smoking' sign, on the wall above Shahrazad, I took a square of nicotine gum from a pocket and stuffed it into my mouth. "Did Momma Portello say anything about Connie Firth's body?"

She jerked back involuntarily.

"There you go again," Shahrazad gulped.

"When Momma Portello was talking to Old Frank, did she mention where Caivano's buried?"

"He's dead too?"

"Love, with the wrong person, can be is dangerous." I chewed for a few more seconds on the gum before going back to take another drink from her well of information. "You know, a man in my business could make use of an insightful and clever woman."

"I don't think so, Mr. Bishop. That's what Doc said when he hired me." She made a sweeping gesture. "And, all it got me was him sharing my bed." Then, Scheherazade crinkled her face, showing even white teeth. "I never knew my father because my mom never married."

"Mine did," I returned, "with many regrets. I don't suppose you've got one of those fluffy-top mattresses?"

"My mom won't tell me my father's name, but she says he's an ex-cop with a gambling problem." Her incisors indented her lower lip, as if she was working up her courage. "Doc said you have a gambling problem."

Half an hour of panic attacks and denials later, I had spat out my nicotine gum and was sprawled on a recliner in Dr. Jubal Lessingham' private office, smoking a cigarette. He was seated behind an army-surplus desk, a dead pipe gripped between his teeth, his fingers fumbling through my cash advance.

"I take it this visit has nothing to do with your printing needs?" Lessingham said, across the pipe stem.

The former medico had a high, wide forehead and brown hair. His mop was brushed back along both sides. He held himself rather stiffly. In so doing, Lessingham conveyed an aura of aloofness. His gray eyes were wide-set. His nose drooped like an eagle's beak. His chin seemed to dangle.

"Last time I was here, you were offering hypnotism gigs," I

said. "When did the psychic phenomena come into play?"

"A few months back. I hold séances on Thursdays. Twenty bucks a seat."

"What's going on with Momma Portello?"

"Did she complain?" he asked, in surprise.

"Salvator's not happy."

Dr. Lessingham rubbed his jaw for a long moment.

"I had concerns when Mrs. Portello came to me," he said, with a sigh. "Tell Mr. Portello I'll stop seeing his mother."

"It's not that easy, Jubal."

"All I did was try to ease her pain."

"You might want to consider refunding her money."

"Consider it done."

"You, also, might find an excuse to refer Momma to another psychic. She doesn't take rejection, well."

"She gets violent?"

"Not with you. But, dropping her cold might put Salvator within Momma's sights. And we both know his views on violence."

"I'll arrange something."

I took a long draw on my cigarette, and blew smoke to the ceiling.

"I understand Reggie Shepherd came to see you, from time to time," I said.

"Ah, the Shadow," Lessingham returned, sadly. "I read about his death. If you're seeking more refunds, I didn't charge for Reggie's sessions."

"Did you have contact with Connie Firth, Walter Osgood Kemp, Gordon Shepherd, Charlene Holland or Willard Fitzroy?"

He waggled a dismissive finger.

"I heard about their deaths," Lessingham said. "But, I've never had dealings with any of them."

"Did Reggie mention any of those people?"

Lessingham shook his head.

"What was your arrangement with Reggie?"

"For every client he brought, Reggie would receive an hour of my time." Lessingham grinned. "You'd be amazed at the people he knew."

"You counselled him?"

"I'm not allowed to do that anymore."

"You asked questions. Reggie answered. Then, you analyzed."

"We chatted."

"What about?"

"Mostly, his crime fighting fantasies." His eyes were sad, and Lessingham moved his head slowly from side to side in grief. "We all have dreams of greatness."

"Did Reggie talk about Cutie?"

"Cutie was Reggie's Professor Moriarty." He smiled wistfully. "How simple life would be if we each had only one evil force to battle."

"You're telling me Cutie was a fantasy?"

"Absolutely."

"About two weeks before Reggie died, he witnessed Connie Firth's and Willard Fitzroy's murders," I explained.

"You're certain this was not another delusion?"

"Both victims are very dead. When I asked Reggie who had done it, he said it was Cutie."

Lessingham rekindled his pipe and puffed for nearly a minute.

"If Reggie actually witnessed a murder," he mused, "I'd be surprised if he did not identify the killer as Cutie."

"Jubal, he wasn't lying."

"Of course he wasn't. The Shadow would never lie. But, to Reggie, Cutie was the ultimate villain. Any crime Reggie witnessed would, invariably, be the work of Cutie. That type of rationalization would've been Reggie's coping mechanism for handling the shock."

"How many times did you meet with Reggie?" I asked.

"Three or four dozen." Lessingham pointed at my chair. "He sat right where you are, completely animated."

"Did he talk to you about anyone besides Cutie?"

Lessingham paused to think.

"His brother, a few times."

"The butterfly?"

"Gordon Shepherd, before his recent death, was an entomologist."

"I guess that translates to butterfly easily enough. How did he get along with brother Gordon?"

"Reggie admired him. But they had not spent any amount of time together in the past twenty years. Reggie was the Shepherd family embarrassment."

"Did you know Gordon Shepherd?"

"Never met the man. My research into Reggie disclosed Gordon's existence."

"What about Dr. Parker?"

"Reggie described him as a wizard with magical powers."

"Did you have any interaction with Parker?"

"None. But, he's known in the medical community."

"Good reputation?"

"He's careful to avoid mistakes in his pursuit of the wealthy."

"Dr. Firth?"

That name rings no bells. What's with all the questions?"

"Dr. Firth hired me to look into his wife's murder. He's not convinced the police will do it honestly."

"Why wouldn't they?"

"Firth thinks they may be involved."

"What do you think?"

"There may be some credence in what Firth says. Did Reggie mention a ledger?"

"The magic red book?"

"Possibly. What did he say about it?"

"It was full of secrets that only the Shadow could fathom."

"Did Reggie say how he got it?"

"A beautiful lady gave it to him and told Reggie to give it to no one unless she told him to."

"Charlene Holland would've fit the bill for a beautiful lady. Did Reggie say how she came by it?"

"I tried to get an explanation. But Reggie refused to disclose the how or why unless I knew the password."

"Password?"

"Apparently the beautiful lady had given Reggie a password whereby he would know who to pass the ledger onto."

"Did he say anything about the Anniston Arms Hotel?"

"It was a castle controlled by a pair of witches."

"Mortise and Minerva Anniston?"

"Reggie claimed Mortise controlled Cutie with a spell."

"Anybody else in Reggie's world?"

"Someone named Eddie, who was a spy."

"What about Buford Reese?" I asked.

His lips folded around the pipe stem, his jaws working ruminatively for nearly a minute.

"Nope," Lessingham said. "I'd remember that name."

"Drax Ravaillac?"

"Ah, his name I recall," he said. "Ravaillac mystified Reggie. He suspected Ravaillac of magical powers."

"Such as?"

"Ravaillac had a death ray."

"Ravaillac is real. So, why isn't Cutie?"

"Cutie could become invisible." Lessingham set his pipe aside. "Remember that fire in the annex to the Anniston Hotel?"

"Yeah. Hundreds died."

"The investigation uncovered accelerant residue," he said. "But, placing blame became problematic."

"How so?"

"A couple of the bed-warmers cooked up a batch of meth-amphetamine. But, while they were testing their product the makeshift lab exploded."

"Do the Anniston's still own the property?"

"I couldn't say," Lessingham returned.

After leaving Lessingham, I stopped for supper at Lone Star Ed's. The special for this evening was a rare Texas delicacy: roasted Armadillo in mint sauce.

Chapter 16

The next morning, I telephoned Precious Heidegger. We exchanged a few words regarding the banking information she had requested. Her side of our conversation was more colorful than mine. But I chalked that up to her enthusiasm for revitalizing our relationship.

After ringing off, I drove to Charlie Trent's home. In order to compensate Kenneth Miller, I would need every nickel. And, Trent's promotion to Captain meant he would be flush enough to pay a long overdue debt. Then there was the knife between the ribs angle. According to Walter Osgood Kemp, Trent had been in bed with Kemp in a business sense. This meant Trent knew a lot more about Kemp's life, and possibly his killer, than I. The trick from my end was getting Trent to talk. From experience that meant inserting the proverbial blade and giving it a good twist.

"What's on your dirty mind, Bishop?" Charlie Trent demanded.

"A word or two in your shell-like," I replied, "concerning that financial transaction we entered into before my retirement."

We were on the front porch of the Trent home; a recently acquired limestone sprawl with a steel roof.

"What transaction?" he snorted.

"The loan you needed," I said, "to pay off the waitress you…"

"Shut up!" he cut in. Then, Trent tossed a worried look over one shoulder. "The wife's inside."

Charlie Trent was enormous. He stood nearly seven feet tall and weighed over three hundred pounds. Trent flaunted a light-brown complexion, probably from sunny weekends on his yacht. His dye-black mop was parted in the middle, leaving a white line of scalp from front to back. His Mexican bandit moustache drooped over an oddly small mouth. Trent's green eyes accurately echoed his snake-like disposition.

"Just want what's due me, Charlie," I coaxed. "Would you

like me to come back? You know. When you're out and your wife isn't?"

There was a long scraping moment as Charlie Trent ground his teeth. Then his sloping shoulders bunched.

"Don't threaten me, your sorry son-of-a-bitch!" he snapped.

"Cut me a check and I'll be on my way," I returned.

Trent pinched his flat nose. In so doing, his wide mouth curved up in clown fashion.

"You making a begging crawl over here means the detective business is slow," he gloated. "How do you like having an empty belly?"

"Now that you're Captain, Charlie, I'm thinking my eating habits'll improve."

"Not from my larder. Not if you put a torch to my balls."

"As enticing as that sounds, you shouldn't step on your friends."

"You and I were never friends."

"Then consider me a longtime confidant. One willing to take a vow of silence — concerning your rancid history."

"Are you threatening me?"

"Right down to your tippy-toes."

I could hear laughter coming from inside the house. Either the television was being run through an enormous amplifier, or the Trent's had guests.

"What say we do this on the back porch?" he gritted. "I'll make my apologies and meet your there."

As Charlie Trent went inside, I strolled around the house and picked a spot, in the back yard, on a grass-embedded flagstone. Then I lit a cigarette. The last time I had visited Charlie Trent, it was at his old place. A wood framed hovel in East Austin. I had been facing an internal affairs investigation for killing the mayor's son. The sadistic bastard had been beating an elderly woman. When I tried to stop the melee, he had pulled a gun. Three rounds from the Mauser ventilated his head. In spite of the evidence, the mayor had taken offense to my actions. Better dead old ladies than a corpse from his bloodline. Charlie Trent had been my partner at the time. His statement would have justified my use of deadly force. But, instead of testifying to what he had witnessed, Trent had claimed no first-hand knowledge of the incident because he had been busy in the cruiser. The net result was my taking early retirement.

Trent waddled out the back door, looking impatient.

"I write you a check and we're done, understand?" he glowered.

He rummaged through his suit, a newly tailored number in Navy blue. A few seconds later Charlie Trent withdrew a checkbook and pen. His jaw muscles rippled, as he opened to a blank draft.

"Surprised I made Captain?" he asked.

"Not with your lack of talent and political connections," I replied.

"You're jealous. Admit it."

"I am, Charlie. I'm also wondering how Walter Osgood Kemp took the news? I'll bet his hand went out and his smile widened."

Trent eyed me for a beat.

"Kemp's dead." He glance back toward the house. "So, whatever you think you've got is moot."

I flicked cigarette ash at the newly appointed Captain of police.

"I was thinking how Herby Mann would make a fine addition to your staff," I told him.

"Once I get things rolling, your pal will be pensioned off."

"You're overlooking the importance of credibility, Charlie," I said. "You'll need Herby for that, once the dust clears on your promotion."

"Mann's been promoted beyond his abilities!" He tore the draft from the checkbook. "This makes us even."

I had an urge to belt Charlie. But I controlled the impulse. My being arrested on a battery charge would do Herby Mann no good. Admittedly, my longtime associate might not see it that way.

"Before you return to your guests," I said, and snatched the paper from his fingers, "tell me who killed Walter Osgood Kemp."

"If I knew that I'd have the bastard behind bars," he growled.

"That would depend on the blackmail potential."

"I don't give a fiddler's fuck what you believe."

"The thing is, I never trusted Ozzie. So, whenever he and I

met, I recorded our conversations." I dropped my cigarette to the ground and heeled it. "Ozzie rambled on and on about you and him and business. He was really giving it to you, wasn't he Charlie?"

Charlie Trent went white. I smiled, letting my fictionalization weigh on his conscience.

"Everybody knows that Kemp was an incessant liar," he growled.

"Relax, Charlie," I said. "Like you said, a dead man's words are moot." I lit another cigarette, took a deep draw, and blew smoke into his face. "Usually, I wouldn't give a rat's ass about the killer of a guy like Kemp. But, in this case the clown who killed him also killed Connie Firth."

"What's your interest in her?"

"The dead lady's husband has me on the clock."

Charlie Trent turned, intending to go into his house.

"Any information I might have, along investigative lines," he said over one shoulder, "would be police business."
I grabbed his jacket, and spun him around. He jerked free, flushing with rage.

"I'm thinking there may be a connection between the killer I'm after and Kemp's church," I said.

"Leave homicide to me and my people," he snapped.

"The trouble is, Charlie, you can't be counted on to give a fair shake." I settled back on my heels. "Which makes me nervous. That, in turn, could start a wild allegation coming down the pipe toward internal affairs. Which could get them asking questions about you." I waggled my cigarette. "You don't want me taking the shoeflies down memory lane."

"Piss off."

"Who financed Ozzie's interest in God?"

He stood, there, glowering.

"If I kill you right now, this ends," he seethed.

"You know me, Charlie. Which means, you know that's a very big if."

He wet his lips like man facing his own mortality.

"With your reputation," Trent said, "nobody'd question my actions."

"Depends on who tells the story. And between you, me and

your maker I'm thinking the tattletale will be me."

He rolled his lower lip beneath his upper teeth as he considered options.

"I don't know who killed Kemp," Trent eventually said. "But, I might know who Kemp was dealing with."

"Oh, there's no 'might' about it, Charlie. You wouldn't have gotten involved with Ozzie unless he identified all the players."

Charlie Trent expelled a long, weary breath.

"Talk to Cornelia Wilson," he muttered.

"The mud wrestler from the Counting House Bar?" I asked, in disbelief.

"Yeah."

"Where in hell would Cornelia get the kind of money Kemp would've needed?"

"You'll have to ask her."

Suddenly, I had an unexpected brainstorm. Although the circumstances of Kemp's death were not Portello style, an angry and jealous man often made mistakes. And the most angry and jealous man I knew was Dominic Portello. Could Dom have passed the money to Connie, thinking she had plans for their future, and then had his heart broken when he heard how she had handed it off to Kemp? Dom could not have used a Portello torpedo to kill Kemp. His brother, Salvator, would find out. Which meant, Dom would've done the killing personally. If he had done it. What did not work, with that theory, were the other killings.

"Any link between Kemp's church and Connie Firth?"

"Cornelia Wilson was her niece," he said.

"How well did you know Cornelia?"

"That's none of your damn business."

"Is there a link between Kemp and a guy named Gordon Shepherd?"

"The bug freak who works for the State?"

"Bingo."

"No. But, I happen to know that he and Cornelia used to be an item."

I could see Dom wanting to hide any connections to Kemp. But I could not imagine Kemp taking up with any woman at the risk of losing Charlene Holland.

"Are we done, now?" Trent demanded.

"Take my advice, Charlie. Put Mann on your team."

Chapter 17

The Counting House Bar was on East Sheffield Street in Austin. It was a two-story brick affair, built around 1870. The structure slouched, in tired building fashion, at the street's terminus. The place was owned by a corporation controlled by Salvator Portello. Naked mud wrestling was its current entertainment... a form of showbiz long past its prime. Nevertheless, muck-covered nudity still had an allure. That evening, the place was packed with a boisterous clientele.

I went to the service bar and elbowed my way onto a stool.

It had been nine hours since my chat with Charlie Trent. Nine hours of working up a storyline to mislead Cornelia Wilson. Nine hours of refining my theory concerning Dominic Portello.

I ordered a beer and, from a bowl, grabbed a handful of soggy pretzels.

There were several people behind the bar, pouring drinks. One was Hispanic. His nametag read: *Ambrose*. I quickly discovered that he was a jovial chap with a seemingly endless supply of humorous stories. Most, of which, concerned his broad and varied love-life.

"I tell you, man," Ambrose chuckled, while we huddled over my beer. "Her pussy was as bare as a baby's ass. Not even stubble."

He was short, heavy, and big-chested. His square face had blunt features and twinkling brown eyes. The latter moved, ceaselessly, beneath black brows.

"Sounds like you had a close shave," I told him.

"No blade, Man. Strictly laser. Hair removal's her profession." His eyes went glassy. "That woman's given herself permanent smiles at both ends."

"Marriage potential?"

His head went back and forth.

"Commitments make me nervous." Ambrose made a sucking

noise with his teeth. "But, I'm thinking she should defoliate my balls."

That crossed my legs.

"Burning light, in the hands of somebody suffering from noncommittal, might barbeque your danglers," I warned.

"Not a chance, man," Ambrose said. "Worse case, it'll bleach my scrotum."

That, too, squeezed my knees.

"Is it possible to speak with Cornelia without your personal pursuits tempting my family jewels toward a hot light?" I asked.

"Nobody working here by that name, man," he returned.

"Her stage name's Connie."

"Oh, Connie's our star," he said, and grinned dreamily. "Just finished a set. You probably saw her when you came in." Then, he pointed to a large kiddie pool filled with mud. "Wrestled Kellie to a three–fall win." His nose twitched with the eagerness of a young hound savoring the backside of a heated bitch. "Talk about pussy fit for the potter's wheel."

"Or a dirty skin crawl."

"Not for me, man," he laughed. "But, a little rinse and it's go-go-go."

I made a sweeping gesture with one hand.

"That go-go-go draws this crowd every night?" I asked.

"It's all good, clean fun. Unless, of course, you get hit with a splash."

"I saw an entry box for a drawing, by the door. But, I didn't see the prize."

"It's a nightly event. The winner helps with the post-match rinse-offs."

"Hands on scrubbing?"

Ambrose gave his head a sloppy shake.

"Strictly hose holding," the bartender replied.

"When will Connie be wrestling again?"

Ambrose glanced at his wristwatch.

"About forty minutes," he said. Then, Ambrose took out rolling paper and a tobacco pouch. "That's why I love this job, man." He tore loose a fold, and tucked away the remaining. "Every night of the week, I pour drinks while watching a show." From the pouch, he loaded tobacco spreading it on the paper in a ridge. "And, should the need arise, I give the girls their after-wash oil-rub." He massaged the tobacco with the paper until he formed a crooked cigarette. "Nothing like velvety skin for those ever important close-ups."

"You do all the rubbing around here?" I asked.

He licked the paper to seal the makeshift cylinder.

"It's the least I can do since I salted the mud," Ambrose returned, with a grin.

I pointed at his drooping cigarette.

"You're the second, this month, I've seen roll one," I remarked.

"Not too many of us left," he confided, after returning the pouch to its keep. "But, it's the only way I get my special blend."

I picked up my glass of beer, sipped, and then put it down. He lit up with a match and puffed out a fragrant cloud. I sniffed and smiled. His special blend was a trek down memory lane to my wayward, if high-flying, youth.

"Any chance I could speak with Connie before her next gig?" I asked.

"You're a nice guy, so I'll give you some advice." He studied the burning coal on the end of his cigarette. "Forget Connie. She'll bring you nothing but heartache — among other low-down and painful ailments."

"I've had my shots."

"Oh, it's nothing like that. But, the big boss has sort of put her on his special lease which don't have a lend covenant."

"How about you give her a call while I continue to overlook your choice in recreational drugs?"

"It's not what you think, man." Ambrose fanned the air with his free hand to disseminate the smoke. "Mostly it's Turkish."

"With just a hint of Maui-Wowee?"

He shrugged.

"Turkish gets a little dry," Ambrose explained. Then he blinked, dully, as his toked brain considered an unpleasant possibility. "You a cop?"

I rubbed the back of my hand against the stubble on my chin. In my years as a police officer I had heard many explanations from joint-smokers. But, dry tobacco was a new one.

"I'm a magazine journalist," I fictionalized. "All I'm after is an interview with Connie Wilson. Strictly business. So there's nothing for the boyfriend to get hot about.""

"Heat ain't the problem."

Meaning?"

"Dominic Portello gets nutso when it comes to her." He took another pull on the smoke, held his breath and then choked out a cloud. "Any one on one, when he ain't around, is strictly *verboten.*"

I nibbled on a pretzel.

"What he doesn't know doesn't count," I returned.

"It will if you get caught."

"I'll take my chances."

"It ain't you I'm worried about. It's the collateral damage."

"You might get hit in the crossfire?"

"It's not that I'm yellow. But, I bleed easily."

The weed he was smoking had worked its magic. So, I shifted gears.

"What's Connie see in Dum-Dee-Dee-Dum-Dom?" I asked.

"If I understood that, I'd understand women," Ambrose replied.

"From your tales of glory, I thought you did."

"I know just enough to avoid the need for tourniquets and emergency surgery." He took another pull, held it until he was nearly blue in the face, and then expelled smoke like a factory chimney. "The rest of my action comes from guesswork."

Not an unwise assessment for a guy whose brain was heading toward the stratosphere.

"What I've got planned will put this dump on the tourist maps," I said.

"That's your story, Man. And, I believe you. But, Dominic Portello ain't the trusting type." With his free hand he took a swing trying to catch something in the empty air. "He once killed a guy for having a bigger dick."

That, as far as I knew, was an untruth. Dominic Portello had killed many people for many reasons. But, nobody was a bigger dick than him.

"Makes a guy fight the urge to measure up," I said, dryly.

"That's why I always make sure I don't hit the head until after Dom comes back from a draining." Ambrose rested his chubby forearms on the bar-top and tilted toward me. "Let me give you another example of what you're up against. One night some guy grabbed Connie by the ass as she crawled from the mud. Not that I blamed him. Many's the time I've wanted to do the same thing." He dragged over a nearby ashtray, and dumped the ash from his smoke. "Dom had the guy hauled into the kitchen where he shoved the offending hand into the electric meat grinder." The bartender's face twisted with revulsion. "Three fingers and part of a thumb topped an order of pizza surprise."

While the meat grinder treatment was not unusual during a Portello temper tantrum, the pizza revelation was news. I made a mental note to avoid take out Italian.

"I'm willing to make this worth your while," I coaxed.

"Didn't you hear my pizza story?" Ambrose asked.

"I swear, my hands will never leave pencil or pad."

"You get caught and they'll be minced and coated with tomato sauce and mozzarella."

He stood erect and looked around while taking another drag on the weed. Then he returned his forearms to the bar top.

"Do us both a favor," he said, "and write about one of the other girls. Kellie, for example. She's got kinks that'll curl your hair."

"Sounds enticing. But, I can't do it." I dipped a pretzel into my beer. "My boss saw Connie wrestling." I took the damp snack out of the brew and watched the salt run. "He's convinced she's heaven on the hoof." I plopped the remains of the pretzel into my mouth, took out my money clip and slipped Ambrose a twenty. "See what Connie has to say."

"Okay, man. But, keep me out of it if you get caught."

Ambrose tucked my bribe into a pocket, went to the back-bar and opened a drawer. From within he took a cellular phone. Then, he punched a number. Moments later he spoke. After a few seconds he rang off and returned the phone to the drawer. Then he came back over.

"Connie says she'll do it," he whispered. Then Ambrose tilted his head toward the nightclub's exit door. "Hang a quick right, after you get outside. You'll see the shed." He dragged out a handkerchief and blew his nose. "There's a bell, in there. When Dom comes in, I'll ring." He returned the cloth to his pocket. "You hear that, you make tracks like there's no tomorrow. Because if Dominic Portello catches you with her, there won't be."

"Is the shed unlocked?"

"Connie'll bring the key."

"She's the key carrier?" I asked, in surprise.

"All the girls have keys."

The implication was unexpected and unpleasant. Unexpected because it meant Connie was part of the go-go-go as far as preferred customers were concerned. Unpleasant because Dom was not the sharing type. So, had he lied to his family about marrying Cornelia? Or, had love made him oblivious to her sideline?

"Does this shed have places to sit?" I asked. "I'll be taking notes."

"It's fully equipped," he confided. "Because it's not really a storage shed."

"Clue me in?"

"That's what we call it should somebody ask." He scratched his nose. "It's actually a getaway for our better paying customers."

That confirmed my suspicions.

"Does Dom know about this side of Connie's life?" I asked.

"I'm thinking not," Ambrose replied. "But I can't say for sure either way." He wet snuffed out his roach. "You ain't plannin' anything beyond what we discussed, now that you know about the shed?"

"Meaning cash and carry?"

"In Connie's case, it had better be cash and haul ass."

I headed out guided by Ambrose's instructions.

There was no difficulty in locating the shed. It was the only other structure on the property. I went over and gave it a quick eyeball. The building was about the size of a one-car garage, replete with a gabled roof covered in shingles. The siding looked like wood-grained plastic. There was no foundation, in the usual sense. A dozen two-by-sixes, positioned on edge, served that purpose. There were no windows. A padlock secured a plywood door. One way in. One way out. And no escape should Dominic Portello come looking.

"Are you the journalist?" a female voice called through the darkness.

I looked back toward the bar and saw the moonlit figure of a tall, lithesome woman trotting toward me.

"My name's Deacon Bishop," I said, when she reached me. "Are you Cornelia Wilson?"

"Connie," she corrected. "Cornelia's old fashioned."

Her eyes were large and dark. They glinted expectantly. She wasn't beautiful in the accepted sense. Her nose was too large and her lips too thin. But, I found her intriguing.

"I think my readers will enjoy the familiarity of your stage name," I told her.

Cornelia was around twenty-five. She was wearing grayish lounging pajamas over-coated by something green and shiny. A gold-colored chain belted the outer garment. On her feet were red sultan slippers.

"I've never been interviewed," she blurted, excitedly.

"In that case," I told her, "I promise to be gentle."

With a giggle, the mud wrestler stepped past and unlocked the door.

"There's no air or heat," she warned, going inside.

"If you get cold, feel free to cuddle."

I followed Cornelia Wilson, and shut the door. The space smelled of unwashed flesh. She stopped and reached up. A chain tug on an overhead light provided a dim glow. Then Cornelia turned and faced me. She wore her hair in a ponytail. It hung in a black rope, dropping past her shoulders.

"Are you really gonna' make me famous?" Cornelia asked.

"I'll do my best."

The shack had been furnished with a wooden table, a straight-back chair, and a bed. Considering what Ambrose had shared, the springy mattress made sense. The table and chair did not. Then I noticed a mirror inset into the tabletop. It carried a dusting of white powder. Probably residue from using nose candy.

"Have a seat," she instructed, pointing to the chair.

"Only if you'll perch nearby."

She giggled again.

"I was warned about journalists," Cornelia said, taking roost on the tabletop.

"You must've been talking to my mother." I sat down and took out my notebook and pen as part of my cover. "Did you always want to be in show business?"

"Ever since I was a little girl," she gushed. Cornelia squirmed closer, her hip touching my elbow. "It's all I could think about."

"Until you hit puberty."

"You're terrible," she laughed.

"I was told you're very sweet and loaded with compassion."

Her smile drooped.

"I try to help when I can," she said.

"Have you a church background?"

"Not much when I was growing up. But, I helped buy one last year."

"My readers are going to love that. Was this church about to close and you jumped in to keep it open?"

"Actually, a man I knew — Reverend Kemp – wanted to open a church to help people living on the street. I got the money he needed to buy the property and convert the building."

"You used your life savings?"

"Actually, my aunt loaned me the money." Her shoulders bobbed. "I'm not sure what's going to happen now. She's dead and so's Reverend Kemp."

I turned several pages in the notebook, pretending I was searching for an entry. Then, I stopped and dragged a finger down the page. "According to my source, you were friends with a man named Reggie Shepherd, alias The Shadow."

A pair of tears tumbled out of her eyes and coursed down her cheeks.

"Poor Reggie," Cornelia whimpered. "He was mad as a hatter. But, he was so sweet." She pulled a tissue from her coat pocket and daubed at the tears. "He's dead, too."

"Was Reggie the inspiration behind your desire to open that church?"

"Reggie introduced me to Reverend Kemp." She sniffed, wetly. "People I know keep dying."

"How did you meet Reggie?"

"I used to date his brother, Gordon. I'm a big fan of Comic Con. So, I took Gordon there. That's when Reggie came over and introduced himself as The Shadow, and Gordon's brother." She shifted in the table. "Reggie promised to be my protector. A tiny man with a lame leg who was willing to lay down his life for me." Cornelia wiped at more tears. "Nobody'd ever promised me that, before or since."

"How much money did you invest in the church?"

"Quarter of a million."

"You must've had a rich aunt."

"Not really. When she heard what I wanted to do she said she had investors who would be willing to help. She was right. Not long after that, I had the money."

"What's your favorite Comic Con character?"

"Shambroza the Golden Witch. I dress up like her for every Comic Con."

"Do you know anyone nicknamed: Cutie?"

"I don't know him, as such. But, last Comic Con, while I was talking to Reggie, he suddenly pointed at a group of six or seven people. Then he whispered, Cutie."

"Reggie didn't explain which person he meant?"

"I asked. But, Reggie yelled: 'the Shadow knows.' Then, he ran away."

"Did you recognize any of the men in that group?"

"Two of them. One was Dr. Parker." She nodded as if Parker's name needed affirmation. "He's very popular, with the ladies. He has a fat farm in Fredericksburg. The other was Drax Ravaillac. His aunt's own the Anniston Arms Hotel, where Reggie lived."

"How do you know Dr. Parker?" I asked.

"He's a friend of Dom's."

"Friend in the business or social sense?"

"Business. They've got some deal going." She shifted on the table, pulling away from me as if trying to separate herself from my question and its implication. "I don't get involved in any of that."

"Drax Ravaillac?"

"I dated him a couple of times." She crossed her legs at the knees. "He's sweet, in his own way. But, those aunts of his have him at their beck and call. It's like he's their robot."

I made a scrawl in the notebook and underlined the entry as if it was important.

"This is just background, for me." I cleared my throat as if having trouble finding words. "Are either Dr. Parker or Drax Ravaillac violent sorts?"

"Not that I've noticed."

Her brow formed vertical ridges.

"Are you going to write about them?" she asked.

"No. I was just interested in the type of men you've had in your life. The readers love the romance angle."

Cornelia Wilson considered and then nodded.

"I guess that's okay," she said.

I made several entries of meaningless scrawls in the notebook.

"I've been told your love-life recently took an upward turn," I said.

"Not that I've noticed," she said, in surprise.

"Your engagement to Dominic Portello."

"Oh, you mustn't write about Dom," she pleaded.

"You're not engaged to him?"

"Dom's told his family we're planning to get married," she explained, in a stilted voice. "But, the truth is we're in what might be called a cash-transaction relationship."

So much for love on the Portello front.

"Is it possible Dom's in love with you?" I pressed.

"Whether he is or whether he isn't, it doesn't change anything," she replied. "When we go out it's cash up front."

From the look on Cornelia Wilson's face, she was shutting down. So, I tried to lighten the moment by bringing up Salvator Portello's mention of Dom's furry friends.

"How do you feel about skunks?" I asked.

"They're truly beautiful creatures," Cornelia gushed, her mood lightening.

"That's not the typical description."

"Only because people focus on their smell."

"It's hard to miss."

"In truth, they're gentle animals who are in need of love."

"Does Dom share your devotion to the little stripers?"

Cornelia nodded.

"That's the one thing we agree on," she said. "He's got an entire ranch devoted to their protection."

I took more notes about nothing in particular.

"Since you and Dominic Portello are not an item, don't you think a relationship with him is a path to a dead end?"

"I hadn't thought of it like that. But, you're right. I'm not doing myself any favors by continuing to see him."

"Just between you and me," I said, "has Dom mentioned anything concerning a woman named Charlene Holland?"

"Not really. Reverend Kemp and Miss Holland were engaged to be married." Cornelia sniffed. "She's dead, too."

"What made you focus your career on mud wrestling?"

"The excitement. That's what my act's all about. Excitement."

"I think I'll take that as my article's opening line."

"Ambrose didn't tell me the name of your newspaper," she said.

"I work for a magazine," I lied. "*Texas Women's Periodical.*"

"How curious."

"What do you mean?"

"A man writing for a women's magazine," Cornelia said. "You don't think that's odd?"

"I write under the *nom de plum*: Agnes Whitehead," I told her.

"Is she your boss?"

I nodded, trying to keep a straight face.

"I guess you could call her that," I said.

"Not many men enjoy working under a woman."

"Depends on the job."

She laughed then, tossing back her copper head. The movement exposed the white column of her throat and the mottling from old bruises. Dom had not changed his procedures since connecting with Cornelia. The throat grab had always been his favorite seduction technique.

"One last thing," I said. "What's your biggest regret?"

"Why?"

"My article's going to make you a woman to be looked up to, by every Texas female. I want them to understand you're like them, in some ways. I want them to understand you're human enough to make mistakes."

"I had an affair with a married man."

"Sounds like something my readers will embrace. Can you give me his name?"

"No," she said. "I don't want to cause any trouble."

"How would you describe him?"

"Insanely jealous. He became so obsessed with me, he actually planned to kill his wife." She looked round the dim untidy room. "He thought by doing so, we'd be together forever."

"Naturally, you refused to participate."

"Of course."

"Married men are a bad investment. I'm surprised you didn't leave town."

"I considered. I still might."

"How did this guy expect to get away with murder?"

"He was going confuse the police investigation by leaving his wife's body in a place where a gangster might be blamed. Then, he would leave clues pointing to somebody not connected to the gangster. He claimed his plan was foolproof." Cornelia held up a long, delicate finger, for emphasis. "Then, to further complicate the situation, he was going to hire a private detective to search for her, as if she'd run away."

"To make it look like he could not be involved?"

"I could not believe what he was planning, at first." Her shoulders rose and fell. "But, when he insisted it was the only way we could be together, I broke off our relationship."

"He sounds like a nut-job."

"I tried to make him see reality. But, he refused."

Cornelia may not have identified her former lover as her deceased aunt's husband: Dr. Paisley Firth. But, her words suggested him.

"This guy's still in the area?" I asked.

She slid off the table.

"I'd better get back," Cornelia said. "I hope you'll send me a copy of the magazine when your article comes out."

I thanked Cornelia Wilson and followed her out of the shed.

Chapter 18

Mexicali Village was a real-estate development in the Fredericksburg area. It was an exclusive span designed for people with money. These luxurious homes sold for a minimum of $1,000,000. Each house rested on a multi-acre lot fronting Lake Jefferson, a manmade stretch of water formed by damming the Colorado River. Other amenities included a clubhouse for boat owners; a swimming pool, sans lifeguard; and, a golf course known for its wet-bar and female caddies.

At around eight o'clock, two nights after my *tête-à-tête* with Cornelia Wilson, I arrived in the village. A few minutes later, following Dr. Parker's instructions, I parked the Buick in front of his moonlit residence. While his cupolaed home was not the largest in the community, I assumed it was not the smallest. Two Mercedes glistened on either side of the front approach way, like moonlit Christmas tree balls. Either Dr. Parker enjoyed a twin driving experience or he was entertaining.

I got out of the Buick. Then I went between the cars and followed a winding concrete trail to a fancy entrance fitted with brass knobs. Flanking the double doors were narrow, pebbled-glass windows. The kind burglars break for surprise entries.

As I snuffed out my cigarette on the stoop, I wondered how a pill-pusher could afford such digs. The health spa, admittedly, would bring in a bundle. And, of course, there were the insurance payouts from the deaths of Parker's wife and brother. Plus, he maintained a private practice outside his clinic. Then there were his fees from the Anniston Arms Hotel. Okay. So a medico with a few money-making investments could afford a miniature Taj Mahal. But, why live alone in such huge place?

I rang the bell.

Half a minute later a dark-haired woman answered the door. She was petite and thin. A plain, blue dress cloaked her compact figure. On her feet were expensive-looking leather pumps. Nylons, in a paisley pattern, encased her shapely legs. The more I stared the more I liked.

"Yes?" she greeted me.

I identified myself and handed her my business card.

"Dr. Parker's expecting you, Mr. Bishop," she said.

The woman of my next fantasy stepped back, pulling the door wide.

"Come in," she instructed.

"You are?" I asked, stepping into the foyer.

She closed the door.

"Mrs. Sanders," she replied.

I guessed Mrs. Sanders to be about forty years of age. A nice time in life, for a woman. Decades of sexual experience. Her passions at their peak. Just considering possibilities put my motor into high gear. Could she be the reason for Dr. Parker's expensive taste in brick and mortar? Possibly. There were no rings on her fingers. Some widows keep their husband's name but shed the marriage trappings. Of course, some widows have killed their husbands.

"Is there a Mr. Sanders?" I asked.

"Presumably," she returned. "But, my husband is dead."

"You're Dr. Parker's housekeeper?"

"I'm his extra pair of hands."

I liked that concept. It conjured pictures of her doing a variety of pleasurably personal tasks. Preferably those involving whip-cracking while strutting around in a leather corset and thigh-high boots.

"Nice place," I observed.

"Beats a cardboard box in an alley," she said.

Mrs. Sanders had a handsome face and jade green eyes. Full lips folded her mouth into a sensuous purse. I tried to keep my nightstick from jumping to attention. But, without success. Her classic beauty was a delight to my naughty eyes.

"You've tested cardboard in a storm?" I quipped.

"I've tried a great many things in a great many places, lightning and thunder included."

I folded my hands in front of my bulging crotch. There was nothing more erotic than rainwater streaming across a woman's naked, lightning-lit body.

"Sounds wondrously shocking," I told her.

"If you'll wait here, I'll tell Dr. Parker you've arrived."

Mrs. Sanders strode off, leaving me in the expansive foyer. With each stride, her heels clacked on the ceramic tiles. The sounds put me in mind of chickens scratching among stones. But, the view was a lot more interesting. The sight of her undulating backside could resurrect a dead man.

While I waited I stuffed hands into trouser pockets, rocked on my heels, looked around at wall hangings of comic book superheroes, and wondered how I was going to explain my previous visit to Dr. Parker. I considered explaining my portrayal of Dr. Hernandez as a case of mental instability. But, that might extend to the current circumstance, which would cast doubts upon my professional credibility. Not that personal aspersions, bandied about by irresponsible females, were unknown. But, when I accuse a man of murder he has to believe I am not going for a punchline.

Mrs. Sanders reappeared. She beckoned with a discrete movement of one hand. I took mitts from pockets, put my dirty mind back to work, and wandered over.

"Dr. Parker will see you," Mrs. Sanders said.

"I'm in the book, in case the next storm leaves you unaccompanied," I returned.

She indicated the adjacent doorway with a tilt of her head. Then, Mrs. Sanders turned and clacked off. My eyes followed for a long moment, enjoying the flexing of her buttocks. Some women had a sexuality no amount of clothing could conceal.

I entered what could only be called the billiard room.

Pub tables and chairs occupied every inch of the perimeter. Centered on the tile floor was a gigantic snooker table topped with blue felt. Colored balls dotted the cloth. Drs. Parker and Firth, bearing expectant looks, stood at one end. Each was holding a cue-stick. Each was clothed in slacks and shirts.

"Who are you really?" Parker asked me. He leaned his cue against the table and strode over. "Bishop, Hernandez or somebody I should have arrested?"

Firth abandoned his stick against a wall and followed Parker.

"Who in hell's Hernandez?" Firth demanded, in a confused

voice.

"This man came to my clinic posing as Willamette Hernandez," Parker explained.

"He told me he was Deacon Bishop."

"I *am* Deacon Bishop," I protested. "As for the Hernandez impersonation, Dr. Parker, it was the only way I could gain access to Mrs. Portello."

Dr. Parker's brows crawled together like two hairy worms.

"I would've accommodated your desires without the need for a masquerade."

"But, not until you'd talked with her husband."

Parker's eyebrows lifted in stunned surmisal.

"Mrs. Portello is having an affair with you?" he asked.

"Absolutely not," I replied. "My amoral tendencies do not extend to seducing mobster's wives."

Mrs. Sanders entered the room pushing a portable bar. She positioned it near one of the pub tables. Then, she excused herself, saying she was leaving for the day. Parker wished her a good evening.

"Mrs. Portello complained after I left?" I asked him.

"Actually," he replied, "your visit sweetened her disposition. Something I had hitherto thought impossible."

"I have that effect on most women."

Firth gave me a dubious look.

"When you called, you mentioned Reggie Shepherd," Parker said.

"I'm paying you to find my wife's killer," Firth complained.

"They are one and the same," was my snappy return. Then, I returned my attention to Parker. "Other than your professional arrangement with the Anniston Arms Hotel, did you have any dealings with Reggie?"

Dr. Parker took off his spectacles, withdrew a handkerchief from a pocket and used it to polish the lenses. His milky-blue eyes squinted at me, and then at Firth.

"You spent hours driving here to ask that?" he asked, position his glasses on his face.

"I have a couple of other things on my mind," I replied.

"How do you know my wife and Reggie were killed by the

same murderer?" Firth cut in.

"Same gun."

Firth nervously smoothed what should have been hair across his naked scalp.

"So you're saying some lunatic is out there killing at random?" he demanded.

"Not at random," I said. "Purposeful."

"But, there's no connection between my wife and Reggie!"

"Reggie told me your wife's killer was Cutie."

"Reggie had trouble keeping touch with reality," Parker said, impatiently.

"That doesn't make him a liar."

"It sure as hell doesn't make him credible."

"Your wife nicknamed you Cutie, didn't she, Dr. Parker?" I asked.

There was a long silent pause.

"I see where this is going," Parker growled. "But, I'm not a killer."

"You're as mad as a hatter," Firth shouted.

"Your wife tagged you with that same nickname didn't she, Dr. Firth?"

Dr. Paisley Firth straightened his posture until he stood erect with forced dignity.

"I've done nothing wrong," he bleated.

"I'm not saying either of you have. But, I'm not a believer in coincidences. You both attend Comic Con, yes?"

Firth's knees began to tremble. He took out a handkerchief and wiped the damp from his hands. Parker wetted his lips.

"A lot of people attend," Firth protested.

"What about you, Dr. Parker?" I asked.

"Of course I go," he replied. "It doesn't make me homicidal."

"Comic Con was probably what Reggie lived for. From what I've discovered, he was quite a character and most attendees knew Reggie. During the last Comic Con, Reggie pointed to a group of people and identified one of them as Cutie. You were in that group, Dr. Parker."

"I may well have been. I gathered with any number of people, any number of times. But, it doesn't make me guilty of anything."

"I agree. My interest is in Cutie. Who, among those who gathered with you, went by that moniker?"

Parker considered.

"Drax Ravaillac, as I recall," he said.

"Anybody else?"

"Nobody jumps out at me."

"Do either of you own a .22 caliber pistol?"

"I may have at some point," Parker said. "But I don't own one, now."

"And, neither do I," chimed Firth.

Parker went over to the pub table adjoining the liquor cart, and sat down.

"Let's have a drink," he urged.

I looked over at him. He indicated the chair across from him, with a pointing finger. I went over and sat down. Firth followed and settled onto the third chair.

"What's your pleasure, Mr. Bishop?" Parker asked.

He leaned over to the cart and picked up three tumblers. Parker set one in front of himself, and then addressed Firth and I with the same consideration.

"Scotch, neat," I replied.

"Same for me," said Firth.

Parker grabbed a bottle of single malt from the cart and poured three times. Then, he set the bottle between us.

I tasted my drink. The smoky liquor trickled down my throat, like nectar. I did not like Dr. Parker. But, he had good taste in booze.

"What else is on your mind, Mr. Bishop?" Parker asked.

"Cornelia Wilson," I replied.

The vertical lines in the middle of Firth's forehead deepened.

"How does she fit with this?" Parker asked.

"You know her?"

"I know who she is. But we're not friends."

"What about you, Paisley?" I asked.

"My affairs are nobody's business but mine," he insisted.

"She's your wife's niece, Correct?"

"What has that to do with anything?"

"You had an affair with her."

"That little bitch!"

"She didn't say a thing to me."

"Then how did you…"

"I'm a great guesser."

"My wife and I had an open marriage. Cornelia was of age. The fact that she was my wife's niece did not make it illegal."

"What Cornelia did say was her affair with an unnamed married man spawned plans to murder his wife."

Firth's upper lip trembled.

"I'd never kill my wife," he snapped.

Parker's face showed doubts.

"Paisley," Dr. Parker said, "you haven't done something stupid, have you?"

"Cornelia Wilson became infatuated, with me, Nathan," Firth said. "She concocted an unrealistic dream, and when I refused to divorce Connie, she threatened to murder her."

"Now is not the time to lie," I said.

The optometrist drew in a breath, audibly.

"I was at home," he said, "when my wife was murdered. My niece, Precious Heidegger, can vouch for that." His voice trembled and he stopped to take a quivering breath. "She was there that night. We ate supper. We talked about her plans and some lunatic who had her thieve a hundred million from the Russian Mafia." He splayed his hands. "Would I make up a story like that?"

I did not appreciate the lunatic label. But, if Firth was lying, he would have selected someone other than Precious to alibi him.

"Just for grins, Dr. Parker," I said, "where were you when Connie Firth died?"

"On that date, about that time, I was listening to Constance Portello shrieking about pain." He interlaced his fingers atop the table. "Earlier, that day, she had received a vitamin B-12 injection, in her left buttock. While I found nothing out of the ordinary upon examining her, she carried on for quite some time about pain and suffering."

"Constance Portello can be a pain in the petuti," I said.

"Nevertheless, I'm certain Mrs. Portello will confirm the incident."

No man, in his right mind, would use Constance Portello in a phony alibi. No man in his right mind would involve her in anything.

"She gets a lot of those injections?" I asked.

"That's none of your business, Mr. Bishop," Parker said, flatly.

Which left only Drax Ravaillac on my Cutie list.

"It seems to me, Mr. Bishop," Parker said, "you've come a long way for nothing."

Not entirely. I would have fantasies about Mrs. Sanders for nights to come. I thanked the men for their time, and left.

When I got to my flop, I parked the Buick in the lot behind the apartment building. But, as I got out, a pair of gunshots chased the heels of two rounds as they buzzed past my shoulder. I hit the ground and jerked out the Mauser. My straining eyes scanned for the shooter. But, I saw only moonlit vehicles and shadows.

There was the crunch of gravel under foot. I twisted, on the ground, until I was facing the sound. Many seconds passed. Then I heard slow but steady approaching footfalls, scattering gravel with each step. I took aim. Then, twenty feet in front of the pistol's sights, I spotted scruffy jeans riding atop pink sneakers. I cocked the Mauser and scrambled to my feet.

"Hold it, Alfie!" I shouted.

He fired his Lugar, from the hip, shattering one of the Buick's windows. I returned fire, dropping Big Nose to the ground. Then, with the Mauser sighted on the fallen man's torso, I closed the distance between us.

"Move and you're dead," I warned, when I reached him.

I kicked his weapon clear. Then, I knelt next to Alfie. With my free hand I touched his throat. But, there was no pulse. I holstered the Mauser, stood up and took out my cell-phone. It was going to be a long night.

Chapter 19

It was the next afternoon before I was released from custody. Shooting Alfie Baker had proved more problematic than expected. My Mauser did not fare as well. Lt. Herby Mann refused to release it until the prosecutor's office officially ruled on the killing. Considering my history and Austin's political atmosphere, that could take a month.

In front of Austin's Homicide Division, I waved down a taxi.

When I arrived at home, I paid the cabbie and went over to the Buick. Its shattered window would require repair. There was also a bullet hole in one of the side panels. That would need putty and paint. Bottom line, my insurance agent would have another conniption fit with the resulting promise to piss on my grave.

I climbed behind the Buick's steering wheel and let the battery give the engine a spin. It purred reassuringly. I put the transmission into gear and rolled out of the parking lot.

Forty minutes later, I was parked on Lawrence Street in front of the Teton Building. George Percy Investigations occupied a hole-in-the-wall, there. I skipped the usual courtesy of knocking, and banged open his office door.

"Bishop!" Percy bleated, as I walked in.

As I approached, he scrambled to his feet screaming denials for everything from his daughter's fatherhood to Alfie's attempt on my life. Based upon the white froth flecking his lips, the pulsing of his supraorbital artery, his bugging eyes, and the spreading wetness at his armpits, Percy was telling the truth about everything.

"Relax, George," I cooed, and took a seat in his customer chair. "I'm here to express condolences."

"Before or after you kill me?"

"I'm feeling real bad about this, George."

His ample backside made a swishing sound as he settled back into the swivel.

"My daughter's in tears," he whimpered. "All she does is cry."

"Some women show gratitude in odd ways."

"Couldn't you have just winged the crazy bastard?"

"You've know my views on solutions to recurring problems."

Percy produced a handkerchief, which became a facial perspiration dauber.

"I'm not blaming you," George Percy said. "It was just like Alfie to try something stupid."

"Had he done anything smart his entire life?"

"Not that I noticed." He blew his nose into the rag. "My daughter's better off without Alfie. I'm better off. Hell, the entire world's better off." He thumped his flabby chest. "But, I'm the one taking the heat."

"What was Alfie working on?"

He returned the handkerchief to a pocket.

"You kill the guy and then you want his contacts?" Percy demanded. "Bishop, that's cold even for you."

"George, your son-in-law didn't drive to my place on his own nickel. Somebody put a ring in Alfie's nose and dragged him."

The portly man made a beseeching spread of both hands.

"Alfie couldn't drive, Deke," Percy pleaded. "He didn't have a license."

"A lack of license doesn't preclude steering-wheel exercises. Who'd Alfie meet this past week?"

"Alfie was a junkie. Who knows who he meets?"

"Junkie's talk, George. They ramble on for hours." I studied him for a beat. "Think back a few days to what was said. Who was Alfie's last inspiration in eloquence?"

Percy fell silent, chewing his lower lip.

"He got a call from somebody about a job interview," Percy said.

"Who in hell would hire Alfie?"

"He looked pretty good on paper. The guy was gifted at making up stuff."

"Why would Alfie be looking for a job?"

"After you and me last talked, I felt a duty to encourage him."

"Did your son-in-law say where he hoped to work?"

"Dr. Parker's fat farm."

That gave me a turn. What would possess Parker to hire a

junkie, considering the inherent risks?

"You know Parker, George?" I asked.

Percy wagged his head.

"Not personally," he replied. "But, I know who he is and his involvement with the Anniston sisters."

"Knowing Alfie as you do, why would he be an opportunity for a man who's trying to leave his mark on millionaires?" I asked. "It's not like Alfie had medical training."

"He knows how to give injections."

I nodded agreeably.

"They say junkies make the best inoculators," I said. "But, that doesn't make Alfie fat farm material. I'm thinking it's far more likely Parker had something special in mind, for Alfie. Something no one else would do."

"Alfie said he'd be doing deliveries."

"Without a driving license?"

"Alfie was never good at accepting limitations."

"I'm thinking Parker sent Alfie to my place."

George Percy hesitated in thought.

"That's an idea I wouldn't overlook," he eventually said.

"How were Alfie's finances, of late?"

"He was flush."

"He had more than what was needed for his nose?"

"He bought my daughter a new cell phone. One of those fancy ones that does everything except wipe butt."

"Did he explain where he got the money?"

"He said he won it on a horse."

That was possible. Not likely. But, possible. A better explanation followed the idea of somebody having paid him to kill me. Parker sounded like a good fit for that. In fact, he was the only player who fit the money-man in this murder-opera.

"What about the inquiries you were to make?" I asked.

"I hate to bring up the matter of money, but we had agreed on a fee for my service," Percy returned, "but I'm up to my ass in funeral expenses."

"I'm a little short on cash, George, due to unexpected expenses." I grinned tiredly into Percy's agitated face. "How about I put a check in the mail when I collect from my current client?"

His arms rose and fell with defeat.

"According to Buford Reese, and I believed him, Mortise Anniston panicked when you found their missing ledger." He paused awkwardly. "She assumed you'd been hired to dig into the hotel's welfare and social security receipts."

"Hired by who?"

"The Feds. The cops. Who knows?"

"Why would that worry her?" I asked.

"According to Buford, there are fifty to seventy walk-offs from the hotel, every year."

"Walk offs?"

"The move into the hotel and then just walk off. When that happens, the hotel is obligated, according to the social services arrangements, to notify the dispersing agency so checks for the missing individuals stop. But, that's not what's being done."

"How long's this been going on?"

"Decades."

"Meaning the hotel's collecting millions in illegitimate claims."

"Not so much illegitimate, as temporarily misappropriated."

"Your interpretation of their crimes or Buford's?"

"Mine. If a walk-off returns, the money due them is remitted."

"Do you still have the ledger?"

George Percy wagged his head.

"Gave it back the day Fillmore Teal left it," he said.

"Mortise Anniston told me your visit to my office had been arranged through Alfie."

"I still had hopes for him," he said. A worried smile twitched the corners of his mouth. "So, I let Alfie have his head with the deal. The downside of my decision came later. Alfie had collected our fee in advance and spent it on nose candy."

I lit a cigarette.

"What's your take on Buford Reese? I asked."

"He's watching, listening, and waiting for an opportunity to line his own pockets. But, he wouldn't have the money to turn Alfie in your direction."

"How did he get along with Alfie?"

George Percy grimaced.

"They were both looking for the ultimate high," he said. "And Buford may have put a flea in Alfie's ear. But, from my experience, Parker had to have been the one jerking Alfie's chain."

"But what's his motivation?" I returned.

"He may have been getting a cut of the services payments."

"Did you run into a guy named Leonard during your dealings with the Anniston sisters?"

"The bus driver for Kemp?" Percy waggled a dismissive finger. "That boy was collecting two paychecks. One from Kemp. Another from the Annistons."

"What was his job for the sisters?"

"From the way Buford Reese told it, Leonard was mostly fetch and carry. Until he boogied after Kemp died."

"Buford's sure Leonard left and isn't dead somewhere?"

"If Leonard had been murdered dead, I'm pretty sure Buford would've been long gone."

After leaving George Percy, I headed back to my office. When I arrived, I found Kenneth Miller pacing the hallway outside my office. He was carrying a plastic evidence bag containing the pistol I had purchased from the pawnshop. I unlocked the door and led him inside.

"Where in hell have you been?" he demanded.

"Just earning a living," I replied. "Is it a match?"

"You got my money?" Miller demanded.

"I got. What did you get?"

He rattled the bagged gun onto my desk.

"It's a match," Miller said.

"You're sure?"

"I don't make mistakes."

"Kenny, you married a woman thirty years your junior."

"You got my money, wise ass?"

I went over to the safe.

After giving the dial a few spins, I pulled open the safe's door and took out what I owed Miller. Then, after shutting the safe, I carried the bundle over. He did a quick count with shaking fingers, like his life hinged upon my payment.

"Registration on the weapon?" I asked.

"Argyle Anniston IV."

"He's dead."

"Not my problem."

Kenneth Miller pocketed his fee and hurried off.

I had the gun. I knew who had originally owned it. And I knew who had last possessed it. Not exactly proof positive for a jury conviction. But, close enough to warrant further digging. I put the bagged gun into my pocket and headed out to the Buick.

Forty-five minutes later, after leaving the pistol with Lt. Herby Mann for ballistics examination, I gave a shave-and-a-haircut tap on the Anniston sister's apartment door. The light behind the peephole darkened. I gave it my best smile. Then the door opened and swung inward, as if by itself. I smelled cologne. A vaguely familiar blend of spice and musk. Not my style.

"I need one small piece of clarification," I said to no one in particular, and stepped inside.

Everything went black.

Chapter 20

When I opened my eyes I was in a hospital bed.

My skull was wrapped with something. I reached up to touch and found a cloth bandage. I dredged through memories, but my last recollection was of arriving home. Between then, and now, I had nothing.

I tried to rise.

This triggered some sort of monitoring system. Immediately, a loud buzzing sounded. Seconds later, a wild-eyed nurse rushed into view. Because of the braces on her teeth and her petite figure, she looked to be about twelve years of age.

"Just lay still, Mr. Bishop," she blurted, in her little-girl voice. "Doctor's on the way."

"Shouldn't you be in school?" I asked.

She tapped the identification badge pinned to her scrub top.

"My name's Molly," she replied. "I'm an R-N."

I could not decide whether that was good or bad. Good to the extent that I was getting treatment for my injuries by a paid professional. Bad to the extent my life was in the hands of a pre-teen wearing braces.

"While we wait for him, and your babysitter," I told her, "could you let me in on what's been going on while I was away?"

"You're at St. David's Hospital because you've been concussed."

I had been a lot of things, in my wayward life, but never concussed.

"Did I have a good time at it?" I asked.

"I shouldn't think so," Milly said. "You've been unconscious for two and a half days."

That explained the stubble on my chin and the nicotine withdrawal symptoms making my tongue tingle.

"Sounds like quite a gathering," I said. "Do we know any of the other partyers?"

"I don't. But, Doc says somebody shot you."

I paused while my hands returned to the bandage to make a fingertip evaluation. No leakage, so I lowered my mitts to the rest of my body paying particular attention to potential damage to my private zone.

"Would you like some privacy?" she asked, as my hands moved about. "You seem preoccupied."

"Is it just my head?" I asked. "Or should I fumble farther down?"

"That's the only place where there are bandages. That thingy sticking in your John Thomas is to pass urine," she replied. "I can remove it, if you like."

I grabbed the plastic insert, jerked it out with a wincing grimace and handed it to her.

"Any other inserts I should be aware of?" I asked.

Molly shook her head.

"But, after you get home, you probably should check John Thomas's base functionalities," she said.

"How bad?" I asked, and returned my fingers to the bandage.

She pulled my hands away.

"You had a successful surgery," the nurse explained. "So, I'm thinking the party crasher was inexperienced with a gun."

"You don't think my luck could've had something to do with it?"

"In the suit you were wearing when they brought you here? Not a chance."

"I'll have you know that suit cost me an arm and a leg."

"When I was a twinkle in my daddy's eye."

Why did every woman I came across have innate insight concerning my shortcomings?

"There must be more to it than that or I wouldn't be wearing a head-rag three days down the pipe."

"The surgeon removed the bullet. What you got on your noggin is temporary leakage control."

"Brains or fluid?"

"In your case, I'm pretty sure it isn't brains."

That was encouraging — sort of.

"Big, medium or small?" I asked.

"The nursing code won't allow me to make those types of measurements." She winked. "But between you and me, you've got nothing to worry about."

A man about my age staggered into my room. He was wearing a smock with a stethoscope in the pocket. He stopped at the foot of my bed leaned over and gasped several times, like his life was about to expire.

"Want to change places before you drop dead?" I asked.

"Be with you shortly," he wheezed.

There was something vaguely familiar about him. But, I could not fit the Medico with a name.

"No rush," I told him. "It's only a head wound. I could live another ten minutes, easy."

"Damn elevator's on the fritz."

"From your desperate breathing and your face's cyanosis coloring, so's your heart."

He raised erect, still breathless, and stumbled toward me.

"I explained Mr. Bishop's situation, Doctor," Molly announced.

"From the looks of him," I told her, "you might want to call a code blue."

When the medico got within arm's length, he grabbed my wrist. The nametag on his white coat read, 'Dr. Jürgen.' I remembered Jürgen. I still owed him money from my last hospital stay.

"Breathe normally," he instructed.

"I would if I had a cigarette," I returned.

"Shush," he said, raising his other arm to stare at a wristwatch.

"Relax. The pounding in my skull feels like it's going to split my cranium, so my ticker has to be working."

"Give a man hope, why don't you?" he complained, still checking my pulse. "Other than the head, any complaints?"

"Worried you won't get your fee?"

"That crossed my mind the moment I saw you." He dropped my hand and lowered his watch-bearing arm. "Did I, or did I not, during our last encounter, tell you to stop smoking?"

"I have."

"Then why do I still smell that poison oozing from your

pores?"

"It's been a recent, albeit reluctant, change in habit."

Jürgen rolled his eyes.

"I can only imagine," he muttered and plugged one end of the stethoscope into his ears. Then he pressed the listening end against my chest. "Deep breaths, please."

I did his bidding until the room began to spin.

"I guess that's as good as you get." Jürgen returned the stethoscope to his coat pocket.

"How bad is it?" I asked.

He turned to the nurse and said, "Call that cop who left his card."

"Lt. Mann?" she asked.

"Yeah. Let him know Mr. Bishop's awake, and cognizant."

"Does that mean you lose the betting pool?"

"If Mann asks about Mr. Bishop's recovery potential, tell him our attorneys are already preparing litigation to collect for our services."

My luck was running true to form.

"Tell me about the bullet," I said.

"Something new for you, Mr. Bishop," he returned. "A .22 caliber."

Molly hurried off, like a kid heading for a party. The medico went to the foot of the bed, grabbed my chart and began scrawling notes. I inhaled, pretending nicotine was in the air.

"How serious was the damage?"

"The bullet lodged in the parietal bone just above the squamosal suture."

"That sounds serious."

"It usually is. But, in your case, nothing important was damaged."

"Norwegian heritage on my mother's side."

He let go a long sigh.

"I suppose we can't blame one country for your shortcomings," Jürgen mused.

"There's a chance I'll be impaired?" I asked.

"Considering your profession, Mr. Bishop, impairment took place decades ago."

"When can I get out of here?" I asked.

"How's your cash position?"

"I'm tapped out at the moment."

"So when I get the court settlement I should expect it to include a monthly influx of ten-dollars?"

"I'm expecting an improvement in liquid assets, soon."

"One can hope. In the meantime, I'll give you the working man's once-over and then arrange your release."

Jürgen gave me a usual examination, including the 'how many fingers' routine. Then, he staggered off muttering something about bankruptcy being his only way out.

Minutes after, I was dressed and standing on the sidewalk in front of the St. David's, flagging down a taxi. After instructing the driver to seek out Pushkin's Tobacco Shop, I settled onto the rear seat. Pushkin's was the only place in Austin selling the ultra-high nicotine English Ovals. After days of unconsciousness, I was gagging for a fag.

I made my purchase. Then I had the cabbie drive me home.

My digs had seen many changes since I first occupied them. During the decades of my residence it had gone from spiffy to spotty and sweet to smelly. But, the rent fitted my budgetary constraints. I unlocked the door, turned the knob and pushed inward.

The familiar stench of burned tobacco hit my nose like a dirty pair of socks. I tried not to wince. But, it was impossible. The place needed cleaning, fresh paint, somebody else's furnishings and several hours of Texas wind.

I stepped inside, turned on the kitchen light and closed the door. Ahead, by way of a ceiling fixture, I could see the doorway to my living-come-bedroom. It was a welcoming sight. I set the lock and strolled across linoleum.

Shocks were part of my way of life. Usually they involved romantic escapades. But, at the moment I was dumbstruck. Never before, on my front room floor, had there been a blood stain of this size. The crinkled coagulation smeared the linoleum in an ellipse a yard wide. I tried to remember who I must have killed. Surprisingly enough, nobody came to mind. And, yet, the blood was there.

I lighted my third Oval and inhaled the nicotine-saturated smoke. Even with a bucket and mop, a mess this size was going to be a ten cigarette job. But, first things first. I would have to rebuild my strength. So I got on the telephone and ordered pizza; heavy on the sausage and pepperoni.

There was a knock on my door.

When I opened it, Lt. Herby Mann strode in. From the look on his face he was either very concerned for my wellbeing or constipated.

"How's tricks, Herby?" I greeted him.

"What in hell are you playing at?" Mann demanded.

So much for friendly concerns.

"A hint would help," I told him.

"You knew damn well I'd want to question you." His voice was angry and rough. "But, what did you do? Check yourself out of the hospital."

"It's not a nice place to hang, Herby. You should've seen what the kid taking care of me shoved up my schlong."

"You know the drill, Deke. When I drive you to a hospital because you've been shot, I expect you to wait there until we talk."

Lt. Herby Mann driving me to St. David's should have been an unforgettable experience. But, I had no recollection.

"Drove from where?"

"Here. If I hadn't stopped by, to read you the riot act over you wasting police time on that damn pistol, you'd be dead."

"That pistol wasn't the gun?"

His head wagged.

"The rifling was close. So, we think it was in the same production series as the gun we're looking for."

"Nice you hate me enough to come by and tell me."

"I had a weak moment."

"You talked to the registered owner?" I asked, feigning ignorance as to who that owner might be. "Maybe he bought a matching pair."

"Argyle Anniston's dead. But you're correct, he did buy a matching pair of pistols with sequential serial numbers. The one you gave me and another that's gone missing."

A slight variation on the story told me by Mortise and Minerva

Anniston. They were certain there had been a pistol which had been stolen. Nothing was said about a pair of guns.

"There's something I want to show you," I said, tottering back into my front room.

Mann followed. When we reached the dried blood I pointed down at it.

"Mine, yours, or somebody I should be charging rent?" I asked.

"Yours."

In many ways, that came as no surprise.

"How'd it get there?" I asked.

"Presumably, when you leaked while I was on my way here."

"Last thing I remember, is stopping at the Anniston sister's apartment."

"As may be. But, this is where I found you and there was no blood trail into your apartment."

"Meaning I got thumped there and hauled here."

"Look at the mess you made. Can you blame them?"

"I don't suppose you compared the other rounds to that from my cranium?"

"Same weapon."

"Then I must be getting close."

"Or you're universally unloved."

Not an unfamiliar concept, usually heard from the female of my species. But, the same gun being used validated my theory.

"Any clues as to who shot me?" I asked.

"None, so far."

"Have you talked to the Anniston sisters about their whereabouts?"

"Not yet. But, I'm told by neighbors they've been spending their days trying to find the nephew an apartment."

"I'm surprised the old girls are turning Drax out. They seemed like the controlling type."

"Apparently he's been sowing more wild oats than his aunts will tolerate."

"Women can be such complainers."

"Now, if you don't mind," Mann said, "I have questions concerning the attempt on your life."

I looked down at the dried blood.

"There's a bullet hole in my bedside table," I remarked.

"I figure the shooter missed with the first shot because you were moving. You probably regained consciousness. But, he hit you with the second and left you for dead."

The aggravating aspect of head injuries is memory loss. When unconsciousness occurs from injury, there is no memory of the event. No remembering the pain. No recollections of the attack. It is like time stopped a few seconds before the event, and did not resume until after consciousness returned.

"When you arrived," I asked, "was there a Nash Rambler parked in my spot?"

"An ugly green thing."

"I dropped off the Buick to be repaired," I told him. "That's the loaner I got."

"I'll have it towed to the forensics' garage for processing." Lt. Herby Mann tightened his lips. "Who have you been talking to about this case?"

"Since the death of Reggie Shepherd I had two meeting with George Percy; one in the accompaniment of his son-in-law Alfie," I said. "I met with Drs. Firth and Parker at Parker's home in Fredericksburg. I spoke with the Anniston sisters. I chatted with Buford Reese and Eddie Walton. And, I had a telephone interview with Gordon Shepherd."

Lt. Mann's upper lip lifted, slightly, as he said, "George Percy's dead."

This was becoming a more complicated homecoming than I had expected.

"How'd George die?" I demanded.

"Same as you nearly did."

"When did George die?"

"About an hour, ago."

"Anything else I should know before you brighten my other eye?" I asked.

Herby Mann cleared his throat loudly.

"Charlie Trent's car was hijacked this morning," he said.

"Any chance he's dead?" I asked. "What went down with Charlie?"

"Two Russians grabbed Charlie but he managed to escape."

"Some days I can't win for losing."

He shook a finger at me.

"Your pal Pushkin's a member of the Russian mob," Mann said.

"Used to be. He's retired."

"Nobody retires from that mob."

"What's Charlie's story?"

"He says he was on his way to church when it happened and has no explanation as to why he was selected." Man smiled. "Road rash looks good on the lying bastard."

"Where's Charlie now?"

"Safe house."

"You don't think Charlie's tale sounds a little hinky?"

"Every time that man opens his mouth, it sounds hinky."

"The Russian mob is sloppy. They rely on overpowering, not smarts. But, they operate on simple terms. Find the problem and kill it. If Charlie'd offended them, he wouldn't have gotten away."

Mann considered a beat.

"People often get away after being grabbed," he returned.

"Not many of Charlie's weight. Top speed for that man has to be a slow turtle waddle. Ain't no way Charlie could outrun a group of pissed off Muscovites, I don't care how slow the car is they're driving."

"A police cruiser happened to be passing, and the Russians took highspeed flight while Charlie was asking for help."

"How does he know his attackers were Russian?"

"His wife's Russian. And we both know she chews his ass in that language most days."

"Did Charlie say why these Russians were after him?"

"According to Charlie, somebody stole a hundred million from a Smolensk bank and dumped it into Charlie's checking account."

"And you call me a crook?"

"Charlie claims he has no idea where the money came from or why. But, his bank said the money was wire transferred from Smolensk and stayed in Charlie's account for about a week." A long, impatient sigh escaped her lips. "At that time, a million from Charlie's account went to a bank in the Cayman Islands. The balance was transferred back to the initializing account in Smolensk."

I did not like the sound of that. Not about the predicament those money transfers put Charlie in. But, how quickly the Russians caught up with him after Precious Heidegger had transferred my requested hundred million.

"Have you traced the ownership of those account?" I asked.

"Unfortunately, the foreign banks have refused to cooperate," Mann said.

"In my opinion Charlie knows more than he's admitting," I said.

"And you don't?"

There should be a law against smart cops.

"Herby, I can't be involved," I countered. "I don't have computer skills."

"You're clever enough to find somebody who does."

"If you think so little of me, why in hell did take me to the hospital?"

Mann's expression twisted into a sullen glare as he said, "A perfect paraphrase of what the mayor said to me when he found out what I had done for you."

"Is there anything else keeping you here? Because I got a mess to clean up and you're slowing my mop action."

After Herby left, my doorbell rang. It was the pizza guy. I paid for my meal and settled down at the kitchen table to enjoy. While I munched, I pondered my next move. And no matter how I weighed the evidence, it all came down to the Anniston Arms Hotel. What I needed was another chat with Buford Reese.

Chapter 21

There were a dozen or so people gathered around the reception desk when I entered the Anniston Arms Hotel. From the shabby look of the membership, they were hotel residents. I strode over to the gathering. Just behind, sprawled upon the floor, lay Buford Reese. Blood had formed a pool beneath his head, leaking from a bullet hole. The air still smelled of burned gunpowder. Well, that, and the bodily exudations from the residents.

I forced my way through the crowd, and squatted next to Reese. My fingers touched his neck not expecting to feel a pulsing carotid. Buford Reese was, indeed, dead. But, not by many minutes. So who, among thousands with plenty of motive, had chosen today to get even? Somebody, I suspected, who had been very close to him.

After standing up, I questioned the tenants as to what had occurred. But they were all bleary-eyed and confused from meds, to the point of being deaf blind and dumb. When my effort to get their names and room numbers resulted in more blank stares, I instructed the bewildered contingent to await the police in their rooms. They trundled off like intoxicated sheep.

"What's happened, Mr. Bishop?"

I looked to my right and saw Mortise Anniston coming through an alcove, apparently after entering the hotel by way of the rear exit. Her clothing was a gray sharkskin suit, white blouse and high heels. Her face offered me a smile. But there were fresh worry wrinkles around her eyes. She continued another two steps and then stopped. As Mortise eyed the departing herd, her teeth nibbled at the inside of her mouth.

"Your hired man is in need of burial," I told her.

Her stare returned to me, her hands clutching a black suede bag.

"Buford's dead?" Mortise asked in what seemed to be feigned surprise.

"There's a new hole in his head," I returned.

Minerva and Drax entered from the same path. Drax was spiffy in crimson and blue. Minerva looked dowdy in brown.

"A bit off your turf, ain't ya Bo?" Minerva asked.

"This place draws me like a magnet," I said.

Mortise shared my words on Buford Reese's demise. But, instead of rushing over to gape at the corpse as I would have expected, the trio huddled together for a quick verbal skirmish. Almost like they had already viewed the remains.

"Suicide is painless," Minerva chipped. "Until the morticians send their bill."

"It wasn't suicide," I said.

"How can you be sure without an autopsy?" Mortise asked.

"The body's there. The gun isn't."

A sardonic smile twitched Minerva's crooked mouth.

"You shoot him, Bo?" she smirked.

"It was on my to-do list," I quipped. "How itchy's your trigger finger?"

"Not worth the trouble."

I took out my cellphone and dialed 911.

While I let the authorities in on the homicide, the sisters and their nephew crept over to the desk. From their respective body language, the trio weren't interested in the peek they gave the dead man. They were merely playing parts in a show.

"Poor Buford," Mortise said, backing away.

"We'll have to bury him," Minerva complained. "How 'bout poor us?"

Drax Ravaillac wandered off several paces and looked around, as if surveying a newly acquired realm.

"This is as good a time as any for me to take over," he observed.

I finished my call to the police and pocketed my cell phone.

"You didn't like him, Bo," Minerva said, taking a step toward me.

"Neither did you," I said. "I was on my way here when he was shot. Where were you?"

"Stop it," Mortise snapped. "Our friend is dead."

"That junkie was no friend of mine, sister dearest."

"I never liked him, either," Ravaillac chimed. "He had shifty eyes."

Mortise turned from the death scene and strode over.

"You came to see Buford, Mr. Bishop?" she asked.

"I'm a big fan of sparkling conversation," I quipped.

"Buford was going to tell you something?"

"Austin is rampant with murders of late." I gave her a wink. "And I think we both know who's pulling the trigger."

Squealing tires announced the arrival of the police.

We looked toward the entrance expectantly, me more so than them.

A uniformed officer rushed in. He asked who reported the incident. I curled a finger and led him over to the remains of Buford Reese. After seeing the corpse, the cop announced the necessity for us to remain until we were released. Then, he radioed dispatch with confirmation of the homicide.

"We're not involved, Copper," Minerva complained.

The officer made a feeble effort to placate her irritation. When he failed, the frustrated cop flatly told Minerva she would remain and cooperate or he would arrest her for obstructing justice. Minerva decided her plans could be delayed.

Several more police officers arrived.

While the officials gathered around the corpse, the agitated trio retired to the hotel's sitting area and huddled on the sofa in another bout of heated conversation. I slipped outside and lit a cigarette.

Forensics arrived with Dr. Fields in attendance. The news services gathered like vultures, attempting interviews with anyone in sight. When asked, I denied all knowledge of the event. Lt. Herby Mann's cruiser jerked to a stop nearby, and he climbed out. When Mann spotted me, he strode over like a man in need of pitted prunes.

"What is it with you and dead bodies?" the lieutenant of police demanded.

"Don't look at me for this!" I snapped.

"Deke, you're like the Angel of Death." His arms flailed the air. "Every time you show up, somebody dies."

"Buford Reese was dead before I got here."

"My guess is, just barely?"

"I didn't shoot him."

"Then how about telling me who did?"

"I'm guessing it's the same Cutie we've been chasing," I growled.

Lt. Mann pulled me along the sidewalk out of earshot to anyone inside, or traversing the hotel entrance.

"I need more than guesses."

"These killings were committed by a .22 caliber pistol. Presumably wielded by the same killer. Agreed?"

"If you insist." A frown ruffled the police officer's brow. "But, the victims came from all walks of life. So, what's your theory on the killer's motive?"

"Initially, I suspect it was to end blackmail. But, as time progressed, witnesses became a problem. So, the field of fire widened."

We looked at each other in silence for some moments.

"Who, among the dead, was the blackmailer?" Lt. Mann asked.

"I think there was more than one. Kemp would be among them. If it helps, I'm pretty sure the Anniston sisters pulled the strings on these assassinations."

"You're claiming a pair of law abiding old ladies became homicidal maniacs?" Mann demanded.

"Well, I wouldn't turn my back on Minerva. But neither she nor her sister pulled the trigger."

"You still think it's some joker named Cutie?"

"Reggie was incapable of lying, Herby."

"Which leaves us where?"

"Pretty much with Drax Ravaillac and Drs. Firth and Parker as the shooter. Each carried the Cutie moniker. Each is still alive, which is probably not the case for Julie 'the Cutie' Caivano." I blew smoke circles at the sky. "But, most importantly, those three have a connection to the Anniston Arms Hotel."

Lt. Herby Mann considered for a moment, his face troubled.

"I don't see a physician and an optometrist going nutso with an automatic," he muttered.

"Can we also agree the first murder was the most telling?"

He nodded. "Typically," Mann said, "in a series of murders, the first is the most important to the killer."

"In this case, Connie Firth."

"Assuming the security guard was second."

"Dr. Firth had an affair with Cornelia Wilson, Connie's niece. According to Cornelia, Dr. Firth actually plotted to kill his wife in order to keep Cornelia to himself."

"If we arrested every man who contemplated murdering his wife, half of Texas would be behind bars."

"Dr. Parker had an affair with Connie Firth."

"Not her first, from what you've said."

"But Parker actually wanted Connie to leave Dr. Firth. A possessive man, still carrying the torch, might've killed Mrs. Firth out of jealousy."

"Did Ravaillac also want her dead?"

"As far as I know he had no animosity toward Connie Firth. But his aunts might have if Mrs. Firth was blackmailing them." I consulted my watch. "Drax intends to succeed his aunts at the helm of the Anniston Arms Hotel. A determined man might be motivated to please those who control his life without question."

Lt. Herby Mann scratched his head.

"Blackmailed over what?" he asked.

"Hidden profits."

"The Anniston Arms Hotel isn't worth the mortar holding it together."

"It perpetuates a multimillion dollar fraud."

"From housing street people?"

I dropped my cigarette butt and toed it into the concrete.

"If the ledger is correct," I told Lt. Mann, "and I think it is, the hotel is skimming about $286,000.00 a month."

His mouth dropped.

"Or," I continued, "if you're a per-annum kind of guy like me, $3,432,000.00 each and every year."

"That's…"

"Well worth killing for," I said.

"Where in hell's this ledger?"

"The sisters have it."

"That being the case, it'll be ashes by now." He nibbled his lower lip for a beat. "Why didn't Federal and State investigators uncover a fraud that size years ago?"

"Because nobody pays attention to street people."

"What about family members?"

"I don't follow."

"If Reggie Shepherd was part of my family, I'd make sure he got his due."

"That's you, Herby. Most families view people like him as baggage to be shed."

Mann looked back at the hotel, his mind working.

"Have you got anything we can prove?" he asked.

I shook my head.

"Okay if I leave?" I asked.

Lt. Herby Mann nodded and headed back to the hotel.

I strolled down the block to the Nash Rambler. After playing with the starter for half a minute to get the engine going, I nosed it toward my office. I had some telephoning to do to set some bait.

Chapter 22

While I sat at my desk sipping coffee, the outer door opened and closed. Seconds later, Rita Portello strolled into view. She was wearing a blue top with white slacks and clattering high-heels. A tempting combination for a dirty old man like me. So much so my heart raced, my hands perspired and my most important asset jumped to throbbing attention.

"Bishop, you bastard," she said, swaying over to my desk.

"If you're here because I convinced Lessingham to stop fleecing Momma," I told Rita, "a thank you will suffice."

"That might be all the time you'll have."

I stood up and began unbuttoning my shirt.

"For some people, I make time," I returned.

"Cool your jets, Bishop. Momma's furious over your meddling."

"It was Sal's idea."

"Sal's pissed because Momma found out he was behind it." A muscle twitched in Rita's cheek. "And Dom's looking for a randy magazine journalist, of your description, who turned Cornelia against him."

I slumped back into my chair, buttoning my shirt.

"Momma I can get around," I told Rita. "She's always had a soft spot for me. Sal brought me into the Lessingham situation knowing the risks. So whatever went south is on him. But Dom being a loose cannon on the prod, worries me." My left eyelid jerked nervously. "Are names being bandied?"

"Meaning yours?"

"I hope your deranged brother's not shipping skunks to the unwary."

"Not that I've been told," she said. "But descenting and selling the fur-balls as pets was mentioned." Rita lifted a hip and took a perch on the edge of my desk. "How do you feel about a cuddly striper keeping rodents at bay in your apartment?"

"I'll pass."

"When I heard about your owie I went to the hospital."

"Sorry I missed you."

"You were still there. But the cop on your door refused me admittance. He said visitors weren't allowed. Something about no one known to you could be trusted not to kill you." She grinned cunningly. "But, he offered to go for a piss if I was there to break your neck."

"That must've been Nagle."

"What's he got against you?"

"The guy has no sense of humor when it comes to his wife and other men."

"What happened to you living like a monk?"

"I do. But, even the most self-denying hate it when a woman looks rejected."

She crossed her legs. The view of her swaying breasts during the movement was brief but nice. I sighed, letting naughty memories race through my dirty mind.

"Bishop, self-denial doesn't include screwing a cop's wife," Rita said.

"I had a weak moment."

"That is your stock in trade."

"Since then, I've taken vows of celibacy."

"I didn't hear any prayers the last time you and I got together."

"For you, I made an exception."

"Exceptions will be the death of you."

Rita Portello smelled of Shalimar and woman. I inhaled deeply and grinned. I still had it despite the debilitating forces of age. Then, my smile drooped as I realized the staidness of her expression underlined the threat implied by her last words.

"Why don't you admit I'm irresistible?" I asked.

"Irresistible might be a little over the top," she replied.

"Mildly alluring?"

"I'm thinking more along the lines of a festering sore."

That rocked me back in my chair.

"You consider me oozing puss?" I demanded.

"No. But I always have the need to scratch whenever you're around."

I leapt to my feet and attacked my shirt buttons.

"Consider me dusted with calamine," I shouted.

"As tempted as I am over the calamine, put your putter back in the bag." She grimaced and moved her tongue along the inside of a cheek. "I'll be spending this evening enjoying a root canal."

Disappointing enough to redo my shirt. But not completely unexpected. Rita had always been very keen on dental hygiene. However, dentists who offer after-dark surgery were as rare as virgins in a whorehouse.

"What's with you and that Sacrarium debacle?" I asked, settling back into the chair.

"After I took your son to Sicily, Sal tried to push me into an arranged marriage."

"Always the matchmaker."

Rita Portello made a vague movement with one hand.

"So, I decided to embarrass my least favorite brother, and the pig farmer Sal had selected as my latest fiancé."

"In church?"

"I figured I could fulfill a sexual fantasy at the same time."

Tic another off the old bucket list.

"According to Sal," I said, "the pig farmer's still ready to *soo-ee*."

Her dark head gave a determined side-to-side shake.

"Sal last spoke with him before the Sicilian Piglet nearly died from an attempted bilateral orchiectomy."

I crossed my legs.

"Sounds painful," I said.

"It wasn't planned," Rita said. "But, the man got it into his head to demonstrate his hog-like passion for Sicilian farm life."

"How much passion?"

"At the time, I was praying for a chastity belt. Fortunately, there was a rusty sickle within reach, and I was able to bring its rusty blade to hand."

"It certainly sounds like rough love."

"When it comes to relationships, one must be cruel to be kind." She stood up. "Which shows how far I'm willing to go for a little jaded fun."

"But for the objections of your brothers, my boys and I

would've made a monogamous commitment years ago."

"You and your dangling boys will never stop oat-sowing." Rita squinted at the bandage on my head. "You're bleeding. Should I call a doctor?"

"Temporary leakage. It does not affect my base functionalities in case you're reconsidering that root canal."

"I'm not the vacillating type."

"Are you sure? Because you look overcome with guilt."

"Did you see who shot you?"

I lit a cigarette.

"I'm pretty sure there were two of them," I replied. "Based upon the cologne kicking my nose at the Anniston sister's apartment, one was Buford Reese. The other I'm expecting to show up later tonight."

"As enticing as my brothers will find the prospect of your death, I'm not about to cancel a dental appointment to watch it happen."

"But, you were willing to stoop so low for jaded fun."

She went over to one of the customer chairs and sat down.

"Just how badly was your brain damaged?" Rita demanded.

"I'm not in la-la land, Rita."

"That would be a first." Rita Portello pursed her lips and considered for a beat. "Who have you penciled in for after I leave?"

"Paisley Firth, Nathan Parker or Drax Ravaillac." I shrugged. "Or, any combination thereof." I took a deep draw on my cigarette and exhaled. "But, my money's on Drax Ravaillac."

Rita squirmed on the chair.

"Drax is hardly a guy for deadly business," she said. "But, he is a hunk."

There was nothing worse than a woman who compared lovers. It was so… shallow. So callous. Particularly, when the better man was sitting in front of her.

"Ravaillac's all flash but no substance," I said.

"You should have his flash," she returned.

"So you're saying only Firth or Parker have homicidal leanings?"

"Of course they don't," Rita said. "Those two are bunnies."

She raised a finger for emphasis. "Now, if you were banking on the Anniston sisters to show, you might have something to worry about."

I arched a surprised eyebrow.

"Deadly?" I asked.

"From what Dom has told me those two old ladies are not above the occasional bloodletting."

"It's nice our senior citizens keep busy." I flicked ash into the glass ashtray on my desk. "And Dom would know the ins and outs of bloodlettings. But how did your brother come by his information? Everyone I've spoken with regard the sisters as saints."

"My family has a business relationship with Mortise and Minerva."

I tilted forward and leaned my forearms on the desktop.

"How does deadly fit in with cleaning fluids and mops?" I asked.

"Our business interests go far beyond janitorial supplies."

"I'm well aware of that," I said, dryly.

"What you might not know is we have a chain of funeral parlors."

My jaw dropped.

"That explains your family tradition of no bodies no crime," I said.

"No comment."

"But, how does your family's embalming diversification relate to Mortise and Minerva Anniston?"

"The sisters use our parlors for the disposal of hotel guest's remains."

Eddie Walton's suspicions crossed my mind. Perhaps there was a murder for insurance scam going on at the Anniston Arms Hotel?

"How many funerals are we talking about?" I asked.

"I'm not sure," Rita said. "My father arranged the original contract with Argyle Anniston IV. So, that must've been shortly after daddy acquired the parlors. Possibly a hundred.

"Is there any way you could get me a list?"

"What's this about, Bishop?" Rita snapped.

"It has nothing to do with your family," I promised.

"Whenever you start digging dirt, it always involves my family."

"This time your brothers have nothing to worry about."

"Forget it. But, I will ask Sal to send over a couple of men for protection."

"From who?"

"The two old ladies who'll be kicking your ass."

"I have every confidence in my being in control of this situation."

"Which underscores the extent of your brain damage." Rita glanced at her watch and then she got to her feet. "I have to go."

I stood up and went around my desk to lean on its top in front of her.

"Have I ever mentioned how fascinating you are?" I asked.

Rita tilted forward and kissed my cheek.

"Every time you're looking for a pity-fuck," she returned.

"Any chance you're feeling a wave of compassion, now?"

"See ya, Bishop."

Rita Portello turned and headed for the door.

"I could be dying," I called to her back. "You saw the blood. This might be your last chance to making an old man happy."

After Rita Portello left, I went back to the swivel chair and sat down. Almost immediately, the outside office door opened and closed.

"I knew my special brand of charm would guilt you back," I called out.

Instead of seeing the love of my life, Dr. Paisley Firth walked into view. There was an angry expression on the optometrist's face, as he strode directly toward me.

"You weren't first among the expected," I told him, suddenly wary.

"Do you know what it's like to be me?" he demanded.

"Not a clue, I'm thankful to say."

"Just once, I'd like things to go my way."

"It's a pisser when things go wrong," I agreed. "Are you here because of my call? Or, is there something besides murder on your mind?"

Firth jerked out a small bore automatic. His complexion was grayish except for flushed spots across his cheeks. His forehead looked to be wrinkled into a permanent frown. As he glared at me, his eyes blinked their wrinkled lids up and down as though the movement required the marshalling all his strength.

"You were supposed to nail Drax Ravaillac for murdering my wife," he snapped.

"Just so we're clear on your visit," I said. "You're telling me you killed all those people?"

"Would I be holding this gun if I hadn't?"

I raised and crossed my leg. Then I calmly extracted the snubby from its ankle holster. Firth getting the drop on me was not according to plan. But, his admission cleared the air.

"In that case, I don't see how you can have a complaint with me."

"Don't you understand? It was to be the perfect crime," Firth shouted. "I would kill Connie. The police would blame those Portello thugs. But, you would follow the clues to Drax Ravaillac." There was a sharp edge of contempt in his voice. "In the end, Ravaillac would be arrested. You would be paid. I would marry Cornelia Wilson."

"I'm pretty sure she's doing a rethink on that."

"Well when I finish with you, that damn journalist who talked Cornelia into leaving town is next on my list."

"Since you're going to kill me, anyway, at least clarify a few points of interest in this case?"

"Why should I?"

"In all fairness, you hired me to find your wife's killer. That fact that you're here and have admitted to doing so, proves the completion of our contract."

Dr. Paisley Firth considered for a long moment.

"What points?" he asked.

"For starters, how did you get your wife to Hillman's Warehouse?"

"I sent Connie an email, under Drax Ravaillac's name, requesting an assignation. I got to Hillman's before her and waited. My wife walked in." A cunning leer spread over Firth's flabby face. "I shot her. Finally, I was free. Finally, I would do what I wanted." His animated expression turned stiff and dour. "Then, everything went wrong. First that damn security guard came staggering out of the shadows. Then those skateboard lunatics started screaming. And, after that, everything pretty headed for hell in a handcart."

My plan for survival was simple. Shoot through the desk and kill a guy who had caused so many people so much pain. That part was straightforward. Even the mayor of Austin would like the idea. The difficulty was getting it done without getting another bullet in my skull.

"Tell me about Kemp's involvement," I said.

"That idiot Reggie told him everything," Firth replied. "About me shooting Connie and the Security guard. About me trying to shoot Reggie and his lunatic friends." The optometrist paused a beat. "Kemp came to my office demanding millions." He let go a soft whimper. "I felt bad about Charlene Holland. But, she was there when I killed Kemp." His shoulders bobbed. "Collateral damage."

"Louie Ayres, Norman Chaves, Warren Suppanen, and Henry Herschel?"

"Kemp believed Reggie," Firth whined. "Who was to say a jury wouldn't believe the other head cases?"

"But, why go to the trouble of making their deaths look like accidents when you had a gun?"

"I ran out of bullets and after that there was a temporary ammunition shortage."

"You hired Alfie Blake to kill me?"

"Of course not. Alfie was Parker's idea. Without you I couldn't fit Ravaillac to the frame."

"And I thought Parker and I hit it off."

"He hated your guts. But, he didn't act alone."

"Please tell me it wasn't his extra pair of hands."

"Mrs. Sanders? Oddly enough she found you irresistible."

I made a mental note to call on her after I killed Parker.

"The brains behind Alfie Barker's involvement was Captain Charlie Trent. It was he who ordered the end to your nosing around."

"How much did Parker pay Alfie?"

"Nothing. Alfie agreed to do it gratis if Parker gave him a job."

"But if you needed me why did you try to kill me at my house?"

"That was an accident."

"How could going to my house to shoot me be an accident?"

"I was in your apartment doing a quick toss intending to leave behind a clue to point the intrusion to Drax Ravaillac. Out of the blue, Buford Reese dragged in a laundry bag with you in it. He had a length of rope draped over his shoulder. So I assumed he was going to string you up. I knew I had to stop him. So, I shot. But, the bullet hit you instead. Buford ran out and so did I."

"You couldn't have called for an ambulance?"

"I thought you were dead."

"Why did you kill Buford?"

"Because, he saw me shoot you. He threatened to go to the cops unless I came across with enough money to set him on easy street."

"How did Gordon Shepherd fit into your killing spree?"

"That was entirely due to the Anniston sisters."

"They pointed and you obliged?"

"He came to them looking for help in killing his brother, Reggie. They shifted him off to me telling him I was already blackmailing them and if he wanted Reggie dead, he'd have to kill me. Well, he did. But, I got away. Then, I went after him."

"Preemptive self-defense?"

"Works for me."

"Were you blackmailing the Anniston sisters?"

"How do you think I could afford a wife like Connie?"

"Why kill George Percy?"

"Alfie told him about the arrangement to kill you with Parker. Percy called on Parker after you killed Alfie. George wanted in on whatever Parker was into or he'd blow the whistle on Parker for hiring Alfie. But, Parker laid that off on me. And there I was. Being shook down by somebody else. I might as well have bent over and pulled my cheeks for a ramrod."

I adjusted the angle of the snubby.

"Wouldn't it have been simpler to deny Parker's allegations?"

I asked.

"Not after I shot Parker in front of George Percy."

Well spotted.

"Why Reggie?" I asked.

"I figured it was time to tie up loose ends," Firth casually replied.

My forefinger took up the slack in the snubby's trigger. But, before I could complete my intentions, the outer office door banged, followed by hurried footfalls. Firth jumped to his feet, facing the sounds. Lt. Herby Mann rushed into my private office. Firth raised his weapon to fire at Mann. I squeezed the snubby's trigger five times. Dr. Paisley Firth crumpled to the floor.

"Another one?" Mann croaked.

"Nice to see you, too, Herby," I said. "What brings you to my little part of hell?"

"I'm here to return your gun."

Chapter 23

Ignacio's, my favorite Venezuelan restaurant, is on West Pompadour in Austin. The dining experience boasts such delights as Pabellón Criollo with fried plantains, rice and black beans as well as Polvorosa de Pollo, a mouthwatering chicken pie. Each dish is lovingly crafted by none other than Ignacio Mendoza, the owner, who, at the moment, has me searching high and low for his wayward daughter.

"Bishop, you bastard!"

The familiar cry came not from Rita Portello, but Precious Heidegger. She continued to blaspheme my parentage across the checkerboard floor until she reached the booth occupied by me and Fillmore Teal.

"I love you, too, Precious," was my calm return.

She rested her hands on the tabletop and tilted toward me, her eyes blazing.

"When I reclaimed the you-know-what from you-know-where," she seethed, "there was a million missing."

"I can explain that," I protested.

"I don't want an explanation, Bishop. I want what's missing."

"Charlie Trent has it."

"Who in hell is Charlie Trent?"

"It was his banking facilities I borrowed during my time of need."

"You idiot!"

"There wasn't a bank in town willing to write an account unless I had cash to deposit." I shrugged. "I had to give you something."

"Where do I find him?"

"Right now he's in protective custody. Apparently, a few Russians have a bone to pick with Charlie over some missing money."

"Damn you, Bishop! If they're here after him, it won't be long before they figure out my involvement!"

"Do you want me to speak with Charlie? He might have a credit card we could tap."

"Never mind!"

With that, Precious Heidegger turned and stalked out the way she had come in.

"Maybe we should give her the money, Bishop," Fillmore Teale suggested.

"Relax. She'll be fine."

"Those Russian mobsters are nobody to fool with."

"But until they get their hands on Charlie Trent they won't find out he wasn't involved. With witness protection in Charlie's future, that could take a lifetime."

"I don't want deaths on my conscience."

"Precious is already on her way out of town," I assured him. "As for Trent, he'll be shipped to some place in the Midwest where he'll die of boredom."

"Did you put him in the soup on purpose?"

"Long term thinking is the key to business success, Fillmore. If Herby Mann retires, I'm out of business. This way Herby'll get promoted to Charlie's job."

A familiar figure wearing a wrinkled brown suit strode into the café.

"On the other hand, Fillmore, don't spend anything," I whispered. "A minor complication just walked in the door."

Fillmore Teale turned and looked at Herby Mann, who was scanning the tables.

"Jesus!" Teale exclaimed.

"Better slip out the back," I told him. "Hang loose until I call you."

Teale scrambled from the booth and legged it out the back door.

When Mann spotted me, he came over and settled into the both across the table. I shoved my plate aside, expecting to hear the worst.

"How's tricks?" I quipped.

"You know why I'm here, Deke," Mann said.

That sounded like the end of my freedom.

"I've got a pretty good idea," I returned. "And let me tell you, Herby. I can explain everything."

He wet his lips, several times.

"I've decided to stay on, with Austin P-D," Mann said.

That was what I had been working for, in my own special way. But, somehow, it sounded so unexpected his words knocked the breath out of me.

"So, you're not here to arrest me?" I asked.

"The Firth shoot was clean. So relax." Herby Mann sat slumped with his chin resting on his chest. "You're completely in the clear — on that."

"On that?" I echoed, with some hesitation.

"Charlie Trent's being put into witness protection. Apparently, he's been taking payoffs from the local Russian mob for years, and with their cohorts from Moscow on Charlie's tail over some financial confusion, he's decided to come clean and testify against them. On a positive note, I've been promoted to Captain of Homicide." He adjusted the lay of his old suit and then straightened his posture, his eyes on mine. "The official notification won't be for another week. But, I thought you'd want to know. Naturally, this change in my fortunes cannot play a part in our future relationship."

I gave him a nervous smile.

"It never crossed my mind, Herby," I told him. "But, you're sure you're not here to arrest me?"

Books by Michael Paulson